THE

GIRL

FROM THE

HERMITAGE

MOLLY GARTLAND

Lightning
Books

Published in 2020
by Lightning Books Ltd
Imprint of EyeStorm Media
312 Uxbridge Road
Rickmansworth
Hertfordshire
WD3 8YL

www.lightning-books.com

British Library Cataloguing in Publication Data
A catalogue record for this book is available from the British Library.

ISBN: 9781785631887

For LMS

PART ONE

1

~~❖~~

December 1941

MIKHAIL SCRAPES A KNIFE against the wall and a strip of yellowing floral wallpaper curls on the metal edge, peeling away from the plaster. Cradling it in his palms, glue side up, he returns to the kitchen. He holds the paper over a pot of water and scratches the knife across the brittle surface. Flakes of paste drop into the liquid. Hissing gas fuels a flame. Mikhail clasps his hands around the warm pot. Heat grows, pricking his palms and fingers. He lingers another fraction of a second before pulling them away. Pressing his warm hands to his cold cheeks, heat transfers through his skin, disappearing into his core.

Using a wooden spoon, he stirs and the flakes disintegrate. The smell, papier mâché, reminds him of his student years at Leningrad Academy of Art. As he waits for it to boil, rubbing his hands together in the warm steam, he thinks of his daughter, Galya. This stale old glue is not enough nourishment for her. He scrapes another strip from the corridor wall and scratches more paste into the pot. Holding it in the steam, the paper softens. The water begins to boil. It is not enough. He is useless.

Above the stained sink, three teacups hang from hooks. He scoops a cup into the broth and envelops his hands around it. The warmth seeps through the thin porcelain. Just as the heat starts to bite, he sets the cup on the kitchen table. He unwraps a newspaper parcel and cuts three pieces of bread, each about the size of a die, and places them in a shallow bowl. He folds paper around the remaining bread, which is smaller than his palm, and sets it aside. Hunger stabs at his stomach.

Taking the broth and bread, Mikhail walks down the *kommunalka*'s dark corridor. As he passes the door of the Kamerovs' room to his left, Vera's eyes meet his. The little girl, covered in several blankets, wears a pink knitted hat. She waves to him.

'Can I get up, Mikhail Tarasovich?' she asks.

'Stay nice and warm in bed, Vera. You must rest. Conserve your energy.'

'I'm bored.'

'Your mother will be home soon, don't worry.'

'Can't I play with Galya?'

'Not now. She's not well. We don't want you to get ill too.'

Vera sighs and her lower lip pouts. Her head, which looks too big for her tiny frame, drops.

Mikhail continues down the hall, past the flat's main entrance on his right, and enters his room at the end of the corridor, leaving the door open behind him. Galya, buried under wool blankets, lies in her bed at the foot of his mattress. Only her brown hair is visible. He sets the cup and bread on a table beside her and presses his hand to her forehead and cheeks. She shivers from his touch.

'Drink this slowly,' he says, propping up her pillow and pulling the blankets around her. He hands her the cup, which has already cooled in the chilly flat.

Galya purses her chapped lips and takes a sip. Limp hair frames her gaunt face. Mikhail pinches one of the pieces of bread in half and gives it to Galya. She puts it in her mouth, leaving it on her tongue; she does not chew. She waits for it to dissolve slowly, making it last. Her hands, streaked with blue veins, cradle the porcelain cup. They look smaller but Mikhail knows this is impossible. Her bones cannot be shrinking.

He stands, walks to the window and pulls back the black fabric covering the glass. Although it is only one o'clock, the light is growing dim.

'Galya, I have to go for more water. It's getting dark.'

She takes another sip and nods.

'Anna Petrovna should be back soon. I don't like to leave you but we need water.' He knows it is dangerous to procrastinate; tomorrow brings uncertainty. It can, and probably will, be worse.

Setting the cup on the table, Galya sinks beneath the blankets and closes her eyes.

Mikhail looks again at the snowy street below, hoping to see Anna. Worry creeps into his thoughts. She has been out longer than he expected.

'I'll be as fast as I can.' But he knows he will move slowly along the icy road.

He kisses her cheek and she smiles.

'Don't worry. I'll look after Vera,' she whispers.

'Stay in bed and rest. And finish your soup.'

He returns to the kitchen, collects a pail and the kettle, and he walks down the corridor.

'I heard you,' calls Vera.

Mikhail stops at the Kamerovs' door.

'Will Mama be back soon?' she asks.

He nods. 'Don't be afraid. Galya is in our room.'

He puts on his heavy coat. His scarf is draped over the radiator, which has not worked in weeks. The wool is still damp and will quickly turn icy cold in the wind. His wife's loosely knit angora shawl hangs on the peg beside his coat. He winds the cloud of creamy soft fibres around his neck, immediately feeling its warmth. The scent of her hair and lilac perfume makes his throat tighten. How long will Roza's scent linger now that she is gone?

'Don't open the door to anyone. Anna Petrovna has a key. I'll be right back,' he says, fastening his buttons.

Mikhail takes off his slippers, slides his feet into tall felt boots and stomps, willing them to warm quickly. He opens the door, steps out onto the landing and hesitates, hoping to hear Anna's footsteps scuffing the dusty stairs. But the stairway is silent. He locks the door and heads down the four flights.

The wind slaps Mikhail's cheeks as he steps out of the building. Few people are out on Mokhovaya Street. Across the road, a fresh layer of snow covers the crumbling remains of a bombed-out building. He looks right and then left, hoping to see the familiar flash of Anna's red scarf. She is not there. He takes a breath and dry, frigid air crystallises deep in his lungs. He pulls Roza's shawl closer to his skin. Head down, he shuffles along the snow-covered road.

The day is slipping away quickly and Mikhail must hurry and return before temperatures drop and the bombs fall. He must not leave Galya for long. His gaze does not linger on the snow-covered corpses along the road. He ignores the pain in his back and his weak muscles. At the end of Mokhovaya Street, he turns right onto Belinskogo Street where a handful of people, dark against the white snow, congregate around a water pump. Carefully stepping across the ice, he joins the queue.

A figure pumps the metal handle, which cries with every stroke. A stream of water fills her bucket and she picks it up. Shuffling on the ice, she slips. Mikhail grabs her, holding her steady, preventing her fall. She pulls her arm away sharply and glares at him.

'Why aren't you at the front, like a real man?'

Her comment stings.

Not waiting for a response, she pushes past him.

The next woman in the queue approaches the pump. She grasps the handle and water cascades from the tap, upending her pail. Mikhail steps forward.

'Hold it,' he says, pointing at her bucket.

A distrustful scowl flashes, partially hidden by her fur hat and scarf.

'I'll pump,' he insists.

She holds the pail while he pushes and pulls the stiff handle. His back and arm muscles ache and warm under his coat. Cold seeps from the metal through his gloves.

'*Spasibo*,' she mumbles without looking up. She takes it, gingerly shuffling along the ice.

Mikhail motions for the next figure to step up and hands her his kettle. She steadies it below the tap and he begins to

11

draw. She places his pail beneath the tap and then fills her own bucket. Mikhail slows as his muscles cramp and tire. The next woman steps forward, placing her vessel beneath the pump, but he steps away, taking his pail and kettle with him.

'Can't you do one more?' she mumbles.

Unable to continue, he shakes his head and walks away, leaving the pump's lonesome whine behind him.

He heads down Belinskogo Street. The woman's question – 'Why aren't you at the front?' – lingers in his mind. She is right, he should be defending his city. But he cannot leave Galya, especially now.

The heavy load pulls his arms as he shuffles along. Unable to go on, he stops, setting the pail on the snow. He stomps his feet, waking up his numb toes. The shawl, icy from his breath, is frozen to his beard. He pulls it, tugging his facial hair. Forcing himself to carry on, he edges closer to home.

Mikhail stops at the archway which leads to his building's courtyard. A pile of corpses is peacefully silhouetted in the evening haze. He takes a deep breath. Pressing his nose into the soft angora scarf, he holds Roza's scent deep in his lungs. No snow has fallen to blanket her. It has been too cold. He exhales and studies the dusky sky, wishing for heavy snowfall. A warm tear slides down his cheek and quickly cools in the frosty air. He shivers, forcing himself to return to Galya.

Anna's scarf is draped on the cold radiator and her boots are beside it. Melted snow puddles beneath her boots.

'I'm back here,' she calls from the kitchen.

He strips off his layers, puts on his slippers and quickly checks on Galya, who is fast asleep. He takes the water to the kitchen and finds Anna sitting at the table. Her dry, papery face is covered with a layer of powder and rouge, and lipstick seeps into the wrinkles around her lips. She seems much older, as if she has aged many years in just a few months.

'I went for water,' Mikhail says, placing the pail beside the sink.

'I saw Director Orbelli at the Hermitage.'

'Oh?' Mikhail sits on the stool opposite Anna.

He has not bothered going to the museum since they finished packing away all the artefacts.

'Many of our colleagues are living in the museum, Misha. Orbelli said we should join them.'

'I don't want to leave the flat. Everything will be stolen.'

Her brow furrows as she scans the empty shelves.

He looks towards the kitchen window, covered in heavy fabric, which overlooks the courtyard.

Anna follows his gaze.

'Roza wanted Galya to live. More than anything.' She reaches across the table and squeezes his hand. 'We'll die here, Misha. We can't survive on our own. There's food at the Hermitage.' She opens a canvas bag and places a newspaper parcel on the table. Patches of moisture seep through the paper. 'Orbelli gave me this.'

The newspaper is still cold from her journey home. Mikhail peels back the layers of damp paper, revealing a dead rat. He does not waste time. Picking up a knife, he slides the rat closer, makes a shallow cut from the chest to the belly and pulls the fur away.

'There is even a school, Misha, for the girls.' She waits for him to respond but he is silent. 'Director Orbelli is sending a car tomorrow. We have to take our mattresses.'

The first time Mikhail skinned a rat, the result was messy. Patches of fur stubbornly clung to the carcass and pieces of hair floated in the soup. Now he makes incisions lengthwise along the rat's body and pulls the fur in strips. It comes away easily, leaving a neat, naked carcass. Cutting deeper, he reveals the rat's organs. He pulls out the guts and collects them on the newspaper. Firmly pressing on the knife, he cuts off the head and drops it beside the organs. The bright red liver and pale intestines quiver on the rickety table. The knife hovers over the tail, which is still intact. He pinches it, wondering how much nourishment could be found in the long, naked tail.

'Misha, what do you think?'

Standing, Mikhail nods and adds more water to the pot on the stove. He lights the gas ring and drops the rat in the pot.

'Misha, there's another thing.' She puts her hand on his shoulder. 'He needs you to do some work.'

This seems impossible to Mikhail. All the masterpieces have been packed up and shipped away. There is nothing for him to conserve, no paintings to be cleaned or repaired. Mikhail stirs the soup gently. The tail curves along the side of the pot.

'Someone, I don't know who, has asked Orbelli for a portrait artist,' she says.

'I'm not a portrait artist. I haven't painted in years.'

As the steam rises from the pot, his stomach groans.

Who the hell would think about having a portrait painted at a time like this?

'Misha, if we go to the Hermitage, you must paint a portrait.'

2

❧

DIRECTOR ORBELLI SITS BEHIND a massive mahogany desk, surrounded by stacks of books and files. Candles flicker from an ornate silver candelabra, casting shadows on the low, vaulted ceiling of his cellar office. Orbelli's full grey beard, which he strokes as he speaks, rests on his quilted jacket and plaid scarf.

'Colonel Shishkin asked me to send him a portrait artist,' Orbelli says.

'But sir, I'm not a portrait artist,' Mikhail says.

'You're all we have. Were you not classically trained at the best art academy in the Soviet Union?'

'Yes. But…'

'But nothing. You must do this. He's an important man. If he is happy with the portrait, it will be very good for the museum and everyone here.'

'I haven't painted in years, sir. I'm better suited to

conservation and restoration.'

Orbelli sits back with his fingers laced together.

'Everyone else has been evacuated. I'm counting on you, Mikhail Tarasovich. If it weren't important, the colonel wouldn't have asked.'

Mikhail has been given his role and Orbelli will not be persuaded otherwise.

'Shishkin wants to meet you. He's sending a car at eleven. He's an influential man, Mikhail. Don't let me down,' Orbelli says, opening a thick leather-bound book. 'Now, I must get back to my research.'

Mikhail's empty stomach knots as he turns towards the door.

The black Emka pulls up in front of the museum promptly at eleven. Snow clings to the fender's elegant curve. Mikhail steps onto the street and a sharp wind whistles across the Neva River, penetrating his coat. He opens the car door and slides into the back seat. The driver mumbles and puts the car in gear. Still feeling the chill from the wind, Mikhail shivers.

He sits, disbelieving his situation. He cannot possibly produce a portrait which will satisfy the colonel. He must come clean and tell the colonel the truth. Yes, he is a trained artist but he has not painted in years. He slumps into the seat.

The car slips along the icy roads through Leningrad, which has become a ghost town. Much of the population has evacuated and the rest stay indoors, hiding. With petrol in short supply, only military vehicles travel along the wide avenues. An abandoned tram sits frozen on the track with its overhead cables disconnected. It is completely entombed in a thick layer of ice. Many shops, boarded up or bombed, are closed. The only people along the road stand in a long queue which snakes from a bakery. Mikhail knows what it is like to stand in the queue, slowly edging towards the woody aroma of the sawdust bread, hoping there is still a ration when he arrives at the counter.

He catches a glimpse of himself in the driver's rear-view mirror. At first he does not recognise his reflection. An untidy beard covers his long, thin cheeks. His eyes protrude from the sockets. He glides his fingers through his greasy hair. He looks as if he has been living in a cave. He brushes dust from his trousers and coat and the car comes to a halt.

He clenches his jaw. He is going to tell Shishkin the truth.

The colonel is shorter than Mikhail had imagined and strangely plump. His healthy cheeks, kissed with a rosy glow, look alive, warm and vibrant. His dark hair, streaked with grey and slicked back, is perfectly groomed.

Shishkin extends his hand. 'Mikhail Tarasovich Senotrusov, I've been looking forward to meeting with you.' He squeezes Mikhail's bony fingers.

'A pleasure to meet you, Colonel Shishkin.'

'I need a portrait painted. Orbelli says you're the best.' He smiles, revealing his tobacco-stained teeth.

Mikhail recognises his chance to set the record straight. 'At the moment, yes, the best in Leningrad.' He takes a breath, preparing to clarify his statement.

'My wife has a birthday very soon. She is everything to me. I want to give her something special.'

Mikhail has missed his chance. The role as the best is his.

A spark pops from a log in the fireplace. Mikhail adjusts his arms, feeling sticky moisture start to grow under his suit jacket, sweater and wool undershirt. He cannot remember the last time he felt warm. Above the mantelpiece, a portrait

17

of Lenin hangs on the wall. One hand rests on his bearded chin, the other grasps his lapel.

'Do you have a wife?' the colonel asks.

'Yes,' he answers but quickly realises his lie, born out of habit, rather than deceit.

A maid enters carrying a tray, sets it down on the spotless, varnished coffee table and pours two cups of tea.

'*Priyanik?*' The colonel motions to a plate of cookies.

Mikhail has not seen anything like them in months. He takes a bite, savouring the allspice and nutmeg as he slowly chews. He heaps two teaspoons of sugar into the strong tea and stirs. The earthy aroma lingers in his nostrils as he takes a sip. Sweetness coats his tongue.

'Now, where were we? Oh, yes. A gift for my wife.' The colonel sits back on the velvet chair. 'I'd like you to paint a portrait of our two sons.'

The tea warms Mikhail's core. He hopes the boys are not young and fidgety.

'How old are they?'

'Maxim is ten and Vladimir thirteen.' The colonel bites into a second *priyanik* and the crumbs fall into his lap. 'It must be ready for her birthday on the thirteenth of January.'

Only two weeks.

'The boys will be here after New Year. So, you can get started on the second.'

'And the composition, is there anything in particular that you'd like?'

'I'll leave it for you to decide, Mikhail Tarasovich. We'll have them dressed and ready. I'll send a car to fetch you at nine.' He leans back and strokes his smooth chin. 'Senotrusov, I've come across that name before. It's not a common name.' He pauses and the fire sputters in the fireplace. 'Ah, yes. I remember. Andrei Tarasovich Senotrusov. He must be your brother.'

'Yes, he is. How do you know Andrei?'

'We have common acquaintances, shall we say. Haven't seen him in ages. How is he?'

'I don't know.' Mikhail shifts on his chair, uncertain of what to say. 'I haven't seen him in years.'

Shishkin does not react or seem surprised. He pauses momentarily as if considering Mikhail's words and brushes crumbs from his lap.

'I can see what I can find out. Perhaps I'll have some information for you when you deliver the painting.' He stands and offers Mikhail his hand. 'I have to get back to work.'

Mikhail pushes himself up, taking Shishkin's hand.

'Have a Happy New Year, Mikhail Tarasovich. Elizaveta will show you out.' He rings a brass bell and exits the room.

Three *priyaniki* remain on the plate. Mikhail quickly grabs a page from the *Pravda* on the desk and wraps them up. Hearing someone clear their throat, he freezes. He looks up and finds a woman in a maid's uniform.

'I'll show you out.' She lowers her gaze and motions towards the door.

Mikhail places the newspaper parcel in his jacket pocket and heads towards the door.

'You must be Elizaveta,' he says.

She nods, retrieves his coat from the closet and holds it for him as he puts it on.

'They aren't for me,' he whispers. 'My daughter is very ill. The *priyaniki* are for her.'

'I understand,' she whispers, opening the door. 'Until next time, Mikhail Tarasovich.'

Mikhail pushes open the door and steps onto the snowy stairs. Snowflakes collect on his coat as he makes his way to the Emka. He settles in the back seat and his thoughts return to the conversation with Shishkin. He should have asked him more about the portrait. He does not know exactly what the colonel wants. Why the hell didn't he tell him the truth? He is not a portrait artist. What if the boys are uncooperative? Anger swells as he pictures the colonel brushing the *priyaniki* crumbs from his lap. Of course, he knows that people in privileged positions live better, but to experience it, feel the fire and taste the sweet tea, is another matter. And there was that unexpected mention of Andrei.

The snow starts falling heavier and it reminds Mikhail of that day, long ago, when he followed Andrei down a path at the *dacha*. Fluffy snowflakes just like these drifted around them. He seemed like a giant to young Mikhail. But really, he was only on the brink of manhood. His long strides took him quickly down the path and Mikhail slid behind, struggling to keep up. They wove through the leafless birch trees, past clusters of slant-roofed, sleepy *dachas*. Mikhail stopped for a moment, out of breath from trudging in the deep drifts. Andrei scooped up some snow, pressed it into an icy ball and hurled it at him. He ducked too late and the snowball smacked his arm. Brushing crystals from his sleeve, he gathered his strength and ran to catch up with his brother, excited to be included.

Together, they crouched down behind a fallen oak tree. Andrei's eyes were fixed on a windowless shed, the Manakovs' sauna. Smoke billowed from the chimney. Mikhail's heart pounded inside his coat. It was the only sound in the snowy, still forest. Their breath clouded together as they waited.

'Why are we here?' Mikhail whispered.

'Larissa.'

Even Mikhail, at the tender age of ten, was aware of Larissa. She was beautiful.

A crack of laughter filled the silence. The sauna door opened and a slender, rosy foot appeared. Larissa darted out, with steam rising off her body. Mikhail giggled and Andrei jabbed his sharp elbow into Mikhail's side. Larissa's sweaty breasts jiggled as she ran, naked and glistening, out of the sauna, throwing herself onto the snow pile.

A larger, hairy foot appeared from the sauna door. A hirsute man flung himself onto the snow beside her, rolling and laughing with pleasure. The boys recognised the voice immediately. Mikhail turned to his big brother, whose mouth hung open with surprise.

It was their father.

'*Kazyol*,' muttered Andrei, picking up a handful of snow and forming an icy ball. He threw it and the ball smashed on his father's bare arse.

Papa looked up, surprised. Mikhail's heart froze, expecting his father to tear Andrei limb from limb.

'Boys, go home,' his deep voice boomed through the trees. 'Now.'

'Go to hell,' Andrei shouted as he calmly turned and walked down the path, full of righteous courage.

On the way home, Mikhail begged him to leave the secret in the forest and not to tell Mama. But Andrei, who saw everything as black and white, pushed him aside. He was determined to set the record straight.

Mikhail's thoughts return to the strangely pleasant exchange with the colonel, who was far more cultured and polished than he had expected. Shishkin is a military man, disciplined and prepared, but he puts Mikhail dangerously at ease. Mikhail shivers. He should not relax. Despite Shishkin's demeanour, he is part of the establishment and could turn Mikhail's life upside down with a single phone call. He is a man who could unexpectedly issue an invitation to the theatre or to prison and neither would be surprising.

As the car crosses the Neva Bridge, the façade of the Hermitage comes into view, scarred and cracked. Patches of render have fallen away from the building, exposing bare bricks. This stubbornly imperial building, which was once Catherine the Great's dream palace, is crumbling from the abuse of the war. The window panes are crisscrossed with diagonal strips of pasted newspaper. The trellis pattern is out of place with the gilded frames and cherubs. Mikhail turns away from the damaged building, focusing instead on the thick ice covering the river.

The Emka comes to a halt in front of the Hermitage. Mikhail steps out of the car and shuffles up the snowy path to the entrance. He follows the corridor to the Hall of Twenty Columns. Dull winter sunlight filters through the windows, reflecting on the rows of massive black granite columns. Beneath his boots, gritty dust and plaster scratches and scuffs the patterned mosaic floor. He passes empty glass display cases, pushed tight against the wall. He enters an internal courtyard and slides along an icy path to an archway where a flight of stairs takes him deep beneath the Hermitage.

Three bare bulbs hang from the low, vaulted ceiling. Groups of people gather along the perimeter of the cellar, clustered around furniture brought down from the Hermitage offices. Near the end of the tubular cellar, Anna and the girls lie on mattresses on the compacted earth floor. Anna has rigged up bedsheets around their area, but Mikhail can see them through the gaps between the sheets. Galya is sleeping, under blankets. Anna is reading to Vera.

'That was quick,' says Anna.

Mikhail takes off his coat and hangs it on a nail in the wall.

'How's my Galya?' He kneels beside her and presses his hand to her hot forehead.

Her eyes open and she pulls away. 'Your hands are cold.'

'I have a special treat.' He removes the parcel from his coat pocket and unwraps the newspaper.

'*Priyaniki!*' says Vera, leaning over his shoulder.

'Shhh,' Anna whispers, firmly pinning the bedsheets shut. 'We only have a few.'

Anna breaks one cookie into three pieces. Taking the smallest for herself, she hands a piece to Vera and nudges Galya.

'Galochka, try to eat,' she says.

Galya stirs and Mikhail helps her sit up. He breaks her piece in half and hands it to her.

'Eat slowly, girls. Don't chew. Make it last,' he says.

'We're so lucky,' Vera says, smiling broadly.

'What did the colonel say?' asks Anna.

'He wants a portrait of his sons. It's a birthday gift for his wife,' he says with a chuckle.

Her eyebrows lace. 'How charming. But it's no laughing matter, Misha. You must be very careful. This is serious.'

'Of course it's serious.' He attempts to compose himself. 'But all of Leningrad is wretched and starving and he's thinking about birthday gifts for his wife.' His laughter returns. 'Beyond absurd.'

'All the same, you must be careful, Misha. Did he give you the *priyaniki*?'

'Not exactly.'

'Misha, it's very dangerous.'

Mikhail shrugs. As Galya takes another bite, his pride swells. He has provided food.

'The colonel knows Andrei,' whispers Mikhail.

'Your brother?'

He nods.

'Is he alive? Where is he?'

'Shishkin hasn't seen him in a long time. He's going to see what he can find out.'

Anna leans closer to him. 'It was a long time ago. Maybe it is best to leave it in the past?'

He pulls away, not responding to her remark.

Mikhail tucks the blankets around Galya and rubs her shoulder. She is so weak. He must keep her alive. He cannot lose her, too.

Several days later, Galya and Vera hover over bowls of soup. They giggle, counting carrot slivers floating in the watery broth. A candle on the table flickers.

'Papa! I have four pieces,' says Galya. 'How many do you have?' She leans over his bowl and stirs, searching for the little orange surprises. 'Seven! You're so lucky.'

Mikhail stirs the soup in his bowl and shreds of pale meat swirl. It smells of stale dishwater. He collects a few carrot pieces on his spoon and transfers them into Galya's broth.

She smiles but her shoulders droop. Dark circles under her eyes contrast with her face. Mikhail is encouraged to see her out of bed and sitting at the table but he can see her beginning to fatigue. He wonders how much longer she will last before she must return to the cellar.

'How many do you have, Anna Petrovna?' Galya asks.

Anna pushes her bowl towards the girls. 'You count them.'

They lean over her portion, searching.

Anna's dark hair, streaked with grey, hangs loose, framing her face.

'Ten, Mama!'

Anna spoons a couple of pieces into Vera and Galya's soup and pulls her bowl back in front of her.

'How did they manage to find carrots? We are so fortunate,' Anna says. 'This is a very good New Year's Eve. I'm glad we're here in the Hermitage. Better than being all by ourselves at home. Don't you think, Misha?'

Mikhail leans his elbow on the table, resting his chin on his palm. He misses the flat but Anna is right, it is warmer and there is more food here. The soup tastes better when you do not know exactly what is in it. He eats a bit of the stringy meat. Slightly sweet and tender, it must be cat.

'Yeh,' he replies.

Last New Year, it was just Mikhail, Roza and Galya in their room. Even with the door shut, they could hear Anna and Ivan in the kitchen with a couple of their friends. Roza and Mikhail had been invited to join the party but declined, wanting to be on their own. They had a simple meal and Galya fell asleep, long before midnight, in her cot at the foot of their bed. Not wanting to leave their room, even for a moment, and go to the kitchen to wash their dirty dishes, they left the plates and cutlery stacked on the bookshelf.

Mikhail and Roza did not even notice the arrival of 1941. Roza suddenly sat upright and grabbed the clock beside the bedside table. 'Misha, it's twelve thirty! We missed it!' She hopped out of the bed, ran towards the window and pulled back the curtain. The glow of the street lights gently lit her naked body. She opened the window and grabbed the Sovetskoye Shampanskoye, which she had stowed between the two panes of frosty glass. Closing it and squealing in the cold, she darted back to bed. Frigid air swirled through the warm room. She quickly dived under the blankets, pressed her cold body against Mikhail and handed him the bottle. 'We have to toast the New Year!'

He pushed the cork with his thumb and it popped suddenly, hitting the ceiling. She shrieked and took a drink straight from the bottle. He kissed her sweet champagne lips.

'Misha?' Anna says, bringing him back to the cold Hermitage. 'Where did you fly off to? You're a million miles away.'

He shrugs, hiding his thoughts of Roza, and takes another spoonful of soup.

Anna turns to Vera. 'So, what do you wish for in 1942?'

'The children are going to plant a garden in the spring. I want a beautiful garden,' says Vera. 'With cucumbers, tomatoes and an apple tree!'

'Is that what your teacher is planning for the spring?' Anna raises her eyebrows. 'That would be nice to have vegetables. Like at your *dacha*, Misha.'

'I hope I can go to school soon,' says Galya, leaning her elbows on the table. 'I want to help in the garden.'

Mikhail sits back, arms folded. A garden takes time. Surely, they will not be here long enough to harvest the vegetables next autumn. It is impossible.

Galya takes the last spoonful of soup and pushes her bowl to the centre of the table. She leans forward, resting her head on her arms, eyelids heavy.

'And you, Anna, what do you wish for this year?' Galya asks, yawning.

'Of course, most important is for Ivan to be safe at the front,' says Anna.

Vera's smile fades and she climbs onto Anna's lap.

'But for me, my dream is to take a bath. I want to sit in the steam of the *banya*, breathe in the smell of birch tree twigs and scrub every centimetre of my body. I miss water. Clean, fresh, hot water.'

'Me too,' sighs Galya.

'And you, Misha. What is your New Year's wish?'

'I want to go home,' he says. And bury Roza properly.

They return to their mattresses in the cellar. Galya crawls under her blanket while Vera somersaults the length of her bed. Anna pulls the bedsheet curtains together, and pins them shut. Once closed, it feels like a tent and it is surprisingly quiet in the crowded basement.

Mikhail lies beside Galya.

'I have something special for you, girlies,' whispers Anna. She pulls her closed fists from behind her back. 'Choose a hand. Vera, you are the youngest, you first.'

Vera taps her right fist and Anna opens it, revealing a beautifully wrapped domino-sized chocolate. The wrapper features a polar bear surrounded by the warm green glow of the northern lights. She recognises the Mishka Na Severe chocolate and her face lights up.

Galya sits up and taps the other fist. Anna gives her an identical chocolate.

'I'll have a bit now, and leave the rest for another day,' Galya says.

Vera hesitates, clearly wanting to eat the whole piece, and shrugs. 'OK I'll eat just *choot choot* too.'

The girls unwrap the chocolates and take a small bite. Savouring the sweetness, they wait for the chocolate to melt on their tongues and re-fold the wrappers around the remaining chocolate.

'Put them here.' Anna opens an old cigarette tin and waits for the girls to drop them into the container. She closes the lid tightly and pushes the box between the mattress and the wall.

Anna must have saved this secret surprise just in case the siege took them to New Year. It seems impossible to Mikhail that during all the weeks of painful hunger scratching and tugging at her stomach that Anna resisted eating the chocolates. He could not have done the same.

'I have gifts too.' Mikhail hands them each a paper scroll tied with a piece of string.

Anna helps Vera ease the fraying lace from the paper and unroll it.

'Mama, it's us!'

Several weeks ago, Mikhail sketched them while they were reading in the flat. Anna was sitting cross-legged on the bed with Vera nestled in her lap. Simple pencil lines outline their entwined figures. Heads down, they focus on the book in front of them.

Galya opens hers and finds a sketch of Misha holding her hand on the beach. He drew this sketch from a photo which was taken on their last trip to the Black Sea. Walking away from the photographer, their bodies are in silhouette.

Galya immediately recognises the scene. 'I remember this day, Papa. Mama took this photo.' Tears well in her eyes and her chin quivers.

Mikhail had hoped the sketch would not bring back memories of Roza but she was the first thing Galya thought of when she looked at the sketch. His shoulders slump with failure.

'It was nice at the seaside,' Galya says, wiping the tears

from her cheeks.

'Misha, the sketches are wonderful,' Anna says, reaching out to squeeze his hand.

She pulls the string from her gift, which is larger than the girls' sketches, and reveals a watercolour he painted years ago, when the garden at the *dacha* was bursting with ripe vegetables. In the foreground, a fat watermelon on a thick stem lies on the ground. Behind it, tomato plants bend from the weight of the plump fruit.

Anna laughs and gets up. Stretching it open, she holds it on the wall. 'This will be our new window. Let's put it up and forget about the snow and the cold. From our window, we will see this beautiful garden.'

The dull winter sun lights the crisscrossed newspaper on the studio window. Mikhail sharpens a pencil to a point and finds a sketchbook wedged between his workbench and the wall. Most of the pages are clean and unused. He opens the book and starts to draw a profile with an angular nose and petite chin. The pencil scratches across the surface of the page and the image grows. Gentle shaded lines form the iris and pupil. He sketches an eye and a brow. He strengthens the line of the chin and starts to form the mouth, which is slightly open but not smiling, as if she is about to take a breath. He stops and looks at the image. Recognising the face, his heart freezes. It is Roza.

Boris enters the studio, waggling his finger at Mikhail. 'Tsk, tsk, tsk! It's prohibited to work on a New Year's Day, Mikhail Tarasovich!'

Boris stands in the centre of the room with his fur hat perched jauntily on his bald head. The tall ceilings dwarf his skinny body. He is surrounded by easels and scores of empty frames leaning against the walls.

Mikhail closes the notebook. 'Oh, you know, just sharpening my pencils to be ready for a productive 1942.' He does not smile at his cynical joke.

Boris opens a tall cabinet next to his workbench, climbs on a chair, and digs into the furthest corner of the cupboard. 'A-ha!' He pulls out an unmarked bottle of clear liquid. 'The pencils can wait, my friend. We must celebrate.' He kisses it and climbs down from the chair. He places the bottle, two glasses and a pack of playing cards on the workbench. 'I've known that this bottle was up there but I wasn't tempted, even on the worst days. Can you believe, there wasn't anybody here to drink with, Misha? More than a thousand people here, and not a single drinking buddy.'

The vodka will sharply burn his empty stomach but Mikhail craves the warmth that follows.

'Oh, my friend, I'm so glad to see you. It's been terrible here. Of course, the bombs and the war is crap. But we have too many women and *babushki* here. All the men have left, Misha. And the old women, they give me a headache, always offering advice and controlling the situation.'

'What situation?'

'Any situation!'

Picturing the *babushki* hounding Boris, Mikhail smiles but it quickly fades.

'Misha, you're so glum.' Boris pushes the bottle to the side and approaches Mikhail's workbench. 'I've heard about the portrait.'

'It's a double portrait, Colonel Shishkin's sons.'

'Are you ready?'

'Ready?'

'Did you pack your supplies?'

Mikhail shrugs and cradles his face in his rough, dry hands.

'Let's sort it all out.' Boris takes several tins of brushes from a shelf and places them on the bench in front of Mikhail. 'Have you thought about the limit of your palette and the medium? What about your composition?' He retrieves a tin from a cupboard and rattles it. 'Shall I mix some dammar varnish?'

Mikhail selects a variety of hog-hair brushes: flats and rounds, thick and thin. 'What if I can't do it? What if it doesn't turn out?'

'Misha, you're talented. I know it is daunting but you can do this. The most important thing is to get everything packed and ready. You don't want to get there and not have what you need.' He takes a large cloth from a closet. 'Be sure to spread this on the floor. You can't make a mess at the colonel's.' He removes a portable easel from the closet and places an oil box in front of Mikhail. 'Choose your colours, Misha.' He quickly returns to the cupboard. 'And you'll want some paper and charcoal for sketches, won't you?'

Mikhail has not thought about the process but nods in agreement.

'The paper in the closet is damp. You'll be better off using the paper you have at your bench.'

Mikhail opens the box and finds three rectangular palettes resting in the grooves. He slides one out. Although faint shadows of colour stain the wood, it is clean and ready for use. His heart quickens, smelling the residue of oil paint and solvent. Boris pushes a double dipper pot in front of him and a bottle of white spirit.

'What time is the car coming tomorrow?'

'Nine.'

'It will still be dark, Misha. Do some sketches of the lads

while you wait for better light. While you are there, you must use your time wisely. Etch the boys into your memory, every detail of their likeness, not forgetting their shape and form.'

'You should be doing this portrait, Boris.' Mikhail's head aches as the magnitude of the task sets in.

'Of course not. I don't have any formal training. The colonel wouldn't ever want me. Besides, Orbelli knows I'd do something wrong or say something inappropriate. He chose you.' He folds the cloth and places it in a bag and packs an empty tin. 'You'll need this for your brushes.' He tosses in a metal double dipper. 'For your solvent and medium.'

The compartments in the oil box are lined with tin and stained with smears of paint. He packs the metal paint tubes and places the brushes in the long, narrow sections. He puts rags and a small bottle of turpentine and white spirit in the box and seals the clasps shut.

'See? You are all sorted.' Boris claps him on the shoulder and looks at the vodka with a sigh. 'Now, let's celebrate, for old times' sake. Like we used to. Remember all the parties here in the studio with you, me and Lev?'

Suddenly, Boris raises his index finger. 'How could I have forgotten?' He darts over to the other side of the studio and crawls beneath Lev's workbench. He empties the contents of a cupboard, pushing a sweater, a box and a pair of shoes to the side. The seat of his wool trousers is threadbare and bulky around his shrinking body.

'Oy my knees! This floor is so hard!' He removes a tin of paint from the cupboard. 'Glory to God! I've found it!' He slides out a glass jar of gherkins. He grins, trying to catch his breath.

Mikhail helps him lift the jar onto the workbench. They place it beside the vodka, glasses and playing cards. The massive jar is much bigger than the litre of vodka.

'What a beautiful still life, Misha!' Boris pushes the gherkins behind the vodka and props the playing cards in front of it. 'What do you think? Should we draw it or drink it?' He jabs his sharp elbow into Mikhail's bony rib cage.

The jar is filled to the brim with stubby, pickled cucumbers. A long, slender dillweed flower curves against the glass jar. Mikhail salivates and his stomach groans.

Boris grasps the lid and attempts to open the jar. His face reddens, straining. The lid does not budge. He slides it towards Mikhail. 'You try. I don't have the strength.'

Mikhail gently taps the lid on the workbench. Boris presses his hands together in prayer, eyes raised to heaven as Mikhail grasps the lid. It shifts slightly and the seal breaks, releasing the sharp smell of vinegar and dill.

'Well, that solves it. He exists!' Boris says, slapping his knee.

Mikhail unscrews the lid.

'We have to make it last, Misha.' He stabs a gherkin with his pocket knife and drops it on a saucer. He cuts it lengthwise and slices it. Screwing the lid back on the jar he pushes it aside. He returns the cap to the vodka and places it beside the jar. 'It may have to last us ten years. We must economise.' He raises the glass of vodka and starts to contemplate his toast. 'Misha, you look terrible. Really, can't you have a good time for just a moment? We have everything we need!'

Mikhail props his elbow on the table and leans his forehead into his palm.

'You're all ready for the portrait. Stop worrying!' Boris waits for a response but Mikhail does not even look at him. 'I heard about Roza, Misha. Is that it?'

Hearing her name, he shivers and folds his arms, unwilling

and unable to speak of her. He shakes his head. 'It's just,' Mikhail begins, '…the idea that this could all go on for ten years.'

'Nobody knows the future, Misha. Not even Stalin. What can we do about it? Nothing.' Boris shrugs and raises the vodka glass. 'For now, let's drink to 1942! May it be a hell of a lot better than last year!'

They tap glasses and drink.

The liquid burns from the tip of Mikhail's tongue straight down his throat and lands in his empty stomach. He sets the glass on the workbench. Warmth travels from his core and into his fingertips, dispelling fears of the future and the portrait.

'It's been too long,' says Boris, rubbing his stomach.

For a few minutes, the men sit in silence.

'Do you ever wonder, Misha, if it is all worth it? I mean, in the end of ends maybe the Krauts will just march in and take over anyway. Who knows? Maybe we'd be better off.'

Boris's dangerous words linger. A vodka haze spreads like a misty cloud rolling in from the Baltic Sea.

3

⊱✦⊰

Vladimir, the elder son, is a handsome, younger version of the colonel. His dark hair is slicked back in the same style and he has an identical cow's lick on top of his head. His body is lean but muscular. Maxim looks as if he is part of an entirely different family. His chubby cheeks, covered with freckles, dominate his round face and his sandy blond, curly hair is like a short, dense sponge.

The perfectly starched white shirts of their Pioneer uniforms contrast with bright red kerchiefs tied around their necks. Maxim's shirt pulls at the buttons. Vladimir's trousers are slightly short, revealing the socks covering his narrow ankles. Although a bit pale from a lack of sun, the boys look healthy and well-nourished. Their skin has a vibrant sheen and they walk with a spring in their step. Mikhail has stepped into a home of abundance. Feeling the warmth of the fire, he strips off his jacket and lays it on the arm of the sofa. He folds the sleeve, attempting to hide the hole in the right cuff, which he has repaired with an ugly knot of unravelling yarn.

Elizaveta enters holding a tray and places it on the table in front of the sofa. On the tray sits a teapot and a bowl of blush red apples. Mikhail immediately takes one. Its waxy skin is smooth in his dry palms.

'Just ring if you need anything,' she says, closing the door behind her.

Mikhail lifts the apple to his mouth and smells the aroma, slightly musty from cellar storage. It reminds him of his father, who ordered him to collect up the fallen apples which littered the ground beneath the apple tree at their *dacha*. No matter how mushy and wormy, his father wanted them all. They could be salvaged and made into vinegar.

'Papa said that you would tell us what to do,' says Vladimir, breaking into his thoughts.

'Yes, of course,' says Mikhail. He takes a bite into the apple. As he chews the sweet flesh, one of his teeth aches, sending a sharp pain into his gum.

Maxim pours a cup of strong tea for himself. He stirs two teaspoons of honey into the steaming cup, leaving a sticky trail on the tray.

'Offer Mikhail Tarasovich tea first. Don't just help yourself,' Vladimir scolds. 'Mikhail Tarasovich, would you like a cup of tea?'

'Of course,' Mikhail says.

Vladimir pours. 'Honey?'

'Two please.' He salivates as Vladimir spoons sweetness into the cup.

Mikhail stirs the tea, smelling the steam. His stomach groans and the boys look at him as if he has just broken wind. He takes another bite of the apple and sips the hot tea.

Maxim grabs an apple and stretches out on the sofa, taking three enormous, quick bites. Juice drips from his chin onto his kerchief. He tosses the fleshy apple core on the tray beside the teapot.

'How would you like to sit for the portrait?' asks Mikhail.

'You're the expert,' Maxim says, scanning Mikhail's greasy hair, misshapen sweater and baggy wool trousers.

Mikhail savours another sip of tea and sets down his cup.

'Vladimir, help me move this chair by the window.' He points to the armchair beside the fireplace. Together they push but Vladimir is doing most of the work. Mikhail steps away, leaving him to put it in place. This is the best position for the chair, where the morning sun will filter through the windows.

'Maxim, please sit here,' Mikhail says, motioning to the chair. 'And Vladimir, you stand beside him.'

Maxim sits and his buttons strain against his belly. He slumps badly which makes him look like a plump midget in an oversized chair.

'Switch places,' instructs Mikhail.

'I don't want to stand,' Maxim moans. 'Will I have to stand here all day?'

'Not the whole time, only when I'm working on you. You can take a break while I paint Vladimir.

Maxim reluctantly stands and Vladimir takes his place.

The red velvet curtains and the boys' kerchiefs complement the midnight blue rug beneath their polished shoes. Mikhail moves a small wooden table beside the chair and places the bowl of apples on it.

'This is nice,' Mikhail says. 'Just relax and I'll set up my easel.'

Mikhail spreads the cloth over the rug and opens the easel's spindly legs. He moves it closer to the chair but not directly in front of them, slightly off to the side. Undecided if the boys will look out the window, straight, or at him, he scratches his head and looks at the empty chair by the window. Is this the best option?

Vladimir glances at his wristwatch and sighs.

'Are you in a rush?' Mikhail says, setting a canvas on the easel.

'No, I just didn't think it would take this long to get started.'

Mikhail opens the box of oil paints and places it on a table beside the easel. He puts the brushes, bristle side up, in the tin and sets it beside the box. Balancing the palette on his lap he takes the tube of zinc white. He opens it and squeezes it on the far-left side. Beside it, he adds ivory black and ultramarine blue. The arc grows along the top of the palette: viridian, raw umber, burnt umber, burnt sienna, alizarin crimson, cadmium red, yellow ochre. He replaces the cap on the final tube and returns it to the box. The ritual of preparing the paint in his preferred order is complete. Although he has not painted in years, he feels ready to begin.

Vladimir sits with his feet slightly apart, flat on the floor. Maxim stands beside him. He shifts from foot to foot and folds his arms. Mikhail places the palette on the paint box and approaches Maxim.

'Put one hand on the top of the chair, the other at your side. But don't lean on the chair. Stand up straight and look at me.'

Mikhail adjusts Maxim's chin, encouraging it up ever so slightly. He places Vladimir's elbow on the arm of the chair and his other hand in his lap.

Returning to his easel, Mikhail clips a sheet of paper to a sketch board and takes a charcoal from the oil box.

Maxim shifts and sighs. 'How many days do we have to do this?'

'Two. Today I'll do some charcoal sketches and a study – that's a quick painting. I'll take it back to the Hermitage where I will make the proper portrait in the studio. I'll come back in a couple of weeks and complete your faces.'

Maxim sighs and Vladimir kicks him gently.

Holding the charcoal lightly cradled between his thumb and index finger, Mikhail focuses on the boys. His wrist moves freely, but in complete control, as the marks form on the textured paper. His shoulders relax as he sketches their facial features. He must etch them into his memory. Not just the physical aspects of their eyes, lips, and bone structure but their essence, their soul. He quickly falls into a trance, moving the charcoal across the page, creating sketches of Vladimir and Maxim.

As the light from the window grows stronger, Mikhail must begin painting. He is in a race with the short winter day. He returns the charcoal to the box, sets a canvas on the easel and considers the composition. How will he place them on the canvas?

Mikhail slides the metal double dipper onto the palette and pours solvent, turpentine, into one section and the medium, dammar varnish, in the other. With his thumb laced through the palette's hole, the wood rests on his left hand. He holds a variety of brushes, bristle side up, between his fingers. Taking a thick, round brush in his right hand, he combines raw umber with a bit of solvent and medium. The viscous paint thins. With only a faint touch of thin paint on the brush, he creates the underpainting, establishing the composition and balance of tonal values. The dry brush rubs across the canvas, leaving the whispery shape and form of the boys. As the ghostly impression grows, Mikhail gains confidence.

'Can I have a break?' Maxim says.

'Just a bit longer, Maxim. Tell me about your mother. I'm painting a portrait for her and I don't know anything about her.'

'She was evacuated back in June. She's in Sverdlovsk with her mother and sister. That's where she's from.'

'Why didn't you go with her?'

'Papa wanted us to stay.'

'It's boring here. All our friends were evacuated,' says Maxim.

'And you, Mikhail Tarasovich, why weren't you evacuated?'

'I was packing up the Hermitage. The city was surrounded just as we sent off the last shipment. There wasn't time.'

Mikhail does not like to recall boxing up the priceless treasures, racing against the Nazi invasion. He feels nauseous remembering how the canvases were removed from frames, pulled off stretchers, rolled up and filed away in numbered crates. He worked in panicked urgency with his colleagues, packing thousands of pieces. All the crates were then loaded into railway wagons and sent east to an unknown location. Mikhail tenses when he thinks of the vulnerable treasures being outside the Hermitage. They could be damaged, destroyed or stolen so easily. Perhaps they already have been.

'Can I have a break, Mikhail Tarasovich? It's hard to stand here.'

Vladimir kicks Maxim's foot. Maxim retaliates with a harder kick to Vladimir's leg.

'Boys! Enough! Have a break, Maxim.'

Maxim grabs an apple from the bowl, and collapses on the sofa.

Vladimir rolls his eyes.

'You're doing fine,' Mikhail says. 'Vladimir, you have the easy part, sitting.'

Mikhail cannot imagine he and his brother, Andrei, sitting for a portrait when they were boys. Fuelled by boredom, they would have quarrelled too. And it all would have ended with Andrei's classic weapon. He would have pinned Mikhail to the ground and coaxed the dog to lick his face. Mikhail's screams of protest would make the dog lick him even more.

'Why are you smiling?' asks Vladimir.

'Was I? I was just thinking of my brother, when we were young.'

'Is he here, in Leningrad?' asks Vladimir.

'No.'

His brush dances across the canvas, adding more detail to Vladimir's lean body and broad shoulders. He mixes a range of flesh tones on the palette, but they are not quite right. He adds a trace of ultramarine, making the tone cooler.

The last portrait he painted was of Roza holding Galya just after she was born, November 1933. There was more warmth to Roza's skin, more cadmium red. Mikhail tried to capture the new mother's mixture of emotions: determined contentment, pure love, and vulnerable fear. The portrait still hangs in their flat back in Mokhovaya Street. He had planned to do their portrait every year but somehow time slipped away. Now it is too late.

'I'm hungry,' moans Maxim, ringing the bell.

'You're always hungry,' says Vladimir.

Elizaveta enters and Maxim asks for a fresh pot of tea and some chocolates.

'Lunch is in fifteen minutes. We're just waiting for the colonel,' Elizaveta says.

Colonel Shishkin sits at the head of a long dining table, his sons on either side, and Mikhail takes the remaining place at the opposite head of the table. Silver cutlery lies on a linen tablecloth. Outside, fluffy snowflakes fall steadily. A fire crackles in the fireplace and a crystal chandelier hangs over the table.

Elizaveta places bowls of *borscht* in front of Mikhail and the others. The aroma of earthy beetroot and garlic rises from the broth. His stomach twists and moans, demanding food.

'Mikhail? Mikhail Tarasovich?' The colonel raises his voice.

Mikhail looks up, suddenly removed from his thoughts.

The colonel points to Elizaveta, standing beside Mikhail. 'Don't you want soured cream?'

Elizaveta stands holding a dish with a spoon resting in a cloud of soured cream. Mikhail nods and she delivers an ample dollop to the centre of his bowl. He gently stirs and the deep red broth stains the cream. He takes a spoonful to his lips and tastes the forgotten flavours of salt and fat. He does not want the mouthful to end.

'Mikhail Tarasovich.' The colonel is staring, waiting for him to respond to his question.

Mikhail looks up from his food.

'What do you think?' Shishkin asks.

'It's delicious.'

Shishkin's smirk tells Mikhail that was the wrong answer.

'Not the soup. The portrait! The boys were telling me that it is going well.'

'Yes, of course, the portrait. The boys are very helpful and we have a satisfying composition. Would you like to see?'

'Not today. I have to get back to the office quickly after lunch.'

Mikhail takes a slice of bread from a basket and rips a piece. It is baked with real rye flour, not sawdust. He dips it into the soup and the broth seeps into the dense bread. As he eats, his stomach quickly feels full, overfull. He shifts on his chair, trying to find a comfortable position. Using the last of his bread, he mops the remaining soup and forces himself to finish. Bloated, his stomach aches.

'We should get back to work,' Mikhail says.

'Now?' Maxim says.

'Don't you want the second course, Mikhail Tarasovich?' asks the colonel.

Mikhail has not eaten two courses at a meal in months.

Elizaveta places a full plate of chicken, boiled potatoes and cabbage in front of him. Fat glistens on the thigh's crispy skin, a sliver of butter is melting into the potatoes. Eight months ago, Mikhail would have eaten this plate of food without any thought. It was nothing special. But today it is exotic and impossible, a figment of his imagination which will burst when he pierces it with his fork. He picks up his cutlery and cuts the meat from the bone. As he raises it to his lips, a pain shoots from his stomach. He cannot eat any more. His stomach, shrunken and unused to the rich food, is full. Reluctantly, he puts down his fork.

'Mikhail Tarasovich, have you listened to anything we've said?' asks the colonel.

'Pardon?'

'The painting. I need it by the tenth of January.'

Mikhail hesitates.

'It can't be later, Mikhail. The courier must leave on the tenth if my wife is to get it in time. I don't want it to be late.'

'It needs time to dry, sir, before you send it. I'll have to come on the seventh and finish the detail of the boys' faces. It will dry better here. It's very cold in the Hermitage.'

Five days. How can he finish this portrait in such limited time?

'Don't be late, Mikhail. I'm counting on you.' He glances at his watch and pushes his chair back from the table. 'I've got to get back to the office.'

The full plate of food sits, uneaten, in front of Mikhail. His stomach churns, struggling to digest the borscht. He cannot possibly eat any more.

'Aren't you going to eat?' asks Vladimir, finishing the last of his cabbage.

'I'm full,' Mikhail says.

Maxim sneers at his half-eaten plate of food. 'Chicken, potatoes and cabbage. Every day is the same.' He tosses his napkin on the plate and pushes his chair away from the table.

The room grows darker as the sun starts to set. Maxim fidgets.

'How much longer?' he moans.

'I'm done,' Mikhail says, setting his brushes bristle side up in the tin.

Vladimir, stretched out on the sofa, looks up from his book.

'You can have a look, if you'd like.'

The boys come around the easel and Mikhail watches their unimpressed expressions. Maxim grimaces.

'It's just a study,' Mikhail explains. 'The faces will be more detailed in the final portrait.'

Maxim shrugs. 'Can we go?'

'Of course. I'll just tidy up my things.'

'See you on the seventh, Mikhail Tarasovich,' says Vladimir. He follows Maxim to the door.

'Until then.' Mikhail nods.

The door shuts. Quickly, he wraps the remaining *priyaniki* in newspaper, slips the parcel in his bag and puts the apples beside them. As he is about to zip it shut, Elizaveta enters the room.

'Take this,' she whispers, handing him a newspaper parcel. 'It's your lunch.' Her eyes dart between the door and his gaze.

He freezes, shocked by her generosity. Greasy patches seep through the paper. He can smell the chicken and his stomach groans.

'Quickly, put it away.'

He nestles the food in his bag and zips it shut.

'*Spasibo*,' he says.

Back at the Hermitage, Mikhail finds Anna, Galya and Vera reading on the mattresses. He sets the bag beside Galya and hangs his coat on a nail. He pulls the bedsheets closed, pinning them shut. Usually, they only closed them at night for a bit of privacy and warmth.

'What are you doing?' asks Anna.

He places the parcel on the mattress.

'Shhh,' he whispers, holding his index finger to his lips.

He flips open his pocket-knife and unwraps the newspaper, revealing the chicken, potatoes and cabbage. Elizaveta gave him Maxim's uneaten food, Mikhail's portion and a few pieces of bread.

Anna gasps.

'Papa, where did you get chicken?'

'Shhh,' Mikhail and Anna whisper sternly.

'Nobody can know, girls. Promise me, you will not tell anyone.' He looks them both in the eye. 'This is top secret.'

He flattens the newspaper, cuts the chicken into pieces and

pushes it towards each of them. Anna divides the cabbage and potatoes.

'Give me less,' whispers Mikhail.

She nods and gives the children and herself more.

They eat in silence, slowly chewing. Black ink from the newsprint stains the meat but they do not mind. It tastes delicious. Their fingers smell of cabbage and chicken fat. Starchy potato clings to their fingernails. They hide behind the bedsheets, muffling their joy.

Mikhail has hidden the apples and *priyaniki* in the studio. Warmed by the excitement of this secret, he reclines and props his hand under his head. He watches Anna and the girls eat, satisfied he has provided a meal. He always had a good job at the Hermitage which gave his family a decent standard of living. They never had a lot but they always had enough. He does not remember noticing and appreciating their simple, sufficient life.

Anna takes the last bite of cabbage. Her expression changes. Her brow furrows and her eyes drop, staring at the greasy newspaper. She looks up and quickly pushes a tear from her cheek.

'How can they have so much when the rest of the city is starving?' she whispers, leaning towards Mikhail. 'How can they live with themselves, knowing that children are starving?'

4

✎❧✎

THE EVENING SKY SLOWLY turns a fiery pink. Wisps of clouds, lit by the setting sun, streak the Leningrad sky, casting a warm glow through the studio windows. Mikhail steps back from the portrait. After two days of painting, he is happy with his progress. Painted in Soviet Realist style, the boys' figures are beginning to take shape. Vladimir sits, straight-backed on the chair. Beside him, Maxim stands, head turned to the artist. The background is roughly sketched and there is much to be done. Although he is tempted to carry on painting, he knows it is not wise in the fading light.

Boris enters the studio carrying a tool box. 'Look at you. You're such a good worker, a real Hero of the Soviet Union.'

'You think it's OK? It's been a long time since I've painted. And it's so cold, the paint doesn't dry.'

'Don't worry. You'll get it done. The colonel will be happy, the wife will be happy. You'll receive a medal for Artistic

Services to our great Soviet State. All will end happily ever after.'

Mikhail cringes at his cynicism and starts to clean the brushes.

'Papa?' Galya and Vera hover near the doorway. Vera's eyes are red and swollen.

'Where's Anna Petrovna?' asks Galya. 'We can't find her.'

'I'm sure she is somewhere,' Mikhail says.

Earlier in the day, Anna had told Mikhail that she was going out. She had not heard anything from Ivan in weeks, so she wanted to see if there was a letter waiting for her at the flat. He had offered to go with her, but she insisted that he work on the portrait. She did not want him to waste precious time.

'Maybe she is in the kitchen?' Mikhail asks.

'We looked. She wasn't there.'

'Maybe she has Fire Warden duty on the roof?'

Galya shakes her head. 'She hasn't come back.'

'We'll find her. Don't worry,' Mikhail says, but his words lack conviction. He scratches his head. She could have collapsed walking to the flat. Or maybe she was attacked. Or perhaps she has simply disappeared. Mikhail pushes these thoughts away. 'She'll be back. I'm sure.' He opens the bottom drawer at his workbench and takes out an apple. Flipping open his pocket knife, he motions for the girls to come closer and sit at his bench.

'An apple!' says Galya, sliding onto the stool.

Boris drags his stool to the workbench and picks up Vera. 'Light as a feather,' he says, swinging her up and setting her on the perch.

She giggles despite her tears.

'I'm guessing, if we eat slowly, Anna will be here before we are done.' Mikhail cuts the apple into quarters and gives a piece to Boris and the girls.

Galya smells the fruit and takes a bite. She savours it and then slowly starts to chew.

'Papa, how many apples do you have?'

'Not telling,' he winks. 'My secret.'

'Where did you get them?' she asks.

'You know, I went to see the colonel. I'm painting his sons.'

She looks at the canvas and takes another bite.

Galya points to Maxim. 'Is this one really this fat?'

Mikhail shrugs. 'Maybe I should make him a bit smaller?'

'How can it be that he is so big?' Galya asks.

Mikhail hesitates and the wind rattles the window panes.

'The boy has connections to the right people in the right places,' Boris says. What can you do? It's the way it is. Now, who wants to see a magic trick?'

Boris takes a twenty-*kopek* coin from his pocket. With a few flourished gestures, he appears to pull the coin from Vera's ear and she laughs. But Galya does not submit to this distraction and stares at the painting.

As the studio grows darker, Boris strikes a match and lights a candle on the workbench. Mikhail wonders if Anna has returned. Will they go down to the cellar and find her coat and scarf on her nail?

'Show me another trick,' says Vera.

'I haven't got any other tricks. That's it,' Boris says. 'Misha, don't you have an anecdote or something? Or, are you just going to sit there and look glum?'

Mikhail pauses, distracted. 'Do *you* think I should make Maxim thinner?'

Boris pops his last piece of apple into his mouth and studies the painting. 'Yes, probably better to make him thinner. More in keeping with the times.' He looks at the study. 'And you could probably do without the bowl of apples, to be on the safe side.'

He stretches his back, leaning from side to side. He is achy from standing at the easel. 'What will I put on the table?'

'Don't know. We'll think of something.'

The girls finish their bits of apple.

'Maybe we should look in the cellar for Anna Petrovna?' says Mikhail. 'I bet she's back.'

Boris takes the candle and they follow him down the long corridor to the wide, sweeping staircase. Their steps scuff through crumbling plaster and gritty dirt on the mosaic floor. They step into the courtyard where snowflakes drift and swirl in the darkness. Slipping between leafless birch trees and down the snowy path, they make their way to the narrow staircase down to the cellar. From the bottom of the stairs they see the watercolour painting that Mikhail gave to Anna for the New Year. Beside it, Mikhail's coat hangs on the wall but Anna's nail is empty. She has not returned.

Mikhail rolls over and his hipbone presses into the thin mattress, colliding with the earth floor. He stretches his stiff back and heavy arms. His head aches. The persistent twisting and churning of his stomach, which has grown worse since the lunch at the colonel's, demands him to wake. He rolls over again and realises Galya is not beside him. Startled, he sits up. The cool cellar air hits his neck and torso.

Galya is curled up beside Vera. Mikhail remembers that she insisted on taking Anna's place beside Vera, to keep her warm through the night. The pair lie together on their sides, their skinny bodies making a C shape under the pile of blankets. He squints, hoping to see Anna's coat hanging beside his, but it is empty. Anna has not returned.

Mikhail reclines and pulls the blanket up to his chin. Someone on the other side of the cellar gets up, blankets rustle, whispers and footsteps towards the stairs. Thoughts of the portrait send a wave of panic through his body. He only has two days to finish the painting.

'Papa, wake up!' Galya grabs his shoulder. 'We have to find Anna Petrovna.'

Beside her, Vera blinks, waiting for his response. 'Are we going to look for Mama?'

Vera's sleepy, sorrowful eyes stare at Mikhail, willing him to get up.

The painting will have to wait. He must look for Anna. If he goes quickly he could be back in time to have a couple hours of work.

'I'll go to Mokhovaya Street,' he says. 'Both of you must stay here.'

'We want to go with you,' says Galya.

'No. You aren't strong enough.' His voice is firm and inflexible.

'I'll look after Verochka. I promise.' She puts her arm around Vera's narrow shoulders and pulls her close.

Mikhail gets up and puts on a sweater and his fur hat. He pushes his feet into his boots and slides on his coat. He shivers and rubs his hands together, hoping to warm his coat. From behind, he feels the weight of a hand on his shoulder and for a fraction of a second he thinks that Anna has returned. But when he turns, he finds Boris.

'I thought you had already left,' says Boris. He's wearing his coat and his fur hat.

'You don't have to come,' says Mikhail.

'There's been a blizzard overnight. You shouldn't go on your own.'

Leningrad is enveloped in fresh snow. Palace Square, blanketed in white and unscarred by footprints, sparkles in the soft morning dawn. Mikhail and Boris pull their earflaps over their ears and tie fraying laces under their chins. Mikhail takes a deep breath and the frozen air penetrates deep into his lungs. Pulling his scarf up around his face, he covers his beard and cheeks.

'It's as if the damn Krauts have brought a frozen hell with them,' Boris says.

Mikhail and Boris trudge across Palace Square. The snow squeaks underfoot. They do not look behind them at the Hermitage's scarred facade and broken windows. Neither do they comment on the colossal, crumbling male figures supporting the Hermitage's damaged portico. Instead, they focus on the route ahead. Their trail of footprints marks a path across the pristine snow. They walk, heads down, protecting their faces from the Arctic wind.

What was once Mikhail's daily route home is now unrecognisable. Many of the buildings have been bombed, scattering twisted and broken debris onto the streets. Snow-covered corpses, silhouettes unmistakably human, litter the wide avenues.

'She's wearing a traditional red scarf and black muskrat coat,' Mikhail says.

Boris nods.

As they walk, they glance around, hoping not to see her bright scarf protruding from the fresh snow. Mikhail's chest aches as the dry, frigid air fills his lungs. His nose numbs. They take the most direct route, following the Moika River, which is how Anna would have walked. Mikhail has followed this route countless times, always knowing his street and his flat would be exactly as he left them. But today, he has no idea what will be left of Mokhovaya Street. Hopefully, he will find Anna in the flat, wrapped in a shawl, smiling and laughing at them for coming after her. 'Of course, I couldn't go out in the blizzard,' she'll explain. 'It was too dangerous so I stayed here.' A perfectly logical explanation. Or maybe she will be around the next corner, knee-deep in snow, heading back to the Hermitage.

They follow the bridge over the Fontanka River and turn right onto Mokhovaya Street.

Midway down the street, Boris points at Mikhail's building. 'Your home still stands!'

Mikhail's frozen cheeks ache as he smiles but Boris's joke does not placate his worries. Usually, he is eager to arrive home but today Mokhovaya Street is eerie and desolate. His building, although unscarred by bombs, seems unfamiliar. Seeing the archway to the courtyard, Mikhail's throat tightens and he clenches his jaw.

He opens the door and they step into the corridor. His eyes take time to adjust after the bright snow. He removes his thick gloves and fumbles for a key in his coat pocket. Turning towards the row of mailboxes lining the wall, he slides the key into the lock.

'Expecting a love letter?' Boris quips.

'Anna was expecting a letter from Ivan.'

The mailbox door opens. It is empty.

'The post can't possibly still be working. What mailman would have the strength to make deliveries?' says Boris.

'She had heard a rumour that a delivery of military post arrived in our area. That is why she came here,' Mikhail says. 'I tried to stop her, but she was determined to check.'

'Mikhail Tarasovich.' A raspy, high-pitched voice echoes

off the concrete.

Opposite the mailboxes, Natalia Alexandrovna stands in her doorway. Living next to the entrance, she is the building's self-appointed guardian. The siege has taken its toll on the old woman. Her tiny body has grown more frail and her back is terribly hunched. As usual she is holding a broom, ready to swat anyone who steps out of line.

'Have you seen Anna?' Mikhail asks.

'Isn't she with you at the Hermitage?'

'She came here yesterday, but never returned.'

She shrugs. 'I haven't seen her.' Her cloudy eyes shift to the floor.

The wind rattles the door behind them.

'We'll go upstairs and look anyway,' Mikhail says, knowing full well that she is not there.

'Boys, as long as you are here could you help me?'

'Honestly, we are in a bit of a hurry. We have to get back to the Hermitage.' says Mikhail, heading towards the stairs.

But Boris pulls Mikhail's arm, takes off his hat and bows from the waist. His bald head shines in the dim light. 'We are at your service, madame. How can we help?'

She opens the door and shuffles into her flat, motioning for them to follow.

'Something terrible has happened. A tragedy,' she mumbles.

They follow her into the dark corridor, which is clouded with a mouldy, rotten smell. Mikhail breathes into his scarf, preferring the smell of his moist breath. The window is covered in sheets of newspaper.

'My granddaughter, Marina. She's…died.'

On the bed, a bundle is bound tightly with emerald fabric. It is about the size of Galya.

'May God forgive me, but I can't lift her and take her to the courtyard. I don't have the strength, Mikhail Tarasovich, and everyone is gone.' She blows her nose in a well-used handkerchief and dabs her eyes.

He remembers Marina. She was the same age as Galya and often played in the hallway, singing to herself. Her voice echoed around the stairwell. When she saw him, she would quickly dart back into her flat. Her rope-like plait trailed down her back.

Patches of moisture seep through the fabric. A cross is embroidered over Marina's heart. As he approaches the bed, a sweet smell clings to Mikhail's nose and throat. Boris takes the feet, Mikhail grasps the head and shoulders and they lift the dense corpse. As Mikhail carries her through the cluttered flat, his throat tightens. Natalia Alexandrovna holds the door as they take Marina to the corridor.

She mumbles as she walks beside her granddaughter. 'May God be with you and protect you. Dearest Marinochka, you were the sweetest and the best. Forgive me. I failed you. What will I say to your mother? How will I explain? She trusted me to keep you safe.'

Stepping out into the street, they trudge towards the courtyard. Mikhail's throat tenses. He hopes to find Roza undisturbed. His legs and back ache as the burden is shared between the two men. At the centre of the courtyard, beside the swings, the pile of corpses is completely blanketed in fresh snow, waiting for spring and the ground to thaw.

Boris breaks the silence. 'Where?'

'Not on the bottom,' Natalia says.

They hoist the bundle and place it on top of the pile. It sinks down into the snow as they release it, the shroud contrasting sharply with the whiteness of its resting place.

Mikhail brushes flakes from the right-hand side of the pile, searching for their familiar bedsheet. He bends and whisks away the powder, pushing snow from white bedsheets and a maroon quilt, until he finally finds a corner of cornflower blue. His Roza. It seems so long ago that she passed but it has been less than a month. Tears well. He pauses. A strange sense of relief catches him off-guard. She is safe now, buried under this thick layer of snow.

Arm in arm, Boris and Natalia Alexandrovna retrace their footsteps through the courtyard. Wiping the tears from his cheek, Mikhail follows behind. The courtyard darkens as the sun moves behind heavy clouds. The day is slipping away and the light is beginning to fade. Mikhail must get back to the Hermitage.

'Thank you, boys.' She does not look at them as she disappears behind her door and turns the lock. Her lonely footsteps scratch across the wood floor.

For a moment, the men stand in the silence.

'And now, to the fourth floor,' says Boris, extending his hand upward as if he is presenting a prize.

The long stairway stretches before them. Mikhail hesitates as hunger pains prod at his stomach. He knows Anna is not in the flat.

'Come on,' Boris says. We've come this far.' He starts climbing and pauses on the third step. 'What are you waiting for?'

Mikhail presses on, aching with each step. The stairway used to hum with life but is now quiet. Arguments, laughter, cooking smells and piano scales once slipped under the doors and mixed in the stairway. Now it is still, except for their footsteps and heavy breath.

As Mikhail inserts his key into the lock, he listens, hoping to hear Anna on the other side of the door. He turns the key; the door unlatches and swings open. They step into the narrow corridor.

'Anna?' he calls, outside her door. He knocks and waits.

'Do you have a key to her room?'

'No.' He heads towards his room and unlocks the door.

A crack of sunlight pierces the edge of the black fabric covering the window, falling across the floor to Galya's bed. Their books line the shelves. His portrait of Roza and new-born Galya hangs on the wall. The shelf of knick-knacks is undisturbed. Everything exactly as they left it but a ghostly melancholy has moved into the abandoned flat.

Mikhail knocks on Anna's door again but there is no sound coming from the Kemerovs' room. He walks towards the kitchen. Shaking the kettle, he is relieved to hear water splashing the sides. He strikes a match and turns the knob, hoping to hear the gas hiss. The ring ignites. He rubs his hands together, warming them with friction and the heat from the flame.

Boris unbuttons his coat and sits on the stool at the kitchen table. 'I would do anything for a cigarette right now. Just one.' He takes off his hat and scratches his head. 'What a nightmare, the whole thing.'

Mikhail peels a strip of wallpaper from the corridor and scrapes the paste into the kettle. Stirring it with a wooden spoon, he glances at his watch.

'What are you in a hurry for? Take a seat and relax. You must be tired.'

Mikhail sits on the opposite stool. 'I knew this would be a waste of time.'

'What can you do? You had to come to look for her. The painting must wait.'

The men sit, listening to the gas ring, waiting for the water to boil, too tired to speak.

Mikhail's thoughts wander from the portraits to the unnatural curve of Natalia Alexandrovna's spine and her raspy voice. Broken-hearted and alone, she is unlikely to survive.

When the water starts to boil, Mikhail stands and pours the liquid into two cups. He sets them on the table and takes a wrapped *priyanik* from his coat pocket. He breaks it in half and places a piece in front of Boris.

'Another gift from our benevolent prince. What a wonderful surprise,' says Boris. He smells the spiced cookie and takes a bite.

'Roza is down there, in the courtyard.' Mikhail tips his head towards the kitchen window. Tears sting his eyes but he swallows hard and refuses to let them fall.

Boris shakes his head. 'She was a good woman.'

Mikhail looks at his *priyanik* and inhales. 'She stopped eating so that Galya would have more.'

For a moment Boris is speechless. 'That is the power of a mother's love.' He sips his tea, wincing.

'I begged her not to do it. But we both knew there wasn't enough for all three of us.' He sits back on the stool, leaning against the wall. 'I couldn't have done it.' A few times, driven by unyielding hunger pains, he got up in the middle of the night and sneaked a few bites of bread. He took more than his share while Roza went without. His shameful secret.

'I just want it to be over and everything can go back to normal,' Boris says.

Normal. The word swims around Mikhail's head. He takes a sip of broth and a bite of the *priyanik*. The spices mask the stale wallpaper paste.

'We never allowed Galya to play with Marina, even though they were in the same class.'

Boris waits for him to continue.

'None of the children in the building played with her. She was always alone.' Mikhail pauses, collecting his thoughts. 'We heard things about Marina's parents. You know, whispers about her parents. Enemies of the people.' Conjuring judgement and fear, the phrase sits uneasily in the kitchen. 'We just wanted to protect Galya.'

Boris shrugs. 'It's normal. All parents want to protect their children. Don't even think about it. It's in the past. Many mistakes have been made.'

Mikhail still feels the weight of Marina's corpse in his hands and her stench in his nose. The memory of Marina's face darting behind the door lingers. She was timid, like a rabbit scampering into shrubs. Her sweet voice was always alone. It haunts him. Her size is so like his own daughter. Shame and regret swells. Marina was just a girl, no matter what.

Mikhail and Boris set out for the Hermitage, brushing the snow from the corpses along the route, searching for Anna. Boris walks along the right side of the street and Mikhail checks the bodies on the left. Some look peacefully asleep. Others are wide-eyed and open-mouthed, frozen in painful shock. Mikhail does not know where else to look for Anna. Foolishly, he believes that she will be at the Hermitage when they return. He has felt this feeling before. It is the exact same absurd optimism which he felt when he realised that his brother, Andrei, was gone.

Years ago, late on a warm summer's evening, Mikhail walked along the wide avenue to Andrei's *kommunalka*, near Finlandsky Railway Station. The white night sky was light at ten o'clock and the air was still and muggy. When he arrived at Andrei's building, there was a pile of clothes and books scattered on the street. Among the books, a photo caught his eye. He picked it up. It was his father, in a swimming suit, flexing imaginary biceps. He and Andrei stood on either side, laughing as the camera snapped the photo. He could remember this day but could not understand why it would be on the street. It was impossible that Andrei would throw this photograph away. Confused, Mikhail looked up as a woman threw another bundle of clothes from a third-floor window. A striped shirt and a pair of trousers fluttered to the ground, settling beside Mikhail. There must be a mistake, he thought. He put the photo in his pocket and headed into the building. Taking the stairs two at a time, he made his way along the smoky corridor to Andrei's room. A family of four lived in one room, a group of pensioners in another. He knocked on Andrei's door and a middle-aged woman opened it. He asked for Andrei and she stared at him, expressionless. 'He doesn't live here,' she said and promptly slammed the door. Mikhail stood, staring at the peeling paint on the door, taking in her words, the slam echoing in his ears. A bulky *babushka* carrying a cup of tea approached and whispered, 'They took him. He's gone.' With a look of disgust, she pushed past.

Shocked by her words, Mikhail was speechless. He was certain it must be a mistake. It was the only explanation. He was suddenly aware of the sweat collecting under his arms; the flat's moist air closed in on him. He ran, flying down the stairs to the wide avenue. Taking a deep breath, he paused for a moment, frozen. His heart beat faster, pulsing blood around his body. He did not look back, he did not run. He headed home, naturally but purposefully, distancing himself from his brother, blending in with the other citizens of Leningrad on an evening stroll. As he walked, he came to understand the gravity of the situation. Andrei was gone. Surely it was a mistake. Anger and fear grew but he quickly buried these feelings. Everything would be fine and Andrei would come home soon.

Mikhail bends and brushes the snow from another corpse, uncovering a flash of red amid the white. His breath quickens as he pulls away the flakes. It is not her. It is a man, old and blue. Mikhail stands, his feet growing numb from the cold. Ahead, Boris beckons from the edge of Palace Square. They are nearly back at the Hermitage. He dreads telling Vera of their useless search.

Hunger pains grip his empty stomach and he forces himself onwards. Mikhail used to travel this same route every day and often passed familiar yet unknown faces. But this time, he does not recognise any of them.

The cellar stairs creak as Mikhail descends deep underneath the Hermitage. He steps gingerly on his numb feet. He pulls off his glove, revealing fuchsia skin, and walks towards their mattresses. He rubs his fingers together, feeling a painful tingle as they warm. His eyes fall to Anna's nail on the wall. It is empty.

Beneath the watercolour of the bountiful garden, Vera and Galya sit together on the mattress. They smile when they see him but then their faces fade to disappointment when they realise he is alone. He pulls off his boots, takes off his coat, and dives under the layers of blankets. His body shivers, trying to create warmth. Galya curls up beside him and rubs his back.

'You didn't find her,' Vera says.

'Everything will be fine,' he says. 'I promise.'

5

꙰

IN THE STUDIO, MIKHAIL BITES a small piece of apple and chews. His teeth ache in their roots. Moving his jaw carefully, he tries to avoid the shooting pain. He cuts another sliver and places it on his tongue, savouring it.

The morning sun intensifies, casting a warm golden light through the studio windows. His legs are sore from walking to Mokhovaya Street. He pulls his stool in front of the easel and perches on it, feeling relief in his legs. His palette, exactly as he left it, is ready for him to carry on. The colours arc around the top of the wood. Below them, a variety of mixed hues fill the palette. He takes a thin brush and collects flesh tones on the bristles. Delivering the paint to the canvas, he concentrates on Maxim's hand.

'Where were you yesterday?' Orbelli says, entering the studio. His words are spoken firmly, his face stern.

'Anna is missing,' Mikhail starts to explain.

Orbelli does not wait for his explanation. 'Colonel Shishkin was here yesterday.'

Mikhail scowls and tenses.

'He wanted to see your progress. I brought him to the studio and you weren't here, Mikhail. Do you know how important this is? You've hardly done anything! It is supposed to be done by tomorrow morning.'

'I understand, sir. I'll finish today.'

'More than a thousand people live here. Don't you understand? It will be much better for everyone if the colonel is satisfied.'

'I understand.'

'He's sending a car tomorrow, nine o'clock. It has to be done.'

Orbelli turns and storms away but his words linger behind him.

Mikhail rolls his shoulders, releasing tension, and takes a deep breath. He skips the brush around the palette, adjusting the flesh tones. With short, smooth strokes he adds definition to the curve of Maxim's fingers.

He studies the brothers, adding more detail: the shadows in the folds of the pioneer scarves, the crisp creases on their ironed shirts, white highlights of their shoes. Once satisfied with their figures, he will move on to the background.

As he paints, he forgets about everything he cannot control. He loses himself, the Hermitage, war and hunger in the viscous paint. He creates a rhythm: palette, canvas, palette, canvas. The brushes keep time, dancing between the two. His mind clears, focusing completely on the portrait. As the figures emerge, a warm sensation radiates from his core. It seems foreign at first, but as it spreads he recognises the feeling, so long lost. It is joy, satisfaction, purpose, endeavour all rolled into one. After months of concentrating solely on survival, the painting has given him something fresh, an escape from his existence, a reconnection with creating, awakening his soul.

Boris slides a bowl of soup and a piece of bread onto the table beside the easel.

'You haven't eaten, Misha. Take a break, you're making good progress.' He looks over Mikhail's shoulder. 'It's beautiful. I think you were right to make this one thinner,' he says, pointing to Maxim.

Mikhail sets his brushes in a tin and dips the spoon into the bowl. The stale smell grows stronger as the broth approaches. A hunger pain jabs his stomach, demanding that he eat. The soup coats his tongue, leaving a sour taste in his mouth. Ever since eating the delicious *borscht* at the colonel's, Mikhail struggles to eat the Hermitage food. His taste buds have woken up. He takes another spoonful, willing them to go back asleep. He pinches a bit of woody bread and eats it.

'What will you put on the table?' Boris points to the canvas.

Mikhail has not given any thought to the table. He chokes down more soup.

'Maybe I should just get rid of the table? He glances at the windows as a sliver of sunlight cuts between clouds and slices through the crisscrossed tape on the windows. He only has a couple of hours more of good light. 'It seems more trouble than it's worth.'

'*Pravda!*' says Boris. He finds an old newspaper in his workbench drawer. 'Just put a copy of *Pravda* on the table. Who could argue with that? Not as pretty as the bowl of apples, of course. But demonstrates the boys are studious and up to date on current affairs.' He lays the folded newspaper beside Mikhail's palette.

'Not a bad idea, Boris,' Mikhail says, nodding.

Boris pats Mikhail on the back. 'Now, quickly, finish, so that we can toast the completion of this work of art.'

Mikhail adds a touch of alizarin crimson to the ultramarine on his palette, creating a deep violet. He applies the paint to the canvas, enriching the shadows of the folds of the curtains. His brush glides from the palette to the painting. His eyes dart seamlessly between them but his head remains still as he adds depth and nuance.

'The light is fading,' says Boris. 'You should stop.'

Mikhail steps back and looks at the canvas. The longer he looks at the painting, the more he sees what is yet to be done. But the race with the sun is over, he is running out of time.

'Mikhail Tarasovich, this is a masterpiece.'

Mikhail shrugs, unconvinced.

'And you say you aren't a portrait artist! Maybe you should be.'

'It's not finished. The faces are the most important part. I have to get it right tomorrow.'

Boris takes his brush and lays it on the palette. He urges Mikhail to stand and pulls the stool over to his workbench.

'Tomorrow will be sorted out tomorrow. For now, let's toast your masterpiece.' He fills the glasses with vodka and spears a gherkin in the jar.

Mikhail takes his place on the stool and leans his elbow on the rough surface.

Boris raises his glass. 'To artistic endeavour!'

They tap glasses and drink. The vodka burns a hot trail from Mikhail's lips to his stomach and he pops a piece of gherkin in his mouth.

'Are you going to write to Ivan and tell him about Anna?'

Mikhail has been so busy with the portrait that he has not thought about writing to Ivan.

'Tell him what? We don't know what to say. For now, I think it's best just to leave it. I don't want to worry him. Besides, he can't do anything to help find her. What's the point?'

Boris nods. He strikes a match and lights a candle on the workbench. A gust of wind rattles the window frame and the flame flickers. A shiver pricks Mikhail's spine.

Boris scratches his chin and reaches for the bottle. 'Under the circumstances, I think another is in order. You formulate the toast, dear friend.'

'You know, she hasn't disappeared. *That* is impossible. Dead or alive, she is somewhere. I propose this toast to Anna.'

Boris raises his glass. 'To Anna!'

The second shot tumbles down his throat, fuelling a fire in Mikhail's stomach.

'My brother, Andrei, has been on my mind lately,' Mikhail mumbles.

'I didn't know you had a brother.'

'Haven't seen him in a long time. I lost contact with him seven years ago. A few months after Galya was born.'

Boris slices another pickle, waiting for him to continue.

'He was probably connected to something. He wasn't a saint. But he wasn't the devil either. I don't know. Who can say what happened?'

The men sit in silence as if waiting for an answer to Mikhail's question.

'Misha, if someone had told me how this would end up, I never would have believed them.'

'You mean the war?'

'I mean everything.' He waves his arm. 'Everything. Can you believe, I was only twenty-two when the revolution came. It was all so exciting. The possibility of change was everywhere. We were creating something new, something different. I believed everything would be better. We all did.' He looks away, the candle reflecting in his glassy eyes. 'But as I get older, I see all the mistakes and each one chips away a little bit of our dream. Like chiselling a huge stone. Who knows what happened to your brother, or Marina's parents? Maybe they were enemies and got what they deserved. Or, maybe not. We'll never know. But I must believe that it will all come right. We'll build something great and uniquely ours. It will be worth all the mistakes.'

Mikhail sits, considering Boris's words. The candle casts eerie shadows on the faceless double portrait.

'What if the colonel doesn't like it?' Mikhail says.

'Don't worry. He'll love it.'

'Boris, about tomorrow. If something should happen…'

'Nothing is going to happen. How can it? Your painting is fabulous.'

'But if it does. I want you to promise me you will look after Galya and Vera.'

'Me? I don't know anything about children.'

'Just think how many children will be orphans after the war. Please, promise me you will look after them.'

'I promise.'

6

MIKHAIL EXTENDS THE LEGS of his easel and sets it upright. Avoiding contact with the wet paint, he secures the canvas in place. He holds his hands in front of the fire, rubbing them together, absorbing the warmth from the dancing flames. Vladimir enters, carrying a tray with a pot of tea and plate of *priyaniki*.

'Where is Elizaveta?' Mikhail asks.

'Fired! Can you believe, the thief was stealing food from the kitchen!'

Mikhail tenses, masking guilt. He opens his oil box and carefully removes the palette from its slot. In the centre of the palette, a variety of cool and warm flesh tones are already mixed, ready to begin.

'Turns out, it all started about a month ago, right under our noses,' Vladimir says.

Wanting to change the subject, Mikhail motions to

Vladimir to help him with the chair. They push it in front of the window and place the table beside it. The day is overcast with heavy dark clouds, and little light filters through the glass panes. Mikhail studies the tableau, disappointed the light is not stronger. Vladimir passes him a steaming cup of tea.

'Are you surprised?' asks Vladimir.

Mikhail looks at him. 'Surprised?'

'Yes. Isn't it surprising that Elizaveta would steal from us?'

Mikhail hesitates, shocked at Vladimir's disbelief. He takes a breath. 'She always seemed to take her duties very seriously.'

'Not any more!' Vladimir's face glows victorious.

'I should get to work,' says Mikhail, biting into a *priyanik*. 'You can sit first and then Maxim. Maybe your father would like to have a look before we start?'

'Impossible. He's not here. Won't be back for a week.'

'But doesn't it have to be sent in time for your mother's birthday?'

'A courier is coming for it in a couple of days. It's all organised.'

The absurdity of the situation slaps Mikhail. The colonel will not even see the painting before it is sent. He may never see it. After all the worry and pressure from Orbelli, insisting how vitally important the painting is for the entire Hermitage, Mikhail realises it is all a ridiculous charade. The colonel will not do anything to help the museum or the staff struggling inside.

Standing beside Mikhail, Vladimir studies the portrait with his hand resting on his chin. He leans in close and steps back. 'It smells,' he says.

'Oil paints are strong. It'll go away in a few days. It's still wet because it's cold in the Hermitage. It's much warmer here so it should dry swiftly.' He motions to the chair. 'If you take a seat, we can get started.'

Vladimir sits and Mikhail moves Vladimir's leg slightly forward, rests his arm on the chair and tips his chin a bit upward. Vladimir avoids his gaze.

Mikhail returns to the easel and picks up the palette. Threading his thumb through the hole, he balances the palette in his left hand, and places several thin brushes between his fingers. With a thin, round brush in his right hand, he adds a touch of solvent, thinning the paint, and then lightens it with a touch of white. With quick, sketch-like strokes he marks the shape of the eye and the position of the nose. Using the marks as a guide, he darkens the eye, gradually layering paint, defining the curve of Vladimir's brow. As he creates the features, he blocks out everything else in the room. He does not feel the aches in his limbs or the sharp hunger pain in his stomach demanding another *priyanik*. His brush moves between the palette and the painting, slightly adjusting tonal values. His resentment and anger towards the colonel settles further in the back of his mind and he concentrates. Slowly, with each addition of colour, he gives the figures life. As the glow of their skin grows, warmth spreads through his core. Vladimir's young, confident yet vulnerable face stares back from the canvas. He has given the portrait a soul.

Vladimir takes a deep breath and exhales with a long sigh.

'Nearly done,' Mikhail says, adding definition to Vladimir's hair.

'It's hard to sit still.'

'I think you'll like the result.' Mikhail steps back from the easel. 'Would you like to have a look?'

As Vladimir stands and approaches the portrait Mikhail notices a cabinet, pushed against the wall behind the armchair. The door is ajar, revealing several bottles of vodka.

'Mikhail Tarasovich, it looks so different now that it has a face. Before, I wasn't sure. None of it looked right. But, now...' He steps back. 'Now, it really looks like me.' He leans in closer, studying the eyes. Smiling, he turns to Mikhail.

'I'm glad you like it.' Mikhail claps the boy on the back. 'Go get Maxim so I can finish.'

Vladimir nods and leaves the room.

Without thought, Mikhail darts to the cabinet, grabs a bottle of vodka and jams it into his bag. Pushing it beneath the box of brushes and a rag, he zips it shut. Adrenaline rushes around his body. After all his hard work, he deserves it.

With shaking hands he pours a cup of tea, which has gone cold, and takes another *priyanik*. The colonel will never notice the vodka is gone, he tells himself, as he eats the last bite of the biscuit. As he chews, he notices an envelope addressed to him on the desk. It must be from the colonel. After all these years, he might finally have an explanation of Andrei's disappearance. Whether it gives details of sordid crimes or grim incarceration, Mikhail is certain the letter will bring bad news. The thin envelope rests heavy on his mind.

Hearing the bickering boys coming down the corridor, he quickly returns to the easel. Lifting the palette, he slips his thumb into position and selects a brush from the tin. Touching up the curtains in the background, his quivering hand hovers over the canvas as they enter the room.

'Good morning, Mikhail Tarasovich,' Maxim says, tying his scarf.

'Good morning,' Mikhail replies. 'Are you ready?'

'Always ready,' Maxim responds unenthusiastically, giving a half-hearted Young Pioneer salute.

Maxim looks plumper but Mikhail knows that is impossible. He could not have gained weight in less than a week yet his buttons seem to strain against his stomach even more. Maxim hovers over his shoulder, studying the portrait. Mikhail expects him to comment on his thinner frame but he does not. Giving a little grunt, he takes his place beside the chair. Mikhail moves Maxim's foot slightly forwards and adjusts his chin and head to match the original pose. He returns to the easel and studies the boy's bored, vacant expression.

'Do you have any hobbies, Maxim?'

'Not really.' He shrugs.

'What's your favourite subject in school?'

'I hate school. It's boring.'

His expression remains defiantly dull.

'There must be something you like. A person? A pet?'

Mikhail waits. Suddenly an excited spark lights up Maxim's face.

'My cat, Sasha!' He smiles broadly.

'Where is he now?'

'Mama took him to Sverdlovsk.'

Mikhail pauses, perplexed by a mother who took a cat with her when she was evacuated but left her children behind.

'Now, I want you to be very still and tell me everything about Sasha.'

Maxim begins with a description of his beloved ginger tom and Mikhail picks up his brush. Using delicate strokes, he starts to form Maxim's eyes.

Nodding his head as he paints, Mikhail pretends to listen to Maxim's feline monologue. But his own thoughts, intrigued by the letter on the desk, drift into memories of his brother. His eyes periodically fall on the envelope lying on the desk and he wonders what news it may contain. Or, perhaps it says nothing at all.

The last time Mikhail saw Andrei, he was sitting at their kitchen table, holding baby Galya as if she were the most precious bundle he had ever handled. He gently rubbed her chin and round cheeks with his knuckle, unable to take his eyes off his niece. Roza put a bowl of soup in front of him and he looked at it reluctantly, not wanting to part with the baby. Roza took Galya from his embrace and laughed. She told him it was high time for him to find a girl and start a family. He muttered something about being married to the party and too busy for love.

The minute he finished his soup, Andrei took Galya back in his arms. He rocked her while they talked into the night. Mikhail does not remember the topics, only the warmth of the kitchen and the peaceful baby in Andrei's arms.

At the end of the evening, they walked together to the door. 'You'll be a very good father. I know you will.' He patted Mikhail's shoulder and they embraced, perhaps a bit longer than usual. '*Poka*,' he said, closing the door behind him.

Mikhail never saw Andrei again.

'Mikhail Tarasovich?' Maxim's raised voice cuts into his thoughts.

He looks at Maxim from behind the easel.

'What about you? Do you have a pet? I've heard about the legendary cats in the Hermitage.'

Mikhail nods but does not tell him about the recent decrease in the Hermitage feline population or the likelihood of cat meat in tonight's soup.

Vladimir lingers beside Mikhail, studying the portrait. Mikhail steps back, rolls his shoulders and bends his aching knees. He puts down the palette and takes a sip of tea.

Vladimir smiles. 'You've been very...flattering to Maxim.'

'What's that supposed to mean?' moans Maxim.

'Nothing,' says Vladimir.

Using a thin brush, Mikhail gently adds a few more freckles on Maxim's cheeks.

'Are you done soon?' asks Maxim.

Mikhail returns the brush to the tin and laces his fingers together in front of him, stretching. 'Yes, I'm done with you. I have a bit more to do on the background.'

Maxim exhales loudly and collapses on the sofa.

Mikhail stands back from the portrait and studies his work. Maxim has a mischievous sparkle in his eye and a wry smile. Although thinner than in real life, there is a sturdiness in his frame. He has managed to capture the contrasting personalities of the boys.

Vladimir stands behind him. 'Um, yes, that is my annoying baby brother,' he says, nodding.

'Do you think your mother will like it?'

'Absolutely. Although she might panic when she sees how scrawny Maxim has become.'

'He's hardly scrawny.'

Vladimir nearly trips over the bag as he takes a seat in the chair. Worried the stolen vodka will be discovered, Mikhail quickly pulls it closer to the easel. He adds more ivory black to his palette, picks up a brush and strengthens the deep shadows in the curtain's folds.

'I'll be a while longer, boys, but you don't have to stay,' Mikhail says.

Vladimir stands. 'Papa asked me to give you a few things.'

He opens the cabinet and places a bottle of vodka on the desk with the letter. He pulls a bag filled with newspaper-wrapped parcels from behind the desk and puts it beside the other items.

'Shall I put these things in your bag?' he asks.

'No!' Adrenaline surges through Mikhail's body as he quickly takes the parcels and bottle.

Vladimir studies him, taken aback by his urgency and quick movement.

'I'll sort it out,' says Mikhail, composing himself. 'And please, relay my thanks to your father.'

The faint odour of dried fish seeps from the newspaper parcels. Galya will be surprised to have one of her favourites.

'Look who's here! He lives!' Boris enters the studio and gives Mikhail a bear hug.

'Thank you, dear friend,' Mikhail says. 'I couldn't have done it without you.'

Boris brushes the comment away. 'Not at all. You are a great painter. I just calmed your nerves *choot choot.*'

Mikhail unpacks his bag, setting the parcels on his workbench.

'What have we here?' Boris says, unwrapping the newspaper. '*Otlichno!*' He takes a deep breath, smelling the ugly, wrinkled fish. 'You got presents. They must've liked it.'

Mikhail recounts the day and Boris shrugs, unsurprised the colonel was absent.

'Had I realised they were going to give me a bottle of vodka, I wouldn't have taken one,' he whispers, setting the two bottles on the workbench.

'No problem. He'll never even notice. You're always worrying about something, Misha. What's done is done.'

He opens his cupboard and pushes aside bottles of solvent and rags. 'Most important, is that nobody else knows about it.' He takes out his quarter-full bottle of vodka and glasses. 'Besides, our stock is nearly finished!' He jiggles the bottle and the liquid slaps the sides. 'Now, we must celebrate your success and the replenishment of our stocks!' He pours, pushes a glass towards Mikhail and raises his. 'To the creative process and its rewards!'

They tap glasses and drink. Boris picks a bit of dried flesh from the fish and eats it.

'Heaven,' he says, pushing the newspaper towards him.

Mikhail pulls the meat from the skeleton. The dry, salty fish mixes with the trace of alcohol lingering on his tongue. Remembering the letter, he takes the sealed envelope from the bag.

'What's that?' asks Boris.

'From the colonel.'

'Let me guess, he's fallen in love with you.' Laughing, he takes a bit of fish.

'Papa?' Galya's voice distracts Mikhail from the envelope. She and Vera hover near the door.

Mikhail opens the top drawer of the workbench and drops in the letter. 'Girls! Come, have a seat,' he says, shutting the drawer. We have some surprises for you.' He unwraps the remaining parcels: a cured sausage, half a loaf of brown bread, four *priyaniki* and two apples.

'Look at this feast!' Boris says. 'Even better than New Year!'

The girls slide onto the stools and Boris pushes the fish towards them.

'One hundred percent better than New Year!' Galya says, as her fingers delicately pick the meat from the minuscule bones.

Boris slices the sausage and places it beside the fish on the newspaper. He offers a piece to Vera, who has said little since her mother disappeared. She smiles, taking a mouse-sized bite and he winks at her.

'We are the luckiest girls in the world,' says Galya, tucking in to the fish.

Boris pours another round of vodka and Mikhail feels his shoulders relax. He slices the bread. The vodka's warmth replaces thoughts of the colonel, Andrei, Roza, the war and the painting. He wants to forget it all, at least for tonight. Laying the sausage on the bread, he wishes he had a bit of butter. He passes the *buterbrod* to Boris. Mikhail's stomach, still burning from the last shot, groans as he reaches for the glass.

Mikhail raises it. 'To a full table, warm hearts, and good company,' he says, smiling at Galya.

He taps glasses with Boris, drinks and bites into the sandwich. He chews, enjoying the satisfying trinity of sausage, vodka and brown bread.

PART 2

1

⚜

May 1979

STEPPING OFF THE TRAIN, Galina pushes away thoughts of the painting, a portrait she has yet to create. The wagon doors rattle shut and the train departs, slithering into the forest. Crisp air fills her lungs.

Several passengers stride towards the platform stairs and disappear down narrow forest paths. She sets her mesh bags and a cake box on a bench, relieving her arms of their weight. Dima promised to meet her at the station but now, standing alone on the platform, she is not surprised her husband has not come. She waits, hoping to see him scramble up the stairs.

Gathering up the bags and pinching the cakebox string, Galina heads towards the exit and descends. She meets the dirt road, which runs perpendicular to the track, and immediately realises her error. Spring rains have turned the road into a quagmire. Her new leather shoes, purchased only last week from a Finnish trader, sink into the mud. Such a fool to wear her new shoes. Prior to her departure from Leningrad, her attention was occupied with the portrait and her son's eighteenth birthday party, which is today. She did not think about her footwear. Although only half an hour by train from the city, the *dacha* is a world away from Leningrad's wide avenues and ornate architecture. Galina presses on, forcing herself to ignore her mud-splattered shoes.

With each step, the bags pull at her arms and knock against her legs. She worries about dropping the cake and her hands ache from pinching the cakebox string. In the distance, beside her single-storey *dacha*, Dima bends, pulls a weed and tosses it into his wheelbarrow. Just as she inhales, preparing to shout his name, he grasps the handles and disappears around the side of the house. She shifts the bags, passing the cakebox between her hands. Dima will not be helping her.

Arriving at the *dacha*, Galina opens the screen door and it falls off the top hinge. It hangs awkwardly. She kicks off her muddy shoes, slides her feet into well-worn slippers and follows the narrow corridor to the kitchen. She sets the cake and bags on the table which is pushed tight against the wall. Turning on the tap, she fills a glass and drinks. Cool and clear, the water tastes much better than in Leningrad, and it refreshes, washing away the frustrations of the journey. From the kitchen window, she sees the apple tree buds and the bright-green shoots on the strawberry plants. Her shoulders relax, her arms lighten. It is good to be at the *dacha*. Summer is nearly here.

'I didn't expect you so soon,' Dima says, pushing the door back onto its hinges and pulling it shut.

Galina refills her glass. 'I said I'd be on the 12.20.'

Even in the small kitchen, there is distance between them. Although they have not seen each other for a few weeks, neither lifts their arms to offer an embrace.

He taps his watch. 'It stopped at 10.30 I guess.' He scratches his chin, smearing a bit of soil on his greying, stubbly beard.

Dima is as reliable as his Vostok watch.

'Everyone is coming soon. We've got a lot to do,' she says. 'Why don't you start by fixing the door?'

'The door is fine. It's been like that for years.'

'Is a working door too much to ask?'

'I'll do it later. Right now, I must dig in the manure.'

'Dima?' a woman's voice calls from the front door.

'I'm here! With Galya!' he calls, scrambling out of the kitchen, mumbling something about peas and beans.

Galina follows and finds Elena Borisovna hovering around the front door, clutching a cardboard box of pea shoots planted in pots.

'Galya!' Elena sets them on the grass and kisses Galina's cheeks. 'Dima has too many beans and I have too many peas so we've agreed an exchange.' Her fingers comb through her unnaturally blond hair and rest on her slender hips.

Galina, anxious to get on with preparations for Yuri's party, gives Dima a stern glance, willing him to hurry.

'I'll get the beans for you,' Dima says, picking up the seedlings and heading around the back of the *dacha*.

Elena takes a deep breath. 'I love spring at the *dacha*. Life begins again. I'll never get used to these Leningrad winters.'

Elena arrived in Leningrad long after the war, one of the thousands who repopulated the city. She never tasted soup made from wallpaper paste or the sweetness of cat meat. She does not bear the scars of the siege. Her wrinkle-free complexion glows. She is a paediatrician and has the stance of someone with authority; a knowing, quiet confidence.

Galina shrugs. 'Leningrad winter isn't so bad when there's heating and food.'

'The winter's too dark, Galya. But I love the white nights when the day stretches longer and longer, replacing the darkness.'

Galina's brow furrows as Elena marvels at the changing of the season. She has only ever lived in Leningrad. For her, the dark winter and long white nights are a simple fact of nature. She glances along the side of the *dacha* and is relieved to see Dima returning down the path. He hands the bean seedlings to Elena.

'May they be abundant.' He gives a ridiculous little bow, as if living in tsarist times.

There was a time when Galina found his sense of humour endearing.

Elena smiles, admiring the spindly plants.

'Elena, we have to get ready for Yuri's party,' she says bluntly.

'Oh, and I should congratulate you both. I can't believe he is already eighteen! Such a milestone!'

'Dima, have you invited Elena to come celebrate tonight?'

'Not yet,' he says.

Must she do everything? Elena and her daughter always come to Yuri's birthday.

'You and Sveta must join us this evening,' Galina says.

Elena looks at Dima and holds his glance, as if surprised or put on the spot. 'Are you sure?'

'Of course,' Dima says.

'Then it's settled,' Galina says, growing annoyed with this unnecessarily long exchange.

'We'll see you later.' Elena gives a hesitant wave and heads down the dirt road toward her *dacha*.

'Now, Dima, leave the garden for now. Get the table sorted.'

'Everything will be fine.' He whisks away her fears with the back of his hand and returns to the garden, murmuring something about the compost heap.

In the kitchen Galina unpacks the groceries: a loaf of Borodinsky rye bread, Rossisky cheese and some pork. Unwrapping the meat, she realises the girl gave her a very fatty piece. She should have demanded a better cut. Weighing the parcel in her hand, it does not feel like two kilos. Unsure of how many friends are coming with Yuri, she worries there is not enough food.

Galina brushes dried mud from her ankle and slides her feet into tall felt boots. Her mud-crusted shoes lie beside the door but she does not have time to deal with them now. She grabs the handle and the door falls off the hinges, nearly hitting her on the head. Cursing, she jams it back into place and slams it behind her.

Clutching a couple of empty bags, Galina pays no attention to the clump of daffodils along the path and the buds coming through on the raspberry bushes as she walks along the side of the *dacha*. She pulls open the cellar doors, which are flush with the grass. A dark stairway slips beneath the *dacha* leading to the cellar. Striking a match on the top stair, she lights a candle and creeps down the stairs. Little remains on the shelves lining the walls: two jars of dill gherkins, preserved tomatoes and a jar of honey. In the far corner, she opens a burlap bag and finds the last of the potatoes. She scoops several into her bag. Dusty soil clings to her skin. Beside the potatoes, a wooden crate contains the remaining cabbages which have

85

been stored all winter. Although they have travelled only a few metres from the garden to the cellar, they look as though they have rolled across the Soviet Union. The outer leaves, brown and wilted, hang limply. She takes one and squeezes it, hoping it is not rotten in the core. Making two trips, she transfers the food to the kitchen.

Galina unwraps the pork and lays it on a cutting board. She cuts away some of the fat, tossing it into a pail, and glances out of the window. What is Dima doing now? In the back garden, he is setting up a long trestle table. She sets down the knife and opens the window.

'Dima,' she shouts, catching his attention. 'It's too cold. Put it inside.'

'We'll have the fire.' He shrugs, resting his hands on his hips.

'We'll catch a chill. Boris is eighty-three, he shouldn't be in the night air.'

'Boris is stronger than all of us put together!' Dima shouts back.

Galina shakes her head. 'Yuri and his friends can sit by the fire after. We'll eat indoors.'

She shuts the window and watches. When he starts to collapse the trestles, she returns to cutting the meat. As she slides the pieces on the metal skewers, the sound of the front door falling off the hinges and the clamour of Dima bringing in the trestles and the table filters into the kitchen.

She rinses her hands under the tap, wipes them on her apron and heads to the front room where Dima is pushing the armchair into the corner. She takes one side of the coffee table and he takes the other and they push it against the wall. He sets up the trestles and they balance the plank on them, parallel to the sofa. Dima pushes it, making sure it is sturdy.

'It must be cleaned,' he says, rubbing his grubby hand across the surface.

'So must you.'

Dima usually spends April through September living at the *dacha*. Forgoing his clean-shaven intelligentsia life in Leningrad he retreats to the forest, taking on a bristly, unkempt man-of-the-woods persona and tending to his garden. Galina does not know exactly how he manages to eschew his responsibilities for so many months, but as the head of the philosophy department at Leningrad State University, this is the schedule he has orchestrated for himself. Officially, he is doing research and working with PhD students. However, she never sees any evidence of students coming and going and he certainly never goes back to the city. The cluster of *dachas* is cut off from Leningrad, without a telephone or regular postal service. She does not interfere or ask a lot of questions and his extended stay at the *dacha* suits her. Life is a bit simpler with one less person in their flat on Prospect Rimsky-Korsakov.

She cannot imagine abandoning her responsibilities and students at the Art Academy. Once she completes the portrait for the staff exhibition and finishes the school year, Galina will move out to the *dacha* and summer will begin in earnest.

'You look like a peasant,' she says.

'And so, the exploitation of labourers continues,' he mumbles. 'You won't be complaining when we have fresh vegetables and the cellar is full.' He returns the door to the hinge. 'Collective farmers of the world unite,' he chants, holding his fist aloft.

It is only when he is out of sight that Galina allows her stern face to crack a smile.

'Knock knock!' a voice calls from the front door. 'We're here! Came early to give you a hand.' Vera, laden with several bags, walks barefoot into the kitchen. 'I'm glad I wore boots. The road is so muddy! Left them at the door.'

Galina embraces her, kissing her cheeks three times. She finds a box of old slippers in the closet and tosses a pair towards Vera's feet.

'Galochka!' Boris says as he enters the kitchen.

She kisses his cheeks. He is a bit shorter than the last time she saw him. 'You look good, Boris, as usual.' She pats his slightly hunched back.

'I'm still here,' he says. 'Where's Dima?'

'In the garden.'

'I need a screwdriver,' says Boris, heading out of the door.

Vera grabs a gingham apron from a peg on the wall and ties it around her waist. 'I brought whatever I found.' She unpacks her bags: three tins of herring, a loaf of rye bread, a bottle of vegetable oil, a few carrots, a cured sausage and a bottle of Georgian wine.

'How did you know?' Galina says, picking up the oil. 'We needed oil and I couldn't find any in our local shops.'

'We had a lot in our shop and there wasn't a queue, so I bought some. Lucky coincidence, I guess. I also got something for us.' Vera hands her a conical newspaper parcel.

Galina gives her another hug. As expected, she finds beautifully wrapped Mishka Na Severe chocolates. Seeing the label, a polar bear surrounded by the glow of the northern lights, brings back childhood memories of the cellar deep beneath the Hermitage museum.

'Whenever I see them I think of you,' Vera says. 'And my mother, of course.'

'Remember how she gave them to us during the war, for New Year? We took a tiny bite and hid them.' Galina slides the chocolates from the newspaper cone into a basket and places it on the kitchen table. 'It took us at least four days to eat this single chocolate.'

'My strongest memory of her is from that night.' Vera pauses and flicks her hand to the side as if pushing the memory away. 'What else needs doing? Shall I cut the sausage and cheese?'

'Cut them thin. We have a lot of people and little food.' Galina places the plate of meat on the table. 'The *shashlik* is done. I'll make a cabbage salad.'

'So, how is Yuri?' Vera takes a knife from the drawer and starts to slice the cheese.

By the serious, inquisitive tone of her voice, Galina immediately understands the real question behind this simple query. Rather than going to university, Yuri has chosen to go into the army. She always planned for her son to follow an academic pathway, and his decision, the first significant, adult decision he has ever taken, has not been easy to accept.

'He's going through with it.'

Having discussed, argued and begged him to change his mind, Galina has failed to persuade him to take her advice. He simply refuses to satisfy his military obligation while studying at university.

'What do you think about that?' Vera asks.

'He feels it's his duty to serve. What can I do?' She shrugs, hoping her curt response will be the end of it.

Standing back to back in the kitchen, the women chop and slice. Galina cuts into the cabbage and is pleased to see the core is not rotten. The leaves are slightly wilted from the long winter but acceptable. Focusing on the rhythmic motion of her knife, she is thankful to escape the worrisome topic of her son's future. Vera hums a lilting tune, a hopelessly sweet love song which always accompanies her when she cooks. Despite this annoying habit, they work well together, never in each other's way or underfoot.

Years ago, when Galina and Vera were young, they baked a birthday cake for Boris. It was right after the war, just after they moved to the new flat on Chekhov Street. They carefully measured the ingredients but their good intentions turned into a disaster. A crisp burnt crust covered the cake's soggy middle so the girls added a thick layer of strawberry jam across the cake and waited for Boris to return. But he did not come. The evening grew darker and eventually they went to bed. The two orphans curled together under thick blankets and Vera started to cry.

'What if…' Her chest heaved. 'What if he doesn't come back?'

Galina understood her fear and draped her arm over her shoulder. 'Don't say such things.'

They lay in silence, hoping to hear the sound of the latch and Boris's footsteps.

In the morning, they woke and went to the kitchen. The cake, still whole, was on the table. Boris was snoring in his room and the girls waited for him to wake. Eventually he made his way to the kitchen, smelling of onions and vodka, and they ate the cake for breakfast.

The front door bangs shut, bringing Galina back into the present.

'Galya,' Boris calls down the corridor. 'I have a surprise for you. Come see.'

She drops the last of the cabbage into the ceramic bowl, dries her hands, and heads to the front door.

'Go outside and see for yourself,' he says. His wrinkles deepen as he smiles and his eyes sparkle mischievously.

Galina opens the door, expecting the awkward drop of the hinge but it glides open smoothly. Shiny silver hinges have replaced the old broken ones.

'I've been looking in the markets for months and could never find the right hinges. And then, just a couple weeks ago, out of nowhere, I found them!' Boris stands proudly, with a satisfied grin.

Galina drizzles the oil on the cut cabbage and grated carrots. Mixing it together, she glances at the empty sugar bowl on the table. She usually adds just a sprinkle of sugar. But then she remembers the jar of honey. She stirs a spoonful into the salad.

'How is everything at the library?' Galina asks.

'We have a new director,' says Vera.

'Oh?'

'Everyone's in a panic, worried that he is going to change everything.' She shrugs. 'It's the oldest library in Russia. What could he possibly change?'

Vera slices bread and carefully lays the pieces in a shallow basket, creating a fan shape. She places it beside the plates of sausage and cheese, both presented in a radial pattern on the chipped china.

'Is everything going well at the academy?'

Galina shrugs. 'I have to paint a portrait for the staff exhibition next month. I'm looking for inspiration.'

'Don't you usually paint Yuri?'

'Yes, but it is for International Children's Day. He isn't a child any more.'

Galina stirs the salad and is just setting it aside when a

giggly shriek cuts through the stillness in the forest. Yuri's voice filters down the muddy track. She heads towards the front door and steps out into the dusky evening. Pulling her cardigan around her bosom, she hopes to see her son coming around the bend. Folding her arms, she waits. A shrill voice disturbs the silence. Galina did not expect a girl. She exhales, disappointed not to hear the usual voices of Yuri's male friends. They catch up with the sound of their laughter and two figures come into sight. Yuri cradles the girl in his long, lanky arms, as he trudges along the muddy road. One of her arms is draped around his neck and in the other hand she holds a bag of beer bottles on her lap. Her feet, in high-heeled sandals, dangle over his arms. Upon arrival, he sets her on the *dacha* step.

'Mama! It's so muddy.' His blond hair is longer than Galina would like. His face is spotty and boyish.

'Happy birthday, my dear.' She kisses his cheek, breathing in stale beer and sweat. He pulls away.

Yuri grabs the girl's hand. 'Mama, this is Masha. Masha, may I present my mother, Galina Mikhailovna.'

'Nice to meet you.' Teetering on her ridiculous shoes, Masha leans forward and kisses Galina's cheek.

'I love the *dacha*!' Yuri says too loudly, taking a deep breath and exhaling. 'I smell the fire! Is it ready? Let's grill the *shashlik*!'

'Papa will sort it out when he comes back from the river. You relax.'

But Yuri is not listening. He races to the *dacha* and opens the front door, immediately noticing the new hinges.

'What happened here?' he says, admiring the shiny metal.

'Boris just repaired it.'

'Boris Nikolaevich, where are you?' he shouts. 'You're our

hero!'

'No need to shout,' says Boris from the armchair in the front room. 'I'm right here. I may be old, but not deaf. Not yet, anyway.'

Yuri rushes towards Boris and embraces him. His arms could wrap around him twice.

'Let's get the *shashlik* and have a drink, Boris!' he says, opening a beer and handing it to him. 'Mama, why is the table in here?'

The table is covered with a linen tablecloth and each place is set with a plate, cutlery and several glasses. The sausage, cheese, herring, bread, pickled vegetables and salad are already on the table, waiting for the guests.

'I thought it would be too cold outdoors,' she replies.

'But it is such a nice night. We must be outdoors!'

Galina looks at Boris.

'I agree. It's a nice evening. Let's enjoy it.'

'But everything is all set up,' she says.

Ignoring her, Yuri directs Masha. The table is cleared, dishes stacked, plates of food temporarily parked on the coffee table. The cloth comes off and Masha haphazardly folds it and lays it over her forearm but it drags on the floor. He collapses the table and removes it, banging the long plank on the door on his way out. Galina winces and catches Vera's worried glance. Boris remains well out of the way, like a king on a throne.

They return and gather up the dishes, cutlery and glasses. On their final trip, they take the food, and Yuri dashes into the kitchen and returns with the plate of pork skewers. Boris stands, holding his bottle of beer, and follows Yuri.

From the kitchen window, Galina and Vera watch as they gather around the fire. Yuri drops a skewer on the grass and quickly picks it up. Cleansing it with a few splashes of beer, he places it on the grill over the flames and Masha giggles, clinging to his arm. Within minutes, Boris is telling a story and their attention is focused on him.

'We should take him a normal chair,' says Vera. 'It isn't healthy for a man of his age to sit on a log.'

Galina pours two glasses of wine and glances at the clock. Dima is taking a long time at the river.

Yuri and Masha laugh as Boris's smile widens. One of his many jokes, which he has probably told countless times, is still funny. Galina sips her wine, watching the tableau.

'Let's join them,' Vera says, tugging her arm

But Galina's feet are firmly planted on the kitchen floor. Today is different from Yuri's previous birthdays. This one marks the end of his childhood. In a couple of months, he will climb on a bus which will deliver him to the military. He will no longer be hers.

2

GALINA AND VERA SIT AT THE TABLE beside Boris, whose cheeks are already reddening from the beer. Vera places a slice of sausage on a piece of bread and puts the *buterbrod* on the plate in front of him. He ignores it, focusing on the punchline of his anecdote. Yuri, tending to the *shashlik* on the fire, and Masha burst out laughing as Boris swells with pride. Dima emerges from the forest path, unshaven, with a towel draped over his shoulder. His wet hair has not been combed and stands at random angles.

'Papa!' Yuri says.

'Happy Birthday! Welcome to manhood,' says Dima as they embrace. 'I've not seen you in weeks. Why haven't you come out to the *dacha*?'

Seeing them side by side, Galina notices how similar they have become, not just physically, but their mannerisms.

Yuri shrugs. 'I've been with my friends, Papa, in the city.'

'You should come out more often. Country air is good for your health.' He claps him on the back and sighs. 'Already a man. Where did the time go?'

'Time flies. Everyone knows that. Now, take a seat. The *shashlik* is ready.'

Dima scans the table. 'One minute. I'll be right back,' he says, heading towards the cellar.

Yuri opens another beer and divides it between himself, Boris and Masha.

'Not so fast,' murmurs Vera, patting Boris's shoulder. 'Eat something.'

He waves her away, taking a sip of beer.

Dima returns with a bottle of vodka and places it on the table.

'Now,' Dima says, pouring a round of vodka for himself, Boris, Yuri and Masha. He stands and raises his glass, waiting for the others to do the same. 'Tonight, we drink to my son who, today, on his eighteenth birthday, becomes a man. Soon, he will bravely serve in our military. We wish him all the best. I know you will make us all very proud. To Yuri!'

Dima shoots a glance at Galina. Her stomach tightens as she reluctantly lifts her glass.

'To Yuri!' everyone cheers and Galina forces herself to smile. They tap their glasses together.

Tipping back the vodka, they drink it in one go. Vera and Galina sip their wine.

Boris sways slightly as he swallows. Vera pushes his plate closer to him and he takes a bite of the *buterbrod*.

There is a rustling of the hedge beside the *dacha* as Elena and Sveta walk down the path, laden with a box of chocolates, a bouquet of daffodils, and a bowl covered with a dishcloth.

They are greeted with a flurry of kisses. Dima darts back

into the *dacha* and returns with two more chairs which he squeezes around the table. Vera brings out a vase filled with water and places the daffodils beside the plate of sausage.

'I brought a beetroot salad.' Elena removes the cloth and puts the bowl on the table. 'How nice to sit outside, in nature.'

Yuri, Boris and Dima smile triumphantly at Galina.

'Absolutely right, Elena Borisovna!' says Yuri.

'*Spasibo*, Elena. You still have beets. Ours ran out months ago,' says Galina, passing the cabbage salad to Masha. 'Everyone, be sure to eat. We have plenty.'

Sveta takes the seat beside her mother. Her cheeks, already kissed by the spring sun, plump as she grins. Her face still has a youthful, soft roundness and innocence. Resting her elbow on the table she leans her chin on her fist, listening. Her curious eyes focus on Boris and Yuri.

Sveta would be the perfect subject of her portrait. Excitement flutters through Galina.

Masha takes a spoonful of cabbage and puts it on Yuri's plate. She passes the dish to Dima and takes a piece of bread from the basket. Dima refills the vodka glasses.

Boris stands, raises his glass and the table goes silent.

'Although we share not a drop of blood, I have always considered Yuri to be my grandchild, my *only* grandchild, in fact. During the war, we never would have dreamed that it would be possible to be here, so many years later, on this beautiful night surrounded by close friends and family, sitting at this splendid table of delicious food, toasting this young man. It would've been beyond our wildest dreams. Tonight, I toast Yuri's mother, Galina Mikhailovna. She's the strong woman who has made this dream come true.'

Galina's cheeks warm as the others look towards her. Every year Boris makes a very similar toast and she knows it is heartfelt. She reaches out and squeezes his hand. Although orphaned very young, she has never felt alone.

'To Galina Mikhailovna,' everyone chimes.

They drink. In the shadow of the toast, a calm passes over the table before the conversation resumes.

'It's so good to see you, Elena,' Galina says.

The two women always say they will get together in Leningrad during the winter months but they never manage it and their paths never cross coincidentally.

'Glad to see you, too, my friend.'

'And Sveta, you've grown so much over the winter. Practically a young lady now.'

Sveta blushes, leaning towards her mother.

'You know, Elena, I need to paint a portrait for the International Children's Day exhibition at the art academy and I'm looking for a subject. Maybe Sveta would like to sit for me?'

'Well...' Elena hesitates and her gaze shifts towards Dima.

'It's an exhibition of work by the academy staff. Paintings, drawings, and sculpture. We do it every year.'

Elena turns to Sveta, who is beaming.

'A portrait? Of me?'

'Why not? We could do it tomorrow if you are free,' says Galina.

Elena smiles. 'I think it's impossible to refuse.'

A few curling slices of cheese, some bread, and a bowl with a couple of pickled tomatoes linger on the table, uneaten. Sveta is sound asleep on the canvas hammock, under several blankets. Galina stands and stacks the plates in front of her. Vera and Elena follow her lead, collecting cutlery and dishes.

'Boris?' Yuri asks, holding up the vodka bottle.

'*Choot choot*. Just a half,' he says.

Yuri pours another round of vodka, emptying it.

'Oh no!' Masha says, grabbing the empty bottle. 'Never leave an empty on the table, it's bad luck!' She casts it aside and it lands on the grass with the others.

Masha's country-bumpkin accent has grown stronger as the night has progressed. At first, she managed to hide her poor grammar and simpleton vocabulary, but the vodka shots have betrayed her, revealing her poor education. Galina cannot believe Yuri would be interested in someone so uncultured.

'I must propose a toast to Galina's father, Mikhail Tarasovich,' Boris says. 'The bravest, most reliable friend a man could ask for. A victim of the siege that will never be forgotten.'

'To Mikhail Tarasovich!' Dima adds, glass aloft.

Again, they tap glasses and drink. A shiver tingles down Galina's spine as she pulls her cardigan around her. It was vodka and a portrait that had killed her father, not the siege. Boris knows this.

'Let's go for a walk,' Yuri suggests to Masha. 'We can go to the river.'

He fumbles around in the darkness for a bottle of beer.

'No swimming, Yuri,' says Galina. 'It's too cold and you've had too much to drink.'

'You worry too much,' he says without looking back. He wraps his arm around Masha's bony frame and she leans towards him, slightly swaying.

Boris sits back and sighs. 'They're so young.'

A dark feeling returns to Galina. If only Yuri would go to university like she wanted. As if reading her mind, Vera rests her hand on Galina's shoulder.

He will be fine. He will serve and return to Leningrad. After all, the country is at peace. It is not like he is going to war. He is just serving his conscription time.

Inside the *dacha*, Boris settles on the armchair in the front room and Vera lays a crocheted blanket across his lap. Galina jams kindling and a crumpled newspaper into the stove, lights it and the flames quickly jump to life. She puts a larger log on the fire and quickly shuts the door.

'Who's having tea?' Galina does not pause for an answer and heads to the kitchen to fill the kettle. Waiting for the water to boil, she fills the sink and starts to wash the plates. She glances out of the window. As the midnight-blue sky slowly turns a deeper shade of black, countless stars, peppered across the clear heavens, shine brighter. Her hands dip into the warm water, rinse a plate and stack it beside the sink. She looks up again. Elena and Dima stand beside the last embers of the fire, talking. Elena nods, shifting her weight from foot to foot, arms folded in front of her. Dima lifts his hand and it rests on her shoulder, tipping his head. Together they walk to the hammock. Dima bends, picking up Sveta and the blankets.

The kettle whistles and Galina turns off the gas.

Dima should not be carrying Sveta. She's too heavy. Galina raises her hand to open the window but they have already disappeared down the path and out of earshot. Spooning tea leaves into the teapot, she regrets not saying something quickly. She fills the teapot with boiling water and places it on a tray beside four cups and saucers.

'I'm going to paint Sveta tomorrow,' Galina says, carrying the tray into the living room.

'Near the lake would be nice,' Boris says.

'That's a good idea.'

'Then it is settled. Tomorrow morning, a trip to the lake,' Boris says.

'You're coming?' Galina asks.

Vera sets her cup down, shaking her head.

'Why not? I haven't done any drawing *en plein air* in months.' The saucer quivers in Boris's unsteady hand.

'Boris, it's too much,' Vera mutters. 'Besides, after all this vodka, you won't be up for it.'

'Of course I will,' Boris says, failing to stifle a burp.

In her bedroom, Galina slides a portable easel from under the bed and lays the beechwood box on the quilt. She flips the brass clasps and opens the lid. She places several metal tubes, neatly twisted from the bottom, in a paint-splattered compartment: raw sienna, yellow ochre, Naples yellow, cadmium red light, cadmium yellow, alizarin, burnt sienna, ultramarine, raw umber, viridian, Pthalo green, zinc white, and Paynes grey. In the slim compartment, she puts a variety of sable brushes, thick and thin, flat and round.

'He shouldn't go tomorrow,' Vera says, standing in the doorway.

'Who?'

'Boris. He really shouldn't go wandering around in the forest.'

'The walk from the train to the lake isn't far. He'll be fine.' She adds a small bottle of solvent, dammar varnish, a double dipper and clean rags to the box.

'And don't forget the walk from the *dacha* to the station. It's too much.'

Galina shrugs. 'What are you going to do? Tell him he can't go?'

She closes the lid and secures the clasps.

Vera pauses to consider the question, then says, 'Then I should go too.'

'Perfect. We need help carrying the picnic.' Galina pushes past and places the easel by the front door, ready for tomorrow. Beside the felt boots, she notices her shoes have been cleaned. She has not had time to clean them. She rubs the soft leather, which is as good as new. Who cleaned them?

3

⚜

BRIGHT SUN SHINES THROUGH the train windows, casting light on Sveta's strawberry-blond hair. Neatly plaited with orange ribbons tied at the ends, her hair shines. Galina used to style Vera's hair the exact same way every morning before school but it did not glisten like this. It was limp and fine. Even though Vera was only ten years old at the time, she would find strands of grey hair among the brown locks.

Yuri and Masha sit just behind Galina. Their whispers prick her neck like pins. They feel too close. In front of her, Boris leans towards the window, eyes closed. His face is puffy and flushed and when Masha shrieks, he winces and cradles his head. Vera sits beside him, seemingly assessing his condition and occasionally shooting him a disapproving glare.

'Sveta, how old are you?' Galina asks.

'Just turned twelve.'

Their childhoods could not be more different. When Galina was twelve, the war had just ended. She and Vera were orphans living with Boris. Every day they walked to school passing bombed-out buildings, constantly reminded of the horrors they had seen, surprised to have survived, thankful to be alive. Vera was only five years old when the war began so she could not remember peace in their beautiful city. She knew nothing but war. Only one thing remained from Galina's pre-war childhood: the *dacha*.

When Galina, Boris and Vera visited the *dacha* for the first time after the war, they feared the worst. Because the *dacha* had been behind enemy lines, they expected it to be destroyed by the retreating Nazi soldiers. As they walked down the dirt road from the station, they passed strange debris littering the narrow strip: wooden crates, sharp pieces of twisted metal, an abandoned car, empty bottles, metal barrels. The road itself and the quaint *dachas* were as she remembered them, but the rubbish scarred the landscape.

Galina grasped Boris's hand as they edged closer to her *dacha*, hoping to find it intact. The front door was ajar and leaves were blowing into the entrance. Boris opened the door wider, calling out to anyone that may have been inside. Nobody answered. He and the girls entered. The front room was strangely empty except for the divan. All the wooden tables, shelves and chairs were gone. Dozens of books were missing from the shelves, not a single page left. Boris guessed that everything had been burned during the cold winters.

There was a pile of dirty dishes stacked in the sink. On the kitchen table was an ashtray full of cigarette butts and two brown bottles. They heard rustling in the back bedroom. Boris shouted, 'Hello?' but no reply followed. They headed down the corridor, past the stained mattress on a metal bed frame in her parents' room. There was another rustling in the back bedroom. Boris told them to wait as he investigated. Suddenly, a mouse darted past and scurried out the front door. The girls shrieked and Boris laughed as they hurried towards him. He pulled back the curtain from the window and the sun streamed through the grubby glass pane. Galina's wooden bed-frame was not there but the child-sized mattress rested on the floor with a dirty ashtray beside it. The oak chest which once stood in the corner was no longer there. The room, usually cluttered with her father's art supplies, was empty. The walls were covered in writing. Thick black pen formed the letters of a language they did not understand. There was a map, painted directly onto the wall above the bed, which was complete with the *dachas*, forest and the river. The other walls were covered in text, long lists or maybe poetry, they never knew.

Galina's parents were dead and their flat destroyed but the *dacha* had miraculously survived. The Germans had spared it in their shameful retreat. It was as if they knew she had sacrificed enough.

Masha shrieks. Galina pulls her gaze from the conifer forest along the railway track and glances over her shoulder. Yuri blushes as Masha clutches his hand. Galina returns to the rhythmic passing of the trees. She had hoped that Masha would go back to Leningrad this morning.

'Why didn't Dimitry Alexeivich come?' Sveta asks Galya.

'Dima? Oh, he's busy in his garden. He's always busy in the garden.'

'Yesterday he brought me a Mishka Na Severe, my

favourite!'

Vera turns towards Galina. 'Next station, right?'

'Yes,' she replies, standing to collect her easel from the overhead rack.

The train slows, comes to a halt and they step onto the platform. Yuri, carrying their lunch basket, takes a deep breath, admiring the forest surrounding the track as Masha swats away gnats. Holding Boris's arm at the elbow, Vera offers support but he pushes her away, placing a straw hat on his head. Galina adjusts the easel's leather strap on her shoulder and grasps the cardboard under her arm. Sveta carries an old quilt.

They follow a narrow path into the forest. Sandy soil and pine needles cushion their steps. A gentle breeze whispers through the trees, stirring smells of sap and moist earth. Dappled patches of shadow dance across the path as they head deeper into the trees. They walk single-file with Boris in the lead and arrive at the sandy shore of the crystal-clear lake. In the distance, a grassy clearing stretches to the water's edge, where white geese swim. The blanket of birds is so dense, it is as if the lake is covered in snow and ice.

'Let's follow the path over there,' says Galina, pointing towards the geese.

'Was that always there?' asks Boris.

'It's a poultry farm. They built it a few years ago,' says Yuri.

'It's far for Boris,' whispers Vera.

But Boris has already set out on the path with Yuri, Masha and Sveta following behind.

'He'll be fine,' says Galina.

Masha's high-heeled sandals sink into the sand as she

teeters down the path, clinging to Yuri's arm. Yuri leans towards her and whispers in her ear. She laughs loudly, throwing back her head.

Galina slows, allowing the gap to grow between her and Masha.

'She's not so bad, Galya. Just young and smitten with your son,' says Vera.

'But the giggling...'

'You giggled too, when you first met Dima.'

Did she?

They make their way to the wide grassy field. The sun is much stronger without the protection of the trees. Galina squints in the bright light. Several low concrete walls along the water's edge form pens for the geese.

'Sveta,' Galina calls. 'Sit here.'

Sveta perches on the edge of the wall. Behind her, hundreds of geese lazily swim, dipping their heads below the water and lifting them out again. The orange ribbons in her hair match the colour of the geese bills exactly and her hair shines in the sun. It's perfect. Galina slides the easel from her shoulder, extends the legs and flips open the box. She rests the cardboard on the easel and tightens the screws, fixing it in place.

Vera spreads the quilt on the grass just behind Galina.

'Let's give her some room.' Boris pulls the quilt further away and settles in the shadow of a clump of trees.

Galina presses the paint tubes firmly, winding them from the bottom, creating an arc of colour along the upper edge of the wooden palette. Taking a narrow, round brush from the box, she looks at Sveta closely. Masha laughs, causing the birds to scatter and swim away, crowding together at the edge of the barrier, honking loudly.

'Yuri, your mother is working. Take a walk,' Boris calls, motioning further along the path toward a sandy beach.

Yuri gives a salute and leads Masha away.

Boris opens a sketch book and a pencil tin. Resting the book on his knees, he studies the lake view and begins to sketch.

Galina mixes raw umber with a bit of solvent. The paint thins, leaving only a hint of pigment on the brush. The sun seeps through her cotton painting smock, warming her back.

'How long will it take?' asks Sveta sweetly.

'We'll take a break for lunch in an hour. Just try to relax.'

'Should I smile?'

'You don't have to. I'll tell you when I am doing your face.'

Her brush dances, partnered with the symphony of squawking geese. The languid ebb and flow of their movements puts her in a trance as she focuses her attention on the emerging portrait. Sveta, peaceful and innocent, sits with her hands folded on her lap. Galina wants to capture the freshness of childhood, the simplicity of the moment, the promise of the future.

'Can we take a break soon?' Sveta asks, without complaining.

Galina looks up from the easel and sets down her brush. 'Yes, of course. I lost track of time. Let's get some lunch.'

They walk up the slope towards the quilt where Vera is reading a book and Boris, stretched out with his eyes closed, is completely still. His sketchbook rests at his side and his head lays at an awkward angle with his mouth partially open.

'Vera,' whispers Galina. 'Is he OK?'

Vera leans towards him, looking for the shallow rise and fall of his chest or a twitch.

There is a horrendous sound. Boris has broken wind.

'Ha ha! You thought I was dead!' He opens his eyes and a mischievous smile emerges.

Vera pulls away, brow furrowed. Sveta jumps back from the blanket, laughing and wafting the air with her hand.

'You both expect me to drop dead any moment. I'm still alive! You don't have to fuss over me.'

Galina picks up his sketchbook. The page is covered with pencil lines, demonstrating the same dexterity and skill he had all those years ago when he taught her to draw. Of course, her father initially taught her but it was after he died that she started spending hours in the Hermitage studio with Boris, drawing countless still life and life studies. Amid her sadness, drawing provided a distraction from the war. On the page, Boris has sketched her at work. In the foreground, she stands at the easel holding her palette in her left hand and wearing a wide-brimmed straw hat. Sveta sits on the wall with the flock of geese behind her. He has captured their motion with his simple lines.

Yuri and Masha return, holding hands. They sit at the edge of the quilt, entwined together, even closer than they were on the train. Suppressing the urge to pull them apart, Galina passes each a boiled egg and a piece of rye bread. She opens a tin of herring and places it in front of Boris. He spears an oily fish, lays it on the bread, making a *buterbrod* and takes a bite.

As Masha peels her egg, she looks towards the easel. 'I thought you'd be finished by now. Poor Svetochka has to sit there all day!'

Galina does not respond and takes a long drink of water from the flask.

'The creative process takes time,' explains Boris. 'The artist must capture the emotional as well as the visual. It demands careful consideration.'

'You did your drawing quickly,' Masha says.

'That's totally different. It's a souvenir, a snapshot of the day. Galina Mikhailovna is painting a study for the formal portrait which will be exhibited at the top art school in the Soviet Union. She must carefully consider the composition, rhythm of shape and form, and etch it into her memory.'

Boris speaks as if he is explaining something complex to a toddler and Masha listens intently, hanging on his every word. Strands of mousey brown hair blow gently from her ponytail as she tips her head to the side. Her bony shoulders curve inward, leaning on Yuri. The thin strap of her cotton dress drops from her shoulder as she nestles her flat chest against his arm. She is plain. Not distinctively ugly or pretty. Just dull. Her looks match her intellect.

'Have you been to our great museums of Leningrad?' Boris asks.

She shakes her head.

'I've been to every museum in Leningrad,' says Sveta. 'And of course, I've been to the Russian Museum and Hermitage.' She bites into herring *buterbrod*.

'Yuri, you must take her there for sure.' Boris smiles. 'You'll find many important treasures.'

'How is it possible that your school never went to Hermitage or Russian Museum?' Galina says, standing up and stretching.

Masha shrugs.

'It's not her fault,' says Boris. 'It's just how it happened. It's no big deal.' He pats her bare foot. 'Yuri will take you and show you everything.'

Masha nods and takes another bite of egg. A crumb of yolk clings to her lip as she chews and it eventually falls, settling on her lap.

'Sveta, we should get back to work.'

Sveta quickly finishes her egg and follows Galina to the water's edge.

Yuri leads the way back to the station with Masha clinging to his side. Every time Galina looks at them they seem even more connected. Sveta skips behind them, following the curve of the path along the shore. The easel's leather strap is draped over her shoulder and she grasps the folded quilt. Galina pinches the portrait by the edge, careful not to smear the wet paint. She avoids low branches, protecting the day's hard work. Boris stops and rubs sweat from his brow with his shirt sleeve. Vera gives her a sidelong glare as if to say, 'I told you so.'

'We're nearly there, Boris,' Galina encourages. She moves closer to his side and he slips his arm around hers, leaning on her for support. She did not expect him to take her arm. His determined gaze remains fixed on the path ahead. His face is flush and he looks frail.

'That painting is going to be perfection,' he says, nodding towards the portrait. 'I'm glad I was here to see it from the very beginning.'

'In a few weeks, you'll come to the exhibition and see the result,' Galina says.

He nods. 'That would be my pleasure.'

Leaning towards her, he wheezes softly. Each step is more laboured and Galina begins to worry. Perhaps this outing is too much. Vera gives her another stern glance and without a word she sidles up to Boris. He slips his arm around hers. Together they press on, through the tunnel of trees.

As the train platform comes into view, relief washes over

Galina.

'Now, be careful on the steps up to the platform, Boris,' Vera instructs.

'I know how to go up a few stairs,' he grumbles.

'There's still a long way to go. We have the train and then the walk back to the *dacha*.'

Galina scowls at Vera.

Boris pats Galina's hand and looks her in the eye. 'This has been a perfect day.'

4

❦

EARLY THE FOLLOWING MORNING Vera and Boris return to Leningrad. Dima and Galina sit at the kitchen table with two steaming cups of tea. After several days of so many people crowded into the *dacha*, the stillness makes the gap between the couple more pronounced.

'I'm going back to Leningrad today,' she says.

He nods but does not look up from his gardening notebook.

'I want to get to work on the portrait and I don't have any canvases here. Time is short.'

'You should just submit last year's portrait. Last year's Soviet child is the same as this year's Soviet child.'

Many of her colleagues do this, recycling their work year upon year, but she enjoys the challenge of a clean canvas and looks forward to creating a new painting for the exhibition. Tatiana Nikolayevna, the department's director, is tired of presenting the same works year on year and specifically asked for new pieces. But Galina does not bother explaining this to him. He would not understand.

'You can go back with Yuri and Masha, when they wake.'

Galina dismisses his comment. She has no intention of travelling with Masha and she wants to get back as soon as possible. She finishes her tea and takes the cup to the sink.

'About my shoes,' Galina starts. He looks up but before he says anything she knows he did not clean them.

'What about them?'

Like a silly schoolgirl, she thought it was Dima who had committed the unrequested kind gesture. This act would be a sign that he noticed her, evidence of his love. But his eyes, distracted with crop rotation and potato yield, tell her otherwise.

From the *dacha*, Galina travels directly to the art academy. She steps off the trolley bus carefully holding the study, which is not yet dry. She squints as the bright sun reflects off the Neva. A gentle breeze blows and she pinches the painting tighter. Across the rippling water, beyond Palace Bridge, the pale viridian façade of the Hermitage graces the opposite embankment. Its gilded embellishments shine in the morning light. This palace gave her shelter when the city was on its knees and it is impossible to walk by without feeling a sense of gratitude and connection to the building. Her stomach tightens as she remembers the musty cellar and watery soup, surviving on the very edge of starvation. For many, it was luck that determined who lived and who perished. But for her, it was the Hermitage that saved her.

Galina turns away and continues down the embankment towards Repin Art Academy of Painting, Sculpture and Architecture. The mustard-yellow building occupies the whole block and Galina feels small beside the grand, columned façade. She opens a diminutive wooden door, which is incongruous in the imposing exterior. Without looking up at the columned balcony and classical statues above the entrance, she enters and crosses the domed vestibule. Knowing her father had studied in this building long ago, she feels his presence. Her wide heels click-clack across the mosaic floor, echoing off the high, vaulted ceiling.

She shares a studio on the second floor with three other members of staff. The windows, which look onto the inner courtyard, are tall but north-facing. Little light penetrates the smudged glass. Her desk, stacked with files and students' portfolios, is pushed into a corner. Beside it, an easel stands near the windows. She drags another easel from her colleague's corner and places the painting of Sveta on it. Tightening the screws, she secures it in place.

Opposite the windows, several clean canvases, prepared by keen students eager to impress, stand upright against the wall. She flips through them and pulls out the largest one. She sets it on the easel and measures – 112 x 80 centimetres. Maybe she should do something smaller? Something quick and easy. She steps back, hands on hips, considering her options.

Galina closes her eyes and returns to the previous day by the lake. She imagines the warm sun on her back and the bustle of the geese. Looking at the blank canvas, she creates a plan for the composition. She will place Sveta to the right of centre with the endless flock of geese filling the space behind her. Inspired, she slips on her painting smock and picks up a piece of charcoal. Cradling it firmly between her thumb and index finger, she lightly sketches Sveta's head and shoulders on the canvas. With every mark, she relaxes, transporting herself back to the water's edge.

She selects her colours and pulls a palette from the cupboard, brushing her hand across the stained surface. Excitement flutters as she glances at the outline on the canvas. She is ready to prepare her palette.

'Galina! Galina!'

She looks up from her painting and turns towards the voice calling from the corridor. The room has grown darker as the afternoon has progressed.

'I thought I heard you down here,' Tatiana Nikolaevna says, out of breath from running down the corridor. 'Vera Ivanovna is on the phone for you.'

Galina sets her brushes on a table, bristles overhanging the edge.

'She's upset. I think you should come quickly.'

For a moment, she is frozen on the spot. Vera never calls the academy.

Galina follows Tatiana, whose chatter fills the empty corridor. But Galina is not listening. Tatiana leads the way into the office and picks up the phone. Out of breath, she waves it insistently, waiting for Galina to take the smoke-stained plastic receiver.

Galina grabs it and presses it to her ear. 'Hello?'

'Galya, thank God I found you,' Vera says.

She waits.

'How can I say it?' Vera says, her voice cracking. 'Boris is dead.'

5

⚘

As GALINA APPROACHES Chekhov Street, she remembers the first time she came here with Boris and Vera. The exterior was pock-marked from years of war but Boris presented it to the girls as if it were a palace. They craned their necks while Vera counted the six storeys.

'Here we'll begin our happy future,' Boris announced. 'Everything is ahead of us!' He opened the door, ushering in the girls. 'Fourth floor! Who's going to get there first?'

They pushed past him and their voices floated up the stairwell.

Despite the rubble, destruction and loss of life, there was a feeling of excitement on the streets of Leningrad in those months following the war. It was as if the whole city, emboldened by its endurance against all odds, collectively sighed with relief.

Today, Galina's hand grasps the same banister as she

climbs the stairs.

'Galochka.' A raspy female voice echoes off the concrete floor.

Olga Andreyevna is standing outside her flat on the third floor, which is just below Vera and Boris's flat. She is carrying a box of Red October chocolates. Her upper back is curved into a hump and she holds her head awkwardly. She has lived on Chekhov Street ever since they arrived. Back then, she always looked fabulous, even in the chaotic years immediately following the war. She wore lipsticks which brought out the pink of her cheeks and simple, fetching dresses. It did not take long for Boris to notice her and the girls always suspected they had had a fling back in the Fifties, but of course it was never discussed, so they were never certain.

'My deepest sympathies, Galochka.' She dabs the corner of her eye with a handkerchief. 'Terrible to lose our dear Boris.' She kisses both of Galina's cheeks. 'I only just heard the news.' She glances at the chocolates in her hand. 'I'll bake some *pirozhki* later, of course.' Her voice, coarse from years of smoking Yava cigarettes, cracks.

They arrive on the fourth floor and pause outside the flat. Olga Andreyevna, out of breath, steadies herself on the iron banister. Her silver hair is styled as it always was. Pulled up into a loose topknot, thin curly tendrils frame her face. Her eyes are cloudy blue, the flirtatious sparkle no longer there.

Galina knocks on the door and Vera soon answers.

'Thank God you're here,' says Vera, kissing Galina on the cheek. She turns to Olga Andreyevna. 'So kind of you to come.'

They enter the flat. To the right, the door to Boris's room is closed. In the main room, several neighbours sit on the divan.

'We'll sort everything out,' Olga says, patting Vera's arm

and joining the other neighbours.

'You must see him.' Vera takes Galina by the elbow and opens his bedroom door. Boris is lying on his single bed. Galina approaches and gently squeezes his lifeless hand, ridiculously hoping for a response, but the fingers are still. His face is expressionless. Soulless.

Vera talks as if she is afraid of the silence but Galina catches only quick snippets: his final moments, how she discovered him, something about the doctor. But mostly she is not listening. Beside the bed lies a copy of *Novy Mir* magazine which Dima had given Boris at the weekend. Galina picks it up and flips through it. A paper is stuck between the colourful pages. She turns it over and finds the sketch which he drew yesterday by the lake. She looks closely at the lines forming Sveta's plump cheeks and wry smile. She studies the figure standing by the easel. Does she really slouch that badly? On the bottom, he has written a title, *Everything's Ahead of Her*, and signed his name in the lower right-hand corner. Maybe Vera was right and the trip to the lake was too much for him.

'Galya?' Vera shakes her arm. 'The doctor has been and signed his death certificate. The morgue will take him soon.'

'Did you tell Yuri?'

'Nobody answered the phone when I called your apartment.'

'I've got to tell Dima.'

Vera's swollen eyes stare at Galina. 'Now?'

'Of course.' She returns the sketch and the magazine to the table.

'But...there is so much to do here. I've only just called the Hermitage.'

She hesitates, taking in Vera's bloodshot eyes and raised eyebrows.

'Galya, he was a loyal member of the Hermitage collective for decades, his whole career. His funeral will be at the Hermitage.'

Yes, of course.

The room feels too warm and crowded. Galina turns towards the window above Boris's dresser. The sky has clouded over, thick and dark. She reaches up and opens the small vent window, letting in a swirl of fresh air.

'Olga Andreyevna and the others are here. They'll help you,' Galya says. She kisses Vera's cheek and heads towards the door.

Galina settles in the empty wagon as the doors rattle shut. Taking a seat next to the window, she leans her forehead against the cool glass and closes her eyes, but the image of Boris's corpse remains. The train pulls away from the station, passing through the network of Leningrad streets. Of course, rationally, she knew that Boris would die at any time, he was old, but his death has slapped her, leaving a burning sting behind. She is an orphan, again.

Her father's death had not been a slap. It was more like a relentless beating with a club. She remembers the weight of him, leaning on her as he staggered down the dark corridors of the Hermitage. He mumbled as he walked. His senseless words were tinged with the vodka and dried fish on his breath. Somehow, she and Vera managed to lead him down the stairs, into the cellar. As they shuffled to their mattresses, she was aware of the disapproving glances and whispers around them. Ashamed, she guided him towards his blankets. She pulled the bedsheet curtains shut and clipped them together, but the nasty comments filtered through the flimsy fabric. The girls curled up together on one mattress, her father was alone on the other, grumbling gibberish about Stalin and Andrei. Galina did not know who Andrei was but she did know, even at eight years old, that you should not speak of Stalin crossly. She huddled close to Vera, willing her father to sleep. Finally, he went silent.

As her shoulders relaxed and a hazy sleep fell around her, a guttural retch erupted from her father. A woman flung back the curtain. 'Drunken fool. We're all trying to sleep,' she said. Another retch, louder this time, emerged from him and he vomited, splattering the contents of his stomach on the floor. A vile, acidic smell clung to the air. Someone holding a candle approached and the flickering light shone on the patch of black vomit. His sunken, unshaven cheeks turned an alien shade of blue. For a moment, she did not recognise him. She had to persuade herself that this was her father. Vera buried her face in Galina's chest and her warm tears dropped on her hand. His body went still and a *babushka* knelt over him. 'That's it already,' she said. 'He's dead.'

Her mother died quietly. It happened one night early in the war, before Galina knew to look for death prowling around. She pressed herself tight into her mother's thin angular arms, relaxing under the warmth of the blankets which covered them.

'My dear Galochka, my sweetie, my bright star, the best daughter in the world.' Her sugary words soothed and Galina's eyes grew heavy. 'I love you more than I could possibly ever say.' She squeezed and her bony arm met the child's ribcage. 'Everything's going to be perfect.'

In the morning, Galina woke, shivering. It was as if her back was against a pile of snow. Her mother's arm laid heavily on her ribs. 'Mama?' she whispered. There was not a reply.

A sharp spring shower taps the train's window pane. Menacing clouds cover the sky and the trees along the railway line bend in the wind. Passing a yellow *dacha*, the sign that her stop is next, Galina stands and scans the bench. Usually she travels to the *dacha* laden with bags but today, she only brings the news of Boris's death.

The train comes to a halt. She steps into the falling rain and dashes under a corrugated metal awning. She looks to the sky, hoping to see a break in the torrent, but the swirling clouds offer no relief. She steps out from the shelter, darts down the platform and descends the stairs, heading towards the dirt track. Weaving around puddles, her beautiful leather shoes sink in the mud. Wet hair blows loose from her long braid, sticking to her cheeks and neck. Out of breath, she reaches her *dacha* and opens the door. It glides open on the new hinges. Boris's final gift.

Galina kicks off her muddy shoes. Water drips from her skirt, forming a puddle on the floor. She pushes hair from her face and peels a saturated jacket from her back. The rain grows heavier, pounding on the roof but she hears something else. Something she cannot quite place. She walks towards the sound, a voice giggling. But not like Masha. It is deeper, more mature, a woman. Galina steps towards her bedroom door and opens it.

Dima's eyes meet hers. An unnaturally blond head turns. Elena quickly pulls up the sheet to cover her naked body.

Nobody speaks. Rain hammers the shingles.

For a moment, Galina forgets why she is there.

'Boris is dead.' She turns and walks out.

A bottle of Armenian cognac, two empty glasses and the vase of wilting daffodils are on the kitchen table, as if forming a still life that is waiting to be painted. Elena brought these flowers to Yuri's birthday party. Galina jams them into the rubbish pail and puts the vase in the sink. Red lipstick marks the rim of one of the glasses. She tosses it into the sink and it collides with the vase, splintering. She pours a shot of cognac and drinks. The strong liquor burns a trail as she swallows. Thunder rumbles in the distance.

'What a nightmare,' Dima says, coming into the kitchen in his underwear.

'Is she still here?'

'Galya, just give her a minute. Until it stops raining.'

'I don't care if there is a hurricane. Get her out of my *dacha*. Now.'

Her eyes fall to a scratch which marks his shoulder.

'Now!' Galina repeats, splashing more cognac in the glass. 'And you. Go with her.'

'We need to talk.'

She turns away and takes a seat at the table.

'Go.' She brushes her hand, dismissing him.

The floorboards creak as Elena and Dima get dressed in the bedroom. Their muffled voices seep through the thin walls. At the front door, the rustles of putting on shoes and jackets are punctuated with insistent whispers. Galina does not turn towards the quick footsteps coming down the corridor into the kitchen. Nor does she make eye contact with Dima when he grabs Elena's cardigan from the chair beside her. He quickly escapes, shutting the door behind them. They are gone.

Galina buries her face in her hands and screams. The sound grows from deep inside, competing with the relentless, driving rain. Her head begins to ache and she stops, feeling the blood course through her body and her temples pound.

Tears warm her cheeks. She breathes deeply and the moist air fills her lungs. She exhales. Inhaling, she screams again and her fingernails pierce her palms as her fists clench. Pain forces her to stop. Her lungs expand as she inhales.

Breathing calms and her fists unclench.

Of course, she is not the first woman to catch a philandering husband. As she pours cognac into her glass she realises that she is not surprised to have caught Dima in this adulterous act. What surprises her is that the woman is someone of her own age, someone she knows and likes. Galina has foraged mushrooms and swum in the river with Elena. They are friends. She always suspected or expected the other woman would be one of his students, fresh-faced, eager to please, and pert. But why is she thinking of this? It does not really matter who the other woman is.

The following morning, Galina wakes with a headache, shivering on the divan and wearing her damp clothes from the day before. Gentle sunlight filters through a gauzy curtain. She glances at her watch. It is just after five. She sits up and her head throbs. The taste of stale, sickly-sweet cognac coats her dry tongue. Slowly, she swings her legs to the floor. The empty bottle of cognac lies on its side at her feet. She picks up the bottle and forces herself to stand. As she walks, sand clings to her bare feet, scuffing the cold, uneven floorboards. As she bends to place the bottle beside the rubbish pail in the kitchen, her temples pound.

She fills a glass with water and drinks. Rinsing her mouth, she spits in the sink, gagging. She strikes a match and lights the stove. Flames lick the kettle.

Her eyes are dry and raw from crying. She forgot how it feels, to cry. To be completely spent, like a rag that has been wrung out and dripped dry. A salty stiffness encrusts the bags under her eyes and her cheeks. She could remember crying when her father died, but not since. Is that possible? It was Vera who was prone to tears. She cried enough for both of them.

Vera.

Galina's stomach cramps and a nauseous wave rumbles in her gut. She should have returned to Leningrad last night to help her.

She pours the boiling water into the teapot and tea leaves swirl. Turning on the tap, she waits for the water to warm and splashes her face. She dries herself with a linen towel, the coarse fibres are rough on her cheeks and forehead. Has she really not cried in so long? The question lingers in her mind as she pours a cup of tea. Come to think of it, she cannot remember the last time she truly laughed, a full-bellied from deep inside, side-splitting roar of laughter. She drizzles a spoonful of honey into the steamy liquid.

Wrapping her hands around the cup, her dry lips purse and she blows, causing ripples across the tea's surface. She takes a sip and looks out of the kitchen window, avoiding Dima's vegetable garden. Yuri's bicycle leans against a slender birch tree. Her heart pauses, then leaps. Does he know about Boris?

She must get back to Leningrad.

In the bedroom, the bedsheets are rumpled with the imprint of their bodies. A blanket puddles on the floor. Disgusted, she turns away and quickly changes into a dry dress. She brushes her tangled hair and quickly plaits a single braid. Her muddy shoes lie beside the front door. The brown leather is barely visible. Giving up any concern with her appearance, she stabs her feet into tall felt boots. She opens the door and sets off for the train station, leaving her shoes behind.

Galina climbs the stairs to her flat on Prospect Rimsky-Korsakov, hoping to find Yuri at home, alone. The mere thought of Masha being in the flat makes her headache even worse. She turns the key, opens the door and surveys the collection of shoes scattered in the entrance. She does not find either the tacky high-heeled sandals nor Dima's shoes. She relaxes and closes the door behind her.

She places some eggs and a loaf of bread, which she bought on the way home, on the kitchen table, and within a few minutes Yuri appears. He leans against the door-frame. His eyes are red and swollen. She embraces him and he bends, placing his head on her shoulder. His tears soak through her shirt. She rubs his back, unsure of what to say.

'Where have you been?' he asks, stepping back from her embrace and wiping his face with the back of his hand.

'At the *dacha*. I had to tell Papa.'

His chin starts to quiver and he looks away, casting his gaze out of the window onto the street below.

'I didn't expect to stay,' Galina says.

He sits on a stool and props his elbow on the table.

'I'll make us some eggs.'

He nods and she takes out a pan. Turning her back to him, she lights the stove and drops a dollop of butter on the aluminium. Yuri sniffles and inhales, his breathing uneasy.

She cracks the eggs into the buttery pan. The sizzle breaks the silence.

'He was very old, Yuri. He had a long, full life.'

Galina passes him a kitchen towel. He wipes his cheeks and blows his nose on the cloth, balls it up and places it on his lap. His lanky shoulders droop inward. She cuts several slices of brown bread, lays them in a shallow basket, and sets it on the table. She lifts the eggs from the pan. The bright runny yolks quiver on the plate as she sets it in front of Yuri. She fixes a portion for herself and sits on the stool opposite.

She dips the edge of her bread in the viscous yolk and realises that Yuri has never experienced death. Given how much death she had witnessed in her childhood, it does not seem possible that he has avoided it until now. But it is true.

Watching him stifle his tears and finish the meal, worry grows. He is still a boy. He is not ready to join the battalion of men.

Galina leaves the dishes in the sink and quickly showers. She finds a black dress, folded neatly in a drawer. The long sleeves and heavy fabric will be too warm for this spring day but it will have to do. Yuri's dark trousers are too short. She lets out the hem and quickly sews it up again. The fabric is faded and leaves a faint line around his ankles. They are still too short, but they will be fine for the day.

As Galina studies her complexion in the mirror, the phone rings and Yuri answers. She can tell by his responses that it is Vera. She quickly finishes brushing a layer of powder on her face and takes the receiver.

'Where are you?' says Vera.

'Home.'

Vera sighs.

'Vera, you called me at home. Of course, I'm here.'

'When are going to the Hermitage?'

'Just now. Yuri's trousers were too short so I had to sort something out. I promise, we're coming as quick as we can.'

'I'm going now. Mourners will start arriving soon.'

'We won't be long.'

'Fine. *Poka.*' Vera hangs up abruptly.

Galina finishes her make-up and heads towards the entrance where the boots catch her eye. Shoes. She needs shoes. She opens the cupboard below the coat-laden pegs on the wall. Pushing extra slippers and old boots to the side, she finds a pair of black shoes. The leather is scuffed and worn. There is a small hole in the sole, where the ball of her foot hits the pavement. The heads of nails are visible in the heels. She takes a tin of shoe polish and a brush and quickly rubs a layer of black over the leather, buffing a shine on the surface. She puts them on, the ball of her foot rests in the hole. They will have to suffice.

Yuri opens the door and they step out of the flat.

'Where's Papa?' he asks.

'Don't know,' she mutters as they head down the stairs to the bus stop.

The simple wooden coffin, propped open, sits at the far end of the room, resting on sawhorses draped in black material. Two Hermitage employees flank either side, shaking hands with mourners as they pass. A string quartet plays slow sombre notes, which echo off the ceilings. The walls are stark white and the room is surprisingly plain for such an extravagant building. The only splash of colour is a Soviet flag hanging on a pole in the corner.

Galina approaches the coffin. Her hand is linked with Yuri's arm, his steps are slow. She presses gently, urging him forwards. Boris's face is covered with a powdery finish, his cheeks strangely pink. Carnations lie in the coffin. She has come empty-handed. It did not even occur to her to buy flowers. The man beside the coffin, one of Boris's colleagues, takes her hand. His face is familiar but she cannot remember his name.

'My deepest sympathies, Galina Mikhailovna. He was a good man, the best of the best, never to be forgotten.' He releases her hand, blinking back tears.

The viola player holds an enduring, low note, dragging the bow slowly across the strings. The vibration continues as he holds the bow aloft. Yuri quivers, attempting to hold back tears. Galina guides him towards Vera, who is standing at the foot of the coffin.

'I can't believe you left me,' Vera whispers firmly. 'To do everything.'

She is right, but Galina makes no apology.

'You weren't alone. Neighbours and his colleagues were here helping you.' Her stomach churns as the egg mixes with last night's cognac. As the room fills, it becomes warm. Moisture clings under her arms, beneath the long-sleeved dress. 'What's done is done, Vera. We're here now.'

Yuri stands beside her like a shadow, his eyes fixed on Boris's lifeless body. Olga Andreyevna approaches and kisses Galina's cheeks.

'Thank God you are here, Galochka. Vera was so worried and upset.' She turns to Yuri and pulls him towards her. He bends, allowing her to smother him with kisses. 'Yurka, my dearest and sweetest boy, Vilena Dmitrievena on the first floor made some very tasty *priyaniki*, the best in Leningrad. Come with me and I will get you one.' Her hands clasp around his. She speaks to him as if he is still a toddler.

Mourners, mostly neighbours and colleagues from the Hermitage, cluster around the room. In the corner, there is a group of younger people whom Galina does not recognise. They are bookish and plain; she assumes they work with Vera at the Leningrad Central Library.

Tatiana Nikolayevna enters the room and approaches the coffin. Her gauzy dress billows around her ample frame, and a long silk scarf, hand-painted with deep red poppies and black swans, is loosely draped around her neck. She lingers at Boris's side and places four carnations in the coffin. Her head tips to the side and she sighs, resting her hand on her chest. She turns and strides towards Galina.

'My deepest sympathies,' she says, kissing Galina's cheeks. 'He was very special, so respected in his field. He made a tremendous contribution with all the Hermitage masterpieces he restored.' She pats the coffin softly; tapping the wood as she glances around the room. Her eyes rest on a group of Boris's colleagues from the Hermitage. 'The greatest generation. They have done so much.'

'Thank you for coming, Tatiana Nikolayevna.'

Galina cannot think of anything else to say. She shifts, relieving the pressure on her foot, which is uncomfortable in the old shoe. Tatiana takes her by the elbow and pulls her away from the coffin to a quiet corner.

'Maybe now isn't the best time, but I want to talk to you about the portrait you were working on yesterday.'

The portrait. Was she painting just yesterday? It feels like weeks ago.

'It has potential, Galya. I like the composition with the ducks in the background. And it is such a large format, so ambitious. The girl is so cute. Who is she?'

'Sveta. Her mother...' Galina hesitates, remembering Elena's wiry hair against rumpled sheets. 'They have a *dacha* near ours.'

'Well, I love it. You must get back to it, after the burial of course. It has to be ready for the exhibition.'

The mere thought of finishing a portrait of Elena's daughter makes Galina cringe.

'I'm not sure. I'm thinking about doing something else.'

'Why? You should finish this one, Galina. Time is very short and it needs to be ready by early June.' She pulls Galina closer, lowering her voice. 'Look, I need new work for this exhibition. If you finish it on time, I may be able to get a private studio for you.'

Tatiana's smoky breath clings to the words.

A private studio. A place to work, uninterrupted. Galina has visited other artists' studios dotted around town but never thought it would be possible for her to have her own.

'Now is the time to mourn Boris. Don't think about work at all. In two days, you will bury him. Then please, try to get back to the painting.' Tatiana Nikolayevna's glance shifts to her wristwatch. 'We can talk about it later. A studio of your own would be very good for you.' She squeezes Galina's arm. 'I'll let you get back to the mourners.' She pulls her close and kisses either cheek. 'I'll see you next week.'

Tatiana Nikolayevna crosses the room, making her way through the crowd. Before she exits, she turns and gives a quick wave and a nod.

The prospect of a private studio lifts Galina. Ambition grows as she considers her future with her own studio, which is much more than four walls, a ceiling and a floor. It is a mark of achievement and respect.

The quartet drones on while the room fills with whispering mourners. Galina speaks to them as they pass but does not fully engage. She nods and appears to listen to their memories of Boris but she feels alone and separate, as if she is in an audience watching a play. It does not feel real. Then her eyes fall on Boris's corpse and she stands straighter, forcing herself to thank another mourner for coming.

Masha arrives wearing a baggy black dress, which, presumably, has been borrowed. The dark colour makes her skin paler and her skinny frame seems lost in the oversized dress. She walks across the room, directly to Yuri. He wraps his arms around her and they stand, intertwined.

Galina feels a familiar leathery touch on her hand. Dima's eyes meet hers. His damp hair is combed back. His face is clean-shaven and smooth. He rests his dry, cracked palm on hers, enveloping it.

He leans forward and kisses her cheeks. 'My deepest sympathies, Galochka. Boris was much-loved, by everyone who knew him.' He squeezes her hand.

His touch brings comfort. She does not pull away.

'I brought you these,' he says, handing her a bag. Through the mesh are her shoes, clean of all the mud.

Galina takes the bag but it hangs awkwardly in her hand.

'Galya, we need to talk.'

'Not here. It's not the time.'

'I didn't mean for it to happen.'

'What am I supposed to say to that?'

'Nothing is easier than to deceive one's self, as our affections are subtle persuaders.'

'Dima, do not quote a long dead philosopher to me now. It's infuriating. And besides, what about your affection for me? Was that not enough to persuade you?'

'Don't you see, Galya? I deceived myself.'

'No,' she says. 'I refuse to engage in some deep philosophical conversation. You deceived me.'

He scratches his head and looks around the room, as if searching for something to say.

'One thing I do know, absolutely for sure, is that she's never to step foot in my *dacha* again.'

He nods, head down, looking at the floor.

'Dima. Say it. Say you agree.'

'Agreed,' he mutters.

She hands him the bag with the shoes. 'I can't take these now.' She turns and strides away from him, the coffin and the mourners. The nail in the heel of her shoes taps the parquet floor. Her pace quickens as she follows the corridor, past display cases full of enamelled treasures and priceless ancient artefacts. She carries on, passing sculptures and framed canvases, into the Hall of Twenty Columns. Flecks of quartz sparkle in the massive granite columns. Making her way through the splendour, she stops at a window which looks out to a courtyard. Weaving through a cluster of birch trees, there is a very faint indentation of a path, from the courtyard door to an inconspicuous cellar door.

During the siege she skipped along this path. Not in the beginning when she was weak, but later, in the summer, after the ice melted and the mud dried. Holding hands, Vera and Galina climbed the stairs out of the deep cellar and hurried along the path, into the Hermitage where they played hide-and-seek with the other children. In a larger, sunnier courtyard they planted a garden. Everyone worked that summer, hoeing and weeding, willing the seeds to flourish in the poor soil. It was as if surviving the first terrible winter had renewed their determination to live.

She walks to the door and rests her fingers on the handle. She turns it, feeling the mechanism release.

'*Nelzya*, it isn't allowed,' the raspy authoritative voice of a *babushka* echoes off the arched ceiling.

Galina withdraws her hand.

The old woman stands with her fists on hips and her feet hip-width apart. She pushes her aside and takes the door handle in her hand, shaking it.

'See, it's locked. You are only allowed in the permitted rooms. There is nothing to see here.' Standing between Galina and the door, she waits for her retreat.

Galina takes one last glance at the cellar door and heads back to the funeral with determined steps. Tatiana Nikolayevna's offer replays in her mind. She pictures herself, alone in a spacious art studio. Sun streams through windows and she is surrounded by her work and the smell of oil paint. She will finish Sveta's portrait and get the private studio. A place of her own.

6

⚓

GALINA ARRIVES AT THE ART ACADEMY early, hoping for a couple of hours of painting while the studio is quiet. The large canvas sits on the easel and the study of Sveta remains beside it. The brushes and palette have been cleaned, presumably by Tatiana Nikolayevna. Galina looks closely at the painting of Elena's daughter.

Why did she not notice? She's such a fool. Thinking back to that night of Yuri's birthday, she saw Dima and Elena by the fire. Dima lingered too long before he picked up Sveta from the hammock but at the time Galina thought nothing of it. She assumes the affair went on for quite some time but has no desire to learn the details. She puts on her painting smock and forces herself to stop thinking about Dima and Elena.

After three busy days at the funeral, Galina relaxes in the solitude of the studio. There is much to be done. Wispy charcoal contours outline Sveta's form sitting on the concrete wall, like a skeleton waiting for flesh. Galina prepares her palette with an arc of paint along the upper rim of the wood. Her strokes gently skim across the canvas, slowly creating Sveta's features. The colours work in harmony, capturing the structure of her face. Sveta begins to emerge. Her slightly almond-shaped eyes, plump cheeks and chin take form.

Galina settles into the rhythm of the brush strokes, which dance between the canvas and the palette. Free from the sadness of Boris's passing, Dima's adultery, Masha's giggling, Yuri's naivety and Vera's tears, Galina focuses on her work. The brush follows her command and she is transported to the day by the lake: the smell of pine needles, the gentle breeze of warm air, the shine of Sveta's hair. This portrait must capture more than Sveta. It must convey the peaceful beauty of one of Boris's final days.

When Galina enters Boris's room on Chekhov Street, she realises the heavy task which she is about to begin. Vera is determined to start going through Boris's belongings and Galina has reluctantly agreed. With robotic coldness, Vera sets an empty cardboard box beside the dresser and picks up Boris's sketch.

Everything's Ahead of Her, she mutters, reading the title he had written on the paper. Her lips tighten. 'Huh.'

Although she has not said so explicitly, Galina senses that Vera blames her for Boris's death.

'I'd like to keep that sketch,' says Galina.

Vera passes it to her, without saying a word or making eye contact.

His room is the smallest in the flat. The single bed sags in the corner. Beside it, stands an oak dresser. With the bulky furniture in the room, there is only a small square of parquet floor in the centre, which is covered with a threadbare Bokhara rug. Galina pulls back the curtains and the evening light filters through the glass. Below, the dull courtyard is dotted with fading daffodils, and tree blossom litters the ground like snow. Children swing on monkey bars, dodging muddy puddles.

On top of the dresser there is a stack of *Krokodil* magazines and several books. Galina thumbs through the cartoon-illustrated covers of the satirical periodical. Ranging throughout the Seventies, they are in a random order and tattered, most probably passed among colleagues and friends and read several times.

'Do you want his books and magazines?' asks Galina.

Vera shakes her head.

'Are you sure?'

She does not answer.

Knowing that Dima and Yuri share Boris's literary tastes, Galina slips the sketch between the magazine pages and puts them in a bag to take home. The spines of the remaining books are organised by genre: the science-fiction classics *Hard to Be a God* and *Monday Begins on Saturday* by the Strugatsky Brothers and *The Amphibian Man* by Alexander Belyaev. Beside them, a cluster of comedy titles: Zoshchenko's *A Man is Not a Flea, Scenes from the Bathhouse* and *The Galoshes* and Ilf and Petrov's *The Twelve Chairs*. She puts all the books in another bag and sets them aside.

Galina opens the top dresser drawer and it slides heavily, moaning. It is filled to the brim. She picks up a tin and opens it: various black and blue buttons and safety pins. She pushes the lid back on the tin, returns it to the drawer and slides it closed. She is not suited to the role of intruder.

'I don't think I've ever been in this room,' she says, as Vera sets another empty cardboard box on the bed.

They moved to this flat shortly after the war. Boris's flat was too small for the three of them and the girls' building on Mokhovaya Street had been destroyed. This two-roomed flat was perfect. The girls slept in the larger room where each evening they collapsed the divan and laid the sheets on the bed. Boris had the small room on the opposite side of the corridor. He always kept the door closed and although he never specifically said, the girls understood that they were not to enter. A rule they always respected.

As Galina pulls the bottom drawer out of the dresser and lays it on the mattress, she feels a wave of shame, like a nosy thief going through his belongings. She sits and the springs squeak beneath her. The drawer is filled with papers. She takes a yellowing, unsealed envelope and looks inside: newspaper clippings. She tips it and the bits of brittle paper cascade onto the bed. She glances through the headlines: 'Soviets First to Berlin!', 'Gagarin Returns to Earth!', 'Stalin Dead!', 'Sputnik Launched', 'Tereshkova First Woman in Space'. It is a time capsule of Soviet achievement. These clips of history do not surprise her. Boris celebrated progress.

She picks up a folder, tied shut with a fraying lace. Inside lay several certificates stamped with the official seal of the Union of Soviet Artists. It is a chronicle of Boris's career.

She picks up a smaller, sealed envelope which is marked 'Julia' in Boris's handwriting. Who's Julia? She slides her finger under the flap and the old paper rips easily. Galina removes three photographs. Boris, young and handsome with a full head of dark hair, stands proudly beside a woman with a bouquet. She turns the photograph over and reads 'Wedding. July 1, 1921' written in lacy script on the reverse side.

'Did you know that Boris was married?' Galina says, handing the photograph to Vera.

Vera takes it. 'He never talked about his life before the war.' She hands the photo back to her and places a handful of socks in the box.

Galina looks at the next photograph, a formal portrait of the same woman. She turns it over. '1920' is written on the reverse side.

The third photograph is a group of women wearing black dresses. In the first row, they are seated with straight backs, serious expressions and hands folded on their laps. A second and third row of women stand behind them. On the back of the photo is written 'State Leningrad Herzen Pedagogical Institute, 1926'. She searches the photograph, looking for Julia and finds her in the second row in the middle.

'She must have been a teacher.' Galina passes Vera the photo.

But she does not stop to look at it. She pushes more clothes into the box and folds the flaps shut.

'Cut me a piece of string, Galya,' she says, motioning to the spool and scissors on the dresser.

Galina pulls several arms' lengths of string and cuts. She threads it around the box while Vera lifts it up. On the underside, Galina twists the string, wraps it around the carton and ties a tight square knot. Vera immediately carries it out to the corridor.

Galina returns the photos to the envelope and opens a brown folder marked 'Galina'. She finds her school reports in chronological order with the most recent on top. She never would have guessed that he would keep these documents this long. Next, she finds a similar file marked 'Vera' with her school reports.

Galina removes a folder, exposing the wooden drawer beneath it. Inside, there are three envelopes.

The first is addressed to her father. 'Mikhail Tarasovich Senotrusov' is written in ornate slanted handwriting which she does not recognise and has been neatly opened with a knife. She pulls out the letter and unfolds the brittle paper. There is a military emblem at the top of the page. It is written in the same elegant script and dated a couple of days before her father died.

5 January 1942

Mikhail,

I have learned news of your brother. Convicted as enemy of the people and sent to Norilsk without right of correspondence. Uncertain of current condition.

Shishkin

Galina immediately recognises this name, Shishkin. He was the colonel who had ordered the portrait of his two sons during the siege. Why would Boris have this letter? Her parents certainly never mentioned that she had an uncle.

Vera places a handful of undershirts in a box and looks around the room. 'Do you see any other clothes? I think that's the last of them.'

Galina returns the letter to the envelope. The next one is sliced open along the top crease and addressed:

Leningrad
The State Hermitage Museum
Anna Petrovna Kamerova

Galina does not pass it to Vera, even though it is addressed to her mother. She pulls out the letter and unfolds it.

4 April 1956

Dear Anna Petrovna,

I hope this letter reaches you in good health. You do not know me, but we share a friend. For many years, I was imprisoned with your husband, Ivan Ivanovich Kamerov. I promised him that I would write to you upon my release so you would learn the truth of what happened to him. He instructed me to write to you at your place of work, the Hermitage museum, and I sincerely hope this letter finds you after all these years.

Ivan and I spent the latter half of the war in a Nazi prison camp in Germany. When allied forces liberated the camp, we set out searching for a Soviet unit to join. When we found the Soviet forces, they did not believe our story of imprisonment. Hence, we were accused of treason and transported to Pechora prison camp. Ivan, already weak from the German camp, did not endure the journey well. He fell ill when we arrived and never recovered. Sadly, Ivan died in the winter of 1946.

Throughout our friendship, he spoke of you and Vera often. When he died, I lost a true friend, and you, a beloved husband. He wanted you to know his fate so I promised to write. I hope this letter finds you in good health.

Respectfully,
Sergei Borisovich Filipov

On the envelope, there is a return address, 6 Leonova Street, Gatchina, a town on the outskirts of Leningrad.

Galina should not have read this letter. She should have passed it to Vera.

'What now?' Vera asks.

Silently, Galina hands her the paper. Sitting beside her on the bed, Vera scans the page. It trembles in her hand and when she looks up, her eyes are moist.

'Vera, I'm so sorry.'

'Why wouldn't Boris tell me?'

'He probably didn't want to upset you.'

'I would have been twenty when this letter arrived. I had the right to know.'

Galina embraces Vera but she pulls away, wiping her cheeks with the back of her hand.

'Vera, maybe this is enough for one day? Let's shut the door and come back to it all later. It's much more difficult than we expected.'

'How am I supposed to live here, knowing that this room hides so many secrets?' Vera says, returning the letter to the envelope.

'Boris wasn't a bad man… He must've had his reasons.'

Vera shrugs, clearly unconvinced.

She was only five years old when her father went to the front and her mother disappeared during the siege. Throughout their childhood, she would occasionally ask Galina about her parents. For her, they were figures from a fairytale.

Galina used to tell her stories of their two families living together in the *kommunalka* in Mokhovaya Street, creating a perfect Soviet tableau. She did not mention the arguments between their fathers. Galina was too young to understand what they were arguing about at the time, but she remembers the men shouting, usually in the kitchen late at night. Perhaps they were just two very different people: Mikhail, an art conservationist, and Ivan, a chemist. Or perhaps Ivan was suspicious when Mikhail helped Anna get a job at the Hermitage. Despite her efforts to embroider the past, she knew Vera was scarred by the unknown fate of her parents. Galina witnessed the death of both of her parents; all is known and etched into her memory. But for Vera, the fate of her parents has been a complete mystery.

'Tomorrow, I'm going to Gatchina. I'm going to find this Sergei Borisovich Filipov.'

'Vera, it was a long time ago. Maybe he isn't even there any more. Perhaps it's better to write to him.'

'Absolutely not. I won't wait another minute.'

Galina should offer to go with her on this journey to Gatchina, but she selfishly hesitates. She will have to give up a day of painting and it is unlikely that Vera will find him. It will be a waste of time that will only end with her heart broken. She is silly and naive to even think he would still be there, after all these years. But she looks so helpless sitting beside her, fidgeting with the letter.

'I'll go with you,' Galina says.

'I know you are busy with the painting. You don't have to.'

She puts her arm around Vera's slumped shoulders.

'I don't want you to go alone.'

Rushing through the crowd of morning commuters, Galina meets Vera at Baltisky Railway Station. The layer of make-up on Vera's face does not hide the dark circles under her eyes. Smudges of mascara stain the handkerchief in her hand. She forces a smile as they kiss cheeks but she says little.

Vera takes the seat beside the window and stares at the labyrinth of empty tracks.

'Boris should've told me,' she snaps. 'So we wouldn't have

to bother with this today.' She speaks with a sharp anger in her voice. 'Maybe this is foolish. Are you sure we should go?'

'What are you talking about? We have our tickets. We're here on the train.'

Vera takes a breath but the train starts to pull away, ending the conversation.

The wagon shifts between the points, finally joining the track to Gatchina. It snakes through the south side of the city, past dreary apartment blocks and lonely commuter stations. As the landscape greens, Galina relaxes into the rhythm of the wheels on the track and closes her eyes.

'Do you think he should've told me?' Vera asks.

Galina's focus returns to Vera, whose furrowed brow waits for a response.

'I'm sure he had his reasons. Let's get there, and see what we find out.'

Vera folds her arms and purses her lips.

'There is no point in being angry at a dead man. None whatsoever. Nothing can change his actions. And now, you're going to nose around in the past. Who knows what we'll find out?'

After Galina left Chekhov Street last night, she re-read Shishkin's letter about her unnamed uncle. When she finished, she folded it, replaced it in the envelope and put it in a file which she kept under her bed. She did not shed a tear for this unknown man and while it was strange to learn of him, she trusted her parents. They would have spoken of him if they wanted her to know. He must have done something wrong. She does not want to learn more about it.

Vera glares at her and turns towards the window, riding silently towards Sergei Borisovich Filiopov. Galina hopes the rural landscape will improve Vera's mood. There is no point arriving angry and she must be polite to this man, who has clearly lived through an ordeal. The letter paints a picture of him, well-educated yet brief and to the point, a man of science. Assuming he was thirty at the end of the war, he will be about sixty-five years old.

They step off the train at Gatchina Warsaw station and stroll into the leafy provincial town where the pace is slower and the sky wider than in Leningrad. Taking advice from a few locals, they make their way down tree-lined roads and paths. Before long, they find themselves standing outside number six, Leonova Street. The four-storey brick building stretches along the road, a typical Stalin-era apartment block. Stepping under the archway, they walk into the courtyard, where a pair of girls sway back and forth on a swing. Locating the entrance, they open the door and climb the stairs to apartment forty-two.

Galina knocks firmly on the door.

'Da?' a man's voice calls from inside the flat.

She elbows Vera, pushing her closer.

'My name is Vera Ivanovna Kamerova. I'm looking for Sergei Borisovich Filipov.'

There is a pause, followed by a grunt.

'One minute,' the voice answers. 'Wait downstairs.'

They look at each other blankly. Could this be him? Was he this easy to find?

They step back from the door and follow the stairs back to the entrance, returning to the dappled sunshine in the courtyard. They wait, for what feels like hours, but is only a few minutes. The door swings open and a man steps out. His eyes meet Galina's and dart to Vera.

'Let's walk,' he says, rubbing his stubbly chin. 'Have you

seen our beautiful park?' he adds, heading down the lane.

'Are you Sergei Borisovich Filipov?' Vera stammers, struggling to keep up with his stride.

'Of course,' he replies.

'My name is–'

'Yes, I can see who you are,' he says. 'You have your father's forehead and eyes. And I dare say you resemble your picture.' He hands her a photograph of a child sitting on a man's knee. 'He had it with him, through everything. So, of course I kept it when he passed. I knew you would come and get it one day.'

Vera's freezes as she looks at the photo. She had only one photograph of her father, which her mother brought with them to the Hermitage all those years ago. She has never seen any photographs of herself from before the war.

Dazed, Vera hands the photo back to Sergei.

He chuckles, pushing it away. 'It's not mine. It's for you,' he says, continuing down the road.

Clutching the photograph, Vera follows him.

Galina breaks the silence. 'My name is Galina Mikhailovna Senotrusova. Please forgive us, but I think we are both a bit stunned that we have found you so easily.'

'Senotrusova?' Sergei pauses. 'From the *kommunalka*?'

Galina nods.

'Unbelievable. I heard about you and your parents as well. Ivan and I had a lot of time to talk. I knew everything about the flat on, what was it? Pravdy Street?'

'Mokhovaya,' Galina and Vera answer in unison.

'Exactly. Mokhovaya.'

The road meets a sandy path which skirts around the edge of a lake.

'Please, sit down,' he says, motioning to a bench.

The women sit and he takes his place beside Vera, who drops her gaze and shifts uncomfortably.

'Sergei, please tell us everything,' Galina says.

'You wouldn't want to hear everything. But I'll tell you enough.'

'Ivan and I met and spent most of the war in a German prison camp. We were both from Leningrad and had studied chemistry at the same university. We always laughed that we had to travel so far to meet each other. We became very close friends. It was impossible to survive without friends. Ivan was desperate to get back to his wife and you, of course. I didn't have a girl to go back to but I knew my mother was waiting and I dreamed of returning to university and completing my studies. When the Americans arrived at our camp with news that the war was over, they gave us food and we regained our strength. We set out to find a Soviet unit and walked for weeks through forests and across streams. Having finished our supply of Hershey chocolate, we were very relieved to finally find the Soviets but quickly realised our situation was much more complicated than we ever imagined. They didn't believe we were captured by the Germans and accused us of treason.

'They put us with the other POWs who had returned. Everyone was malnourished and dressed in rags. We were there a couple of months, and suddenly they loaded us into a cattle wagon. It was so crowded, you could hardly sit. No toilet, no food. We travelled for days. The further north we went, the colder it became and the less the sun penetrated the cracks. I'll never forget stepping out of that wagon at Pechora. The air was clear and fresh, tinged with the smell of freshly sawn pine. But it was cold. By this time, it was winter. Being from Leningrad, we thought we knew and understood cold but this was something worse. And of course, we weren't dressed properly for such conditions. One guy didn't even have shoes. He stood barefoot on the snow. At first, he danced between his two feet, picking one up and then the other but they must have numbed or something because he stopped and stood still on the snow. They put us to work hauling massive trees to the mill, which was in the camp. Backbreaking work. And so cold. We were only there a few days and your father fell ill. They had no mercy for the weak. One day he stayed behind while the rest of us went out to work and when I came back he was gone. They must've taken him out and shot him.'

A pair of mallards waddle through the reeds and take their place expectantly in front of Sergei. They quack and march along the path, waiting for a bit of bread.

'How can you beg when you are both so fat?' Sergei says to them.

Vera wipes her eyes with her handkerchief.

'When you sent this letter to the Hermitage, did you get a response?' Galina asks.

'No,' he says. 'And I just left it. I figured that Anna had given up, maybe found a new fella. I didn't blame her for wanting to leave it all in the past. I promised Ivan I would write and I did. I wasn't going to do anything more.'

Vera sits beside him silently, lost for words.

'Anna disappeared during the siege,' Galina explains. 'The letter was delivered to her colleague, Boris Nikolaevich, who was our guardian at the time. But he didn't tell Vera about it. We only found it after he died. So, this is all very strange to us. While clearing his things, we found a file with many secrets. We don't understand why he would have hidden this information.'

Sergei takes a cigarette and matchbox from his shirt pocket and strikes a match. Shielding it from the wind, he lights it and takes a drag. He sits back on the bench, holding the filterless *papirosa* between his tattooed fingers.

'Probably, he wanted to protect you. He didn't want you to be connected to a prisoner, an enemy of the people. Even now, it's the same. There can be a stigma. How old were you, when that letter arrived?'

'Twenty,' says Vera.

'You were young, your whole life was ahead of you. Think back to every application that you filled in: university, Komsomol, your first job. A spoilt biography, relations to prisoners, could be a stain on your record.' He takes a long pull of the cigarette and exhales. 'He didn't want you to lie. He didn't want you to worry. If you didn't know, you wouldn't have to hide.'

Galina's shoulders feel lighter as she relaxes, taking in Sergei's words. His explanation was so logical. It was as if Sergei knew Boris. And perhaps this explanation applied to her own parents as well. Maybe they didn't tell her about her uncle for the very same reasons.

'So, what about you, Sergei? How did you end up in Gatchina?

'It isn't easy for any prisoner when they get out. I wasn't a young man any more. The life I had dreamed of had passed by. The university didn't want me. I wasn't allowed to return to Leningrad. My mother had died during the siege. I had nothing. But another former prisoner helped me. His brother was a factory manager here and gave us both jobs. Of course, I would have preferred to be a chemist, as I had planned, but that was a young man's dream.' He takes a long drag and exhales a cloud of smoke. 'But this isn't bad. It's a beautiful town. And I even found a girl. *Zhizhn prekrasna* – life is wonderful,' he says flatly.

The ducks quack loudly, parading in front of them. The drake tilts his head and his iridescent feathers shine. He shakes his tail feathers vigorously and marches back into the water with the female following behind.

Sergei Borisovich stands and stretches his arms. 'Girls, I have to get back. My shift is starting soon.' He gives a quick wink to Vera, pats her shoulder. She sits, stone-faced and still, as if in a daze.

'You can follow this path around the lake, but Gatchina Palace at the far end is being restored. It was badly damaged during the war. We're still cleaning up the mess the Germans left behind.'

'Thank you, Sergei Borisovich,' Galina says, standing up. 'You've been very helpful.'

He nods, flicks his cigarette butt into the lake, and heads down the path.

The women sit in silence. Gentle ripples flutter across the water.

The words *enemy of the people* linger. The first time Galina heard this phrase, she was a young girl following a chain of children which snaked around, surrounding the classmate with a long blond plait. They chanted, 'Enemy of the people. Enemy of the people.' The girl's cheeks reddened as she covered her ears and looked down at her shoes. No matter how hard they grabbed and pulled her thick braid, she remained silent and trembling. Galina did not really understand why they were being so cruel. A few days later, she realised the girl lived in her building in the ground-floor flat with her grandmother, Natalia Alexandrovna. Marina was her name.

They take his advice and follow the path along the lake. They do not speak. Galina glances at Vera, searching for a reaction, but she remains stone-faced and silent.

Galina stops and takes Vera's hand.

'Are you all right?'

Vera shrugs. 'Fate took away my parents and I got on with life.'

'Fate gave us Boris.'

She nods, looking away.

'He wasn't perfect, Vera. Nobody is.'

'I know. But I had created all sorts of explanations in my head. Part of me even believed my parents were together and had created a new life without me. It sounds crazy, I know.'

'It's not crazy.'

'The stories I dreamed up are nothing like the truth.'

'You were only little, Vera.'

'I still think of them. I study the faces of people on a bus or on the metro. I scrutinise men in the chemistry section of the library, searching for my father.'

'You can stop searching.'

Vera nods but there is something about the way she tilts her head and rests her hand on her chin which indicates dissatisfaction or denial. She inhales and combs her fingers through her hair.

'His story just doesn't seem right...'

Sergei Borisovich's story is perfectly plausible, but Galina does not insist. Instead, she squeezes Vera's hand. 'Shall we get back to the train? Or, would you like to get a closer look at the palace?'

'Let's get back. I've had enough war damage for one day.'

7

⚜

THE FOLLOWING DAY, Galina returns to the art academy and slips on her painting smock. She selects a variety of brushes from a canister and slides her thumb through the hole in the palette smeared with warm and cool tones which she blended in her previous painting session. She studies the portrait. Sveta is so similar to Elena. The more Galina works on the portrait, the more she sees the resemblance.

Galina has not been back to the *dacha* since the day she discovered them together and she has not spoken to Dima since the funeral. The portrait is a welcome distraction. While she is busy painting, she can avoid sorting out her marriage. And the painting gives her more time with Boris. It is as if she can feel him at her side, encouraging her while simultaneously lightening the atmosphere. Glancing at the clock on the wall, she feels the pressure of time. She must deliver it to the exhibition hall in two hours. There is no time for delay.

Galina focuses on the study and returns to the day by the lake. The geese are paddling and squawking. Sveta's cheeks glow in the warm sunlight. The oil paints glisten. Boris is nearby, settled on the blanket. The air is tinged with the scent of feathers and mucky soil. Taking a brush loosely between her thumb and index finger, she gently touches the bristles to the palette and lifts it to the canvas. The dance continues.

The paint is still wet when Galina delivers the portrait to the exhibition hall. She has only just completed the final, finishing touches.

'My dear, we have been waiting for you.' Tatiana Nikolayevna ushers Galina towards the wall at the entrance of the exhibition. She stands back, hand on hip.

Galina leans the painting against the wall and takes her place beside Tatiana Nikolayevna.

Sveta shines.

Her face, aglow in the sun, conveys a relaxed, healthy girl. Carefree. Well-nourished. Strong and healthy.

'What a beauty,' says Tatiana Nikolayevna. 'There is an innocence in her face. An angel. *Obyazatelno*, she must come to the exhibition opening.'

Galina has not given any thought to the opening and she certainly has not invited Elena and Sveta.

'You have invited her, haven't you?' Tatiana Nikolayevna does not wait for her response and motions to a handyman, who scurries over, carrying a tool box. 'This portrait must hang here,' she instructs. 'It will be the first painting of the exhibition.'

He nods and goes to fetch a ladder.

'Are you satisfied with it, Galina?'

She tilts her head. 'Boris was with me that day, when I

painted by the lake. And...'

'I completely understand.' Cutting Galina off, Tatiana whisks her hand to the side, as if dismissing her words.

But of course, Tatiana Nikolayevna does not know the whole story. She does not have any idea who Sveta is. She is unaware that the long walk to the lake probably killed Boris. She looks at the portrait and sees a girl on a beautiful day. She does not see what Galina sees.

'After the exhibition, we'll get your new studio organised. There is one available very near to your flat. It will be perfect.' She rubs Galina's arm. 'Everything will be fine, you'll see.'

Picturing herself in her own private studio, pride swells. But then, a little voice in the back of her mind says, 'We'll see...'

The handyman climbs up the ladder and fixes two wires to the picture rail.

'Now, go home and get ready,' Tatiana instructs. 'The exhibition opens in two hours and you have paint in your hair.'

Galina kicks off her shoes and slips into the familiar comfort of her slippers. She walks into the kitchen, lays her shopping on the table and fills a glass with water from the tap. As she drinks, her shoulders relax and she sits on the stool, feeling her legs release. After several days of standing at the easel, her back is tight and achy. She unpacks the items from her bag: a frosty packet of *pelmeni*, sour cream and a wedge of Rossisky cheese.

A hunger pain forces her to stand and fill a pan with water. She sets it on the hob and lights the ring. Waiting for the water to boil, she glances out of the window into the courtyard. Yuri's loping gait catches her eye as he approaches the entrance below. Masha is at his side. She opens the *pelmeni* box and weighs it in her hand. If she had known Masha would be here, she would have bought two boxes. She sighs and takes a jar of gherkins from the cupboard. As the water starts to boil, Galina drops the dough parcels into the bubbling water, and Yuri opens the door.

'I just put on some *pelmeni*. Are you hungry?' she calls from the kitchen.

'Always!' he replies. 'And Masha too. Is there enough?'

'We'll sort it out.'

They enter and take a place on either side of the kitchen table. He opens a bottle of beer on the table's edge.

'Yuri, don't do that. It leaves a mark,' she scolds.

'What mark?' he says, rubbing the scratch.

He takes a long drag of beer straight from the bottle.

'Are you going to offer Masha a drink? Or just have it all yourself?'

He lifts the bottle. 'Want some?'

'*Choot choot*,' she replies.

He pours some beer in a glass.

Galina drains the *pelmeni* and divides them between three plates which she places on the table. She sits on the stool between Yuri and Masha, opposite the wall. He opens the soured cream and spoons several dollops onto the parcels. Masha takes a more modest portion and Galina scrapes the remaining cream from the sides of the jar.

'How's the portrait?' Yuri asks between bites.

'I finished it just in time,' Galina replies as she cuts a *pelmen* in half, revealing its meaty centre. She pushes it into the sour cream and raises it to her mouth. 'The opening is tonight.'

The sound of cutlery on violet-rimmed plates replaces conversation.

'Mama, we have to talk to you about something.' His eyes meet Masha, sitting opposite. 'About the future.'

'Yes, you're leaving soon, two weeks, isn't it? You are about to get the shortest haircut of your life,' Galina says. 'Would you like to have a party before you go?'

He shifts on the stool and sets down his fork.

'We'd like a party.' He reaches across the table and takes Masha's hand.

'And what are you going to do while Yuri is gone, Masha? What are your plans?'

'That's what we want to talk to you about,' Yuri says. 'Masha's future.'

Masha disappears into her concave shoulders.

'Mama, we've decided to get married.'

Galina drops her fork and gasps.

'Aren't you going to congratulate us?' asks Yuri.

'Why?' stammers Galina.

'Because we are in love! Isn't it obvious?' he says. His voice grows louder and more urgent. 'And...' he hesitates. 'And we are having a baby.'

Galina turns to Masha, who is looking down at the remaining *pelmeni* on her plate.

Masha raises her gaze, forcing a smile. 'I'm pregnant.'

'Are you sure?' asks Galina.

'Of course,' says Yuri. 'Masha went to the polyclinic and everything.'

'No, I mean are you sure...' She takes a breath. 'Are you sure you want to have this baby?'

Neither Masha nor Yuri reply to this question.

'You're so young,' Galina says. 'It's a big decision, Yuri. Marriage is hard. Raising a child is hard. And you're leaving for the military. Don't you think it is too much? Too soon?'

Masha pulls her hand away from Yuri. Resting her elbows on the table, she buries her head in her hands. Her shoulders hunch forward, jerking as she tries to fight back tears. Her young boyish frame looks too weak and helpless to give birth to a child. And she certainly cannot raise one.

'Mama, Masha's been thrown out of her house. Yesterday, we told her mother and she went crazy, shouting and swearing. She isn't normal at the best of times, but this news made her go berserk. Masha needs a place to stay. We're getting married before I go and we'll put her on the list for a new flat. But for now, I'd like her to stay here in my room.'

Galina is well aware of how the housing list works. It could take years for Masha to get a flat.

'Mama?'

Her son waits for her response. She has never said no to him. Not ever. She has always given him what he wished for and done what he wanted. She has doted on him, unflinchingly for eighteen years. He expects her to agree. He knows it is impossible for her to say no to him. But this…she remains silent.

'Mama?'

'Of course,' Galina says. 'Masha can stay in your room with the baby until she gets a place of her own.' She takes the last *pelmen* from her plate and chews the rubbery dough. She swallows and it joins the knot of worry deep in her stomach.

PART 3

1

❦

October 1999

GALINA DABS A SLIVER of white paint from the tip of a thin brush onto the canvas, creating a reflection of light on a plump, ripe tomato. Hanging on a rough vine, the fruit is surrounded by a parade of tall dahlias. Magenta and orange blooms dot the canvas and thick-stemmed sunflowers droop in the autumn sun. In the foreground, a ripening pumpkin lies on the grass. She stands and walks over to the plump vegetable. Bending, she grasps an ugly weed and pulls it from the soil. Casting it into the compost, she returns to her stool. She studies the painting as colourful leaves drop from the trees around her. Satisfied that it is complete, she picks up a brush and writes, 'Senotrusova 99' in the lower left hand corner.

Since Dima's passing in 1992, Galina has taken over

the gardening responsibilities. While he was focused on maximising the amount of vegetables he could harvest, she concentrates on colour, mixing vegetables and flowers into a bright kaleidoscopic patchwork. In the first year, most plants were eaten by bugs but year by year, the garden has improved. And now, in her seventh season, the garden is a masterpiece.

'Babushka?' her grandson's voice calls from the *dacha*. 'Where are you?'

'I'm here, in the garden, Igor,' she calls to him.

He usually arrives on Fridays around this time, so she is not surprised to hear his voice. She soon sees him, walking along the path beside the *dacha*, carrying a bundle of rope. His lanky frame and loping gait is a stinging reminder of her son, Yuri. It is impossible to look at Igor and not think of Yuri.

'I bought a new hammock.' He leans down and kisses her cheeks.

He unclips the sun-bleached canvas hammock from the birch trees. Galina did not realise they needed a new one.

'How old is this anyway?'

She hesitates. 'I don't remember exactly. Maybe twenty years?'

'Can't be! I'm nineteen. It's much older than me.'

Galina puts her hands on her hips as she searches her memory.

Boris made it during a long, dark winter, with the help of Olga Andreyevna, his friend in the flat below, who had a sewing machine. The bright red canvas had the look of a Soviet banner and it was never completely clear where Boris obtained the fabric. When spring arrived, he brought the finished article out to the *dacha*, fixed the rigging around the trees, and hung it up. Over the years, she had spent many hours reading or napping on the soft fabric.

'Well, thirty years, I guess,' she says.

Igor untangles the new hammock and lays it on the ground. The net of white rope is strung through two varnished bars at either end. He clips one side to the birch tree and then attaches the other. Pushing on it, he tests its strength. Galina feels the rope between her index finger and thumb, already missing the supple caress of the canvas.

'Ladies first,' he says, holding the hammock at an angle and motioning for her to have a seat.

She eases her backside onto the ropes and lies back, swinging her legs onto the netting. Igor gently pushes and it sways.

'Perfect,' he says.

Galina smiles even though the ropes dig into her shoulder blades. Sunlight filters through the trees, casting dancing shadows over her body. She relaxes in the gentle movement.

'Was it expensive?' she asks. He should not have spent money on such an unnecessary item.

But before he can answer, they hear footsteps on the path. A man approaches and stands beside Igor.

'I knocked on the door and there wasn't an answer. I hope you don't mind the intrusion, but I took the liberty to follow the voices and come around the side.'

Feeling exposed lying in the hammock, Galina sits up. Igor takes her arm and helps her up.

The man, who is considerably shorter than Igor, offers his hand, introducing himself as Vladimir Ivanovich Peskin. Igor shakes his hand, introducing himself and Galina.

Peskin is well-spoken and his beautifully tailored suit fits his athletic frame perfectly. His sandy blond hair is short, his shoulders broad. He stands with his legs slightly apart, arms hanging at his side, relaxed but vigilant. There is a formal, military air about him, which is out of place next to the shabby *dacha*.

'Again, apologies for the intrusion,' Peskin says, as his eyes meet Galina's. 'I'd hate to interrupt.'

'How can we help you?' asks Igor.

'My parents' *dacha* is two doors down, next to the Skiratovs'.'

'Of course – Peskin,' she says, remembering the name. 'I haven't seen your parents in years.'

Galina does not know the Peskins very well but she walks by their *dacha* when coming from the train station. It is always closed tight, neglected and unused.

'How are your parents?'

'They're OK, stopped coming out here years ago. I think they prefer to be at home, where it is more comfortable.' He takes a deep breath, savouring the clean air. 'It's so peaceful out here. I miss it.'

He looks around, surveying the garden. There is a long, awkward pause.

'What brings you here today?' asks Igor.

'We are thinking about renovating the *dacha*.'

Galina and Igor exchange glances, still uncertain why he has come.

'We'd like to build a bigger *dacha*. You know, my wife and kids want *all* the modern conveniences.' He rubs the back of his neck and shifts his weight; his hands settle in his trouser pockets. 'Frolov and Skiratov, on either side of you, are both interested in selling.'

Peskin points to the *dachas* sandwiching Galina's.

She pauses, frozen.

'Mr. Peskin, this *dacha* is very special to my grandmother,'

Igor says. 'It's been in her family for decades.'

'I do not want to sell it,' she says.

He scans the garden and his eyes fall on the easel.

'Are you an artist?' he asks, approaching the painting. Igor and Galina follow.

'Babushka taught at the Repin Academy,' Igor explains. 'She's retired now, but still exhibits.'

He studies the painting and smiles. 'Very sweet.' He slides his hand into his breast pocket and pulls out a slim, gold case. 'Please, let me know about your next exhibition. I'd love to see more of your work.' He hands Galina his card. 'Your pension from the academy must be very small.'

His comment strikes Galina as overly personal. All pensions are small and have not kept up with soaring inflation. She takes the white card. The text is bold and modern with an embossed gold logo.

'If you ever change your mind and want to sell, let me know.' He glances around the garden, taking in the path into the forest and the thick hedge bordering the Frolov's. 'I won't take any more of your time.' He shakes Igor's hand again, lingering for a moment. 'Sorry to disturb.'

Igor starts to walk with him along the path.

'No need to see me out, thank you,' Peskin says as he heads towards the dirt road.

Igor reclines onto the mesh.

Galina slips the card into her dress pocket and folds the discarded hammock into a neat rectangle. Surely, there is something she could make with this fabric, it seems a shame to throw it away. She tucks it under her arm.

'Babushka, we didn't even ask this New Russian how much he would offer.'

Galina does not like this phrase 'New Russian', which

describes the post-Soviet wealthy. She equates it with corruption and dangerous mafia men who would do anything for money.

She pushes the hammock. Why would she ask the price if she did not want to sell?

Igor sighs. 'We live from one salary to the next.'

'We survive.' She shrugs.

Igor rests his hands beneath his head and closes his eyes, presumably dreaming about money that he has never had. His face relaxes as the hammock sways.

'Some women from the St Petersburg International Women's Club are coming to my studio on Monday morning. Maybe I can sell a few paintings.'

'That's fantastic.'

'Igor, I'm not good at this sort of thing. And my English is bad. Of course, there will be a translator there from the club, but I don't trust her. Your English is good. Maybe you can help with the prices? It's not comfortable for me to talk about the price of my art, like haggling over a chicken in the market.'

He takes a diary from his shirt pocket and checks his plans for Monday morning.

'I can go to work a bit late on Monday. No problem.'

'Oh, and Melissa has returned from her holiday in America. I'll start cleaning her flat again on Monday.'

Igor turns towards the hedge, rubbing his forehead.

'The pay is good, Igor.' Galina hesitates, waiting for him to look at her. 'And it's just her, not a big family. Easy money.'

'It must be nice, to be rich. A New Russian.'

'I prefer well-educated, cultured people,' Galina declares. 'I'm not impressed with all this money.'

'But we worry about money all the time. There's never

enough. Wouldn't it be nice, not to worry?'

'Everyone worries about money. Even this Mr...' she glances at the card, 'Mr Peskin, General Director, RosStroi.'

'RosStroi?' Igor glances over her shoulder at the card. 'Their signs are on building sites all over town.'

The thought of selling the *dacha* makes Galina queasy. She loves her cottage. Not only is it a reminder of her parents and her childhood, it has come to symbolise something more for her, a constant that has weathered the war and Soviet collapse. Despite all the changes, the *dacha* remains. She cannot imagine life without this little piece of green heaven.

'Well, Mr. New Russian Rostroi Peskin will have to build his *dacha* elsewhere. I'm not selling.' She says these words with confidence and clarity. However, she too is tired of being a financial burden on her young grandson.

'I have some business ideas too, Babushka.' He shrugs. 'Maybe something will work out.'

Late on Sunday night, Galina and Igor return to St Petersburg. Arriving in their building in Prospect Rimsky-Korsakov, they find the lift broken. Between them, they lug an enormous bag which contains jars of preserved fruit and vegetables from the garden. Igor sets the bag at the bottom of the stairs, rolling his shoulders, preparing for the climb with the heavy load. 'Igor, I'll take one handle, you the other.'

'No way, Babushka. I can do it.'

'I'm stronger than you think.' She takes one of the handles. 'Let's go.'

He grabs the other and their footsteps scuff the cement stairs as they climb. They stop on the landing of the second floor and put it down for a short break. The bulb in the corridor has burned out and the stale smell of cigarettes lingers in the air. Lipstick-stained butts overflow from an ashtray on the floor beside flat twenty-six. Galina's heart beats quickly as she catches her breath. She takes the handle, determined to reach the flat.

'Are you sure?'

'Fine,' she answers firmly, ignoring her aching back and shoulder.

They arrive on the third floor. Igor inserts the key and turns it three times. Click, click, click. The door opens and they heave the bag into the flat. As they enter, Galina stumbles over something in the middle of the corridor. She looks down to find a pair of tall, flame-red boots. The heels are at least ten centimetres, ending in an impossibly narrow point. How anyone could walk in such footwear, Galina could not imagine.

'My Igor! You're here!' Masha meets them in the doorway, throwing her arms around Igor, shrieking with excitement. 'My boy! All grown up!'

'Mama?'

He bends, arching over the bag of preserves and wrapping his arms around her tiny frame, which is clad in a tight leopard-print dress.

'We didn't know you were coming,' he says.

'I know! I wanted it to be a surprise!' She pulls Galina into an embrace and kisses both cheeks. 'It's been too long, Galina Mikhailovna.'

Galina waits for Masha to release her and pulls away. She unzips her coat, struggling to take it off in the crowded, narrow entrance.

Masha helps Igor pull the bag into the flat. 'What the hell is this?'

'Preserves. We're coming from the *dacha*.'

'No way.' She unzips the bag and picks up a jar of jam. 'Nobody makes preserves any more! I can't believe you hauled this bag all the way from the *dacha* on a train. Are you crazy?'

Masha's aubergine hair is carefully styled into a mountain of curls which tremble when she tips her head from side to side as she talks. Her sentences end in a higher pitch, as if everything is the most exciting thing she has ever said. She's thin, which is accentuated by her tight Lycra dress, but there is something different about her. Standing in the dim hallway, Galina cannot quite work it out exactly.

'Can we come in, Mama?' Igor motions for her to step aside.

'Of course!' She moves towards the kitchen. 'I'll put on the kettle.'

Igor takes Galina's jacket and hangs it on one of the many hooks, already laden with coats and bags.

He looks at her blankly, shrugging his shoulders as if to say, 'Why is she here? Where has she come from?' and most importantly, 'How long will she stay?'

They settle around the kitchen table. Igor at one side, Masha opposite, Galina between them, facing the wall. Galina transfers some strawberry jam into a glass bowl and sets three teaspoons on the table. Igor pours the tea into the violet-rimmed porcelain cups. Masha takes a spoonful of jam. Her dark brown lipstick stains the spoon as she pulls it from her lips. She smiles and deep wrinkles form under her thick layer of foundation. She slurps her tea.

'I'm so happy to be here!' she says, glancing around the little kitchen. Her eyes rest on the collection of pottery, displayed on top of the cupboard: the chubby, oversized teapot decorated with orange polka dots, a tall pitcher with a hand-painted firebird, and brass samovar with floral enamel handles. 'Oy, it's like a Soviet time capsule!' She chuckles and her shoulders hunch. Her low-cut dress gapes, revealing deep cleavage. She does not comment on the new Philips electric kettle, Moulinex toaster and Tefal pans.

At that moment, Galina realises what has changed. Masha was always flat as a board, even after Igor was born. And now, she has plump breasts, perfectly round like cantaloupes stuck onto her skinny body. Masha shimmies.

'You noticed my gift!' She shimmies again. 'My Vasily gave them to me! Can you believe it? A couple of years ago for New Year's he promised to buy me tits! After all those years of being as flat as a *doska*. Oh, it was a dream come true.'

Igor blushes, shifting in his seat, unwilling to admire his mother's new bosom. He studies his cup of tea. Galina, on the other hand, cannot stop staring at them. Of course, she has heard of such surgical procedures, but she has never seen it in the flesh. The unnatural perfection is perplexing.

'And the funniest thing,' Masha continues, caressing her spherical breast. 'Vasily is no more. He's with someone else now, but I still have the tits! It's the best gift in the universe. Even better than jewellery, which can be easily misplaced or stolen! I'll never lose these!'

She bubbles like a freshly poured glass of Sovietskoye Shampanskoye on New Year's Eve.

'So, what brings you to Peter?' Igor asks.

'Business.'

'What kind of business?'

'I represent the company of Mary Kay Cosmetics.' Her lips carefully wrap around the foreign words, unnecessarily rolling the 'r'. 'Galina Mikhailovna, have you heard of Mary Kay?'

Not waiting for a reply, Masha springs from her seat and darts towards the main room. They hear her, rummaging through her things and she returns with a baby-pink plastic bag. 'Mary Kay' is written in stylish gold script.

'I brought you some gifts, Galina Mikhailovna!' Pushing the jam to the side, she sets three dainty tubes on the kitchen table. 'We have a very easy, yet effective regime of skincare management.' She points to one of the tubes with her manicured finger nail. 'This is first, the cleanser. It will deep-clean your skin. I see you have problem areas across your nose and forehead. I know it has always been that way but this will solve it all. Your skin will be cleaner, healthier and fresher. Then you need this one – a toner. Most Russian women don't know about this one and that is why our skin is so bad. The toner closes all the pores. And then this, you moisturise. I gave you a special one for *babushka* skin. When you start using this, you will see immediately a big difference, I promise. And when you run out, you just call me and I'll send you more.' She whisks the products away in a flash of coral nail varnish and returns them to the bag. 'And this is a very cute baggie for you. So convenient!' Her smile widens as her head tips to the side.

Galina sets the bag next to the wall, forcing herself to smile. 'Thanks.' She returns the bowl to the centre of the table and dips her spoon into the jam.

'I'm here in St Petersburg for three days. We're having a Mary Kay conference. Even our vice president of Russian marketing is going to be there!'

'Oh,' Igor says.

'So, what about you, Igor, where are you working?'

Galina sighs and shifts in her chair. These days, all conversations eventually lead to money.

'Pony Express.'

'Pony Express? And what is this? Pony? Like a horse?'

'It's a courier service. I do all the computer programming.'

'The pay is low, like everywhere?' She scans his brown plaid shirt.

Galina has dutifully ironed this shirt for Igor at least two hundred times over the years. Sure, the collar is starting to fray a little but it still looks OK.

'I have plans to start my own business, importing computer equipment and setting up websites.'

'Yes, websites are very important. You should do this business, Igor. It could be profitable,' Masha says.

This is the first Galina has heard about Igor's business plans and she has no idea what these websites are all about. He sits taller as he speaks, clearly eager to impress his mother.

'Igor, you need more fashionable clothes, and a haircut.' Masha sips her tea. 'Yes, maybe a leather jacket? And of course, I have some men's products for you as well,' she squeals. 'And what about you, Galina Mikhailovna? Your pension must be very small.'

'We survive. I sell paintings, when I can. We get our vegetables from the *dacha*.' She glares at Igor and he nods, sealing a silent pact not to mention her cleaning job with Melissa.

'How nice it is to be back in our cosy flat,' Masha says.

Our. This word drops into the kitchen like a poorly flipped pancake.

Galina remembers back to the cold January of 1993 when she came home to Masha's note, quickly written and left on this very same kitchen table. It read: Going to Moscow. Staying with best friend Dina. She'll help me find work when I get there. xx

At the time, Galina was not surprised by this note. Ever since the resignation of Gorbachev and the implementation of economic reforms, Masha, usually completely unaware of political events, had grown restless. Pacing the flat, it was clear she wanted something, anything, more. More fashionable, quicker, happier, better. Her note was a declaration of change, a dissolution of their union. Out with the old, in with the new. Masha had never mentioned Dina before and Galina was very sceptical of this Moscow adventure. She fully expected Masha to return broke within the year. But she did not return. She stayed away, sometimes calling on New Year's Eve and occasionally on Igor's birthday.

Galina reacted to the collapse of the Soviet Union quite differently. She understood change was inevitable and necessary but she preferred a more wait-and-see approach. She learned the vocabulary and concepts of the new Russia: inflation, privatisation, capital vouchers and foreign currency fluctuation. But the sweeping changes overwhelmed and frightened her. *Perestroika* was endured rather than welcomed.

With Masha's departure to Moscow, the flat became more comfortable. There was a relief that she was gone. She had never fitted in with their bookish ways and it was easier to feed two mouths rather than three on Galina's ever-shrinking, unreliable salary. Only fourteen years old when his mother left, Igor rarely mentioned her. Seemingly unaffected by her departure, he threw himself into his studies and did odd jobs to earn money for the household.

'We sold your bed a long time ago,' Galina says. 'We needed the money, and the space.'

'It's just a few nights. We'll bunk together, Galina Mikhailovna. You don't mind, do you?'

Galina and Igor head to the studio in the dim morning light. Masha trails behind, pulling a wheelie suitcase.

'I don't understand, Mama. Don't you have to be at the conference?'

'I'll get to the conference. I'll just be a bit late. I think these ladies will love to see some of my special Mary Kay pampering products. This is a fantastic opportunity for them to shop for a new painting and sample some of my creams and scrubs.'

They know it is pointless to argue. It would be impossible to keep Masha from a group of wealthy foreign women. Throughout the fifteen-minute walk to the studio, Masha prattles on like a tour guide, pointing out all the changes that have occurred in the past seven years.

'Very convenient to have this new shop here. I think they must be selling very many nice foreign products. Oh, and this kiosk! Remember it used to sell only vodka and newspapers? And now it has everything: chocolate, ice cream, macaroni, nylons, can openers, colanders, Tefal pans. A successful local business. And so many nice foreign cars in your neighbourhood. I never would have expected to see so many Fords and Volkswagens here. In Moscow, of course, there are more Mercedes, but don't worry, I'm sure they will come to Peter, eventually.'

They enter a courtyard, which is surrounded by six-storey buildings.

'Look at this courtyard,' says Masha. 'It used to be so beautiful. There were flowers and a nice play area for the children. I remember bringing Igor here many times as a baby.'

The chains of the swings have been cut and the seats

stolen. The ladder for the slide, bent and disconnected, hangs uselessly to the side. A man lies on a tilting roundabout, either sleeping or dead.

'It's the same in Moscow. Our courtyard is full of drunks and hooligans.'

They enter the building and crowd into the lift which takes them to the sixth floor. At the far end of a dreary corridor, they unlock the studio door. Easels stand near the tall windows where the light is best. The scuffed floor, which has not been varnished in years, is paint-splattered. Canvases, exhibition posters and drawings hang on the walls. Jars of brushes line the shelves above Galina's desk. Igor opens a small window and a chilly morning breeze flows into the room. The heavy scent of oil paint and solvent circulates.

Masha immediately commandeers a table and pushes it to a prominent place by the door. She opens her suitcase and removes a baby-pink cloth with gold edging. With a flick of her wrist, it unfurls. She sets up two display stands filled with pink bottles, and fans out a stack of business cards. She drags a chair behind the table and sits, checking her make-up in a hand-held mirror, waiting for the women to arrive.

Galina pulls two easels close together and rests a landscape on each. She props up four smaller still life paintings against the legs on the floor.

Igor motions to a rack of canvases in the corner, where dozens of paintings are filed away. 'What about some of those? It is best to have a wide selection.'

'The others aren't for sale. I was thinking $300 for the little paintings and $500 for the larger ones.'

If she sells all the paintings, that would be $2,200, more than double Igor's monthly salary. They need the money. She could finally buy a new winter coat, boots and a nice New

Year's gift for Igor.

'Galina Mikhailovna, put your prices higher and then you can haggle down,' Masha advises. 'These women want a deal, or at least to feel like they got a deal. Maybe put another hundred on the prices and you can adjust it down, if they ask. You can't go higher once they're here.'

It seems greedy. Discussing prices makes Galina's stomach churn.

'She's right. And the more you have out, the more you could sell.'

'You must always understand your worth,' Masha says knowingly.

Dima would have launched into a long, philosophical discussion on such a statement.

'Fine. Let's say $400 for the smaller and $600 for the larger. But not the other canvases. They aren't ready.'

The door buzzer announces the group's arrival.

'They're here!' says Masha, scuttling behind her table.

Buzzing them in, Igor opens the door and waits for the lift to arrive.

The first batch of women enter the studio, marvelling at the high ceilings. All four women have neatly styled dark hair which hangs just past their shoulders. Their skin is tanned, teeth gleaming white, rings gold. Stylish, colourful silk scarves are loosely tied around their necks. They speak constantly, hands gesturing. Pausing by the windows, they look down on the courtyard. Heads shake, manicured fingers point at the man on the roundabout. They shrug and stride towards the paintings. Gathering around Galina they take her hand, smiling broadly. Musky perfume mixes with the smell of oil paint.

Igor greets the next women at the door. More casually

dressed than the first group, they wear jeans and puffy jackets. One has a baby strapped to her chest which she gently bounces and caresses. Her face is plain and she does not wear make-up. The woman beside her is chubby. Appliquéd autumn leaves cascade across her rusty orange pullover. They speak even louder than the first group and their chatter is punctuated with bursts of laughter and glimpses of their perfect teeth. Relaxed but confident, they gather around Galina.

'Dobray ootrah,' they say, without rolling the r.

'Good morning,' Galina replies, attempting a bit of English, conscious of her tea-stained teeth.

More women arrive and the studio fills with many languages. The room warms.

The leader of the group, a skinny Russian woman named Natasha, stands beside the paintings. She introduces Igor and Galina in English.

'Natashichka!' Masha calls, crowding just in front of her. 'Please, allow me one moment. Could you please translate for me? I have very new and exciting products from Mary Kay Cosmetics. Come visit my table at the rear of the studio, when you have a moment.'

Natasha scowls and pushes her aside, stepping in front, muttering something about limited time and another studio to visit. But Masha holds her ground. Standing straight, leopard-clad chest proud, she waits for her translation.

Natasha relents, translating and pointing towards the entrance. The women chuckle and Masha jogs in her high-heeled boots back to her table, where she waves and motions to the products. Natasha returns to her introduction of Galina, who understands a peppering of English words as she speaks: artist, Leningrad blockade, Repin Academy. She introduces Igor and he steps forward, greeting the women in halting English.

With the introductions complete, the women are free to move around the studio. Like bees in a hive, they circulate, chatting and laughing as they meet. A couple of women approach Igor, pointing to a landscape on the easel. He shakes his head and smiles. Galina notices a petite woman, wearing a beige rollneck sweater and three gold necklaces, hovering near the rack of canvases in the corner. She pulls a canvas from the rack, looks at it, pushes it back and grasps another.

Igor is busy with the other women, so Galina approaches her. 'No. Sale,' she says, attempting a bit of English as she returns the painting to the rack.

'Sale?' the woman asks, pulling out a large canvas and setting it against the wall.

Sveta's smiling face greets Galina like a friend emerging from a rush-hour metro crowd. It is the portrait of a beautiful spring day, one of Boris's last.

'No,' Galina says, shaking her head, pushing it back into the rack.

The woman pulls it back out and speaks, but Galina does not understand.

Masha appears by her side.

'Galina Mikhailovna, she offered one thousand!'

She looks at Masha sceptically. Surely, she must be mistaken.

'I know numbers. I can haggle prices in many languages. Trust me, she's offering one thousand.'

'No. No sale,' Galina stammers.

The woman says something else but they do not understand.

'Igor!' Masha calls loudly across the buzzy room, urgently motioning for him to come over.

He approaches and the woman speaks to him, gesturing at the portrait.

'Babushka, she is offering one thousand two hundred. She says it looks like her daughter, that's why she likes it.'

'No, it's not for sale.'

Masha suddenly shrieks, pulling on Igor's arm. 'I remember that day, Igor! You were conceived on that day, right over there, in the forest,' she says, pointing off the canvas.

Igor blushes, caught between his mother and the woman, who is now waggling her finger at him.

'Mama, not now!' he says firmly. 'Babushka, she is offering a lot of money. Are you sure, you don't want to sell?' His eyes fix on hers.

'I can paint a portrait of her daughter, if she wishes. This one is not for sale.'

Igor explains this to the woman, but she shakes her head, hands him her card and weaves her way through the crowd to the exit.

Galina has not looked at this portrait for years and seeing it today immediately precipitates painful emotions: Boris's passing, Dima's philandering and Yuri's departure for the military. This is the summer when everything changed. Although this painting conjures a complicated reaction, she cannot part with it.

She pushes it into the rack and looks at Masha, who has returned to her table. She is counting change into a woman's hand and handing her a shiny Mary Kay bag.

Galina is a world away from 1979.

2

***

SITTING AT HER KITCHEN TABLE with a cup of tea, Galina counts the US dollars. She sold three paintings, but the women demanded lower prices and she earned only $600. The hundred-dollar bills are sturdy and crisp. The twenties are flimsy and worn. She studies the portrait on the twenty. Who is Jackson, anyway? She counts five twenties, folds them in a piece of paper and buries them deep in her handbag. She places five twenties in her wallet. The rest, she rolls into a tube and wraps a rubber band around it. She can earn good money from her paintings, but it is very difficult to find opportunities to sell. Perhaps Melissa will help her organise a Christmas exhibition, like she did last year.

Climbing up on a stool, she drops the money into the *samovar* on top of the cupboard. Hearing it fall into the brass vessel, she relaxes. This will be for a winter coat and a New-Year's gift for Igor. Hopefully, she will have a bit of savings left in case there is some sort of emergency.

She quickly writes a note:

Igor,
    Went back to the dacha. *Too crowded with Masha here.*
Was planning to go back anyway. See you Friday.

Love,
Babushka

Melissa's flat is located on the Fontanka Embankment, very near the trolley-bus stop. The salmon-pink building has been recently refurbished and a security guard sits behind a desk near the lifts. His chubby head seems to attach directly to his shoulders and he nods sombrely as Galina enters the building. The entrance is cleaned regularly and is always spotless, even on a slushy winter's day. The lift delivers her to the top floor and she unlocks the door to Melissa's flat. She enters carefully, mindful that a Russian Blue cat might try to escape. Leila greets her, as expected, and rubs her sleek body along Galina's leg.

The flat smells of Dolce Vita perfume and cigarettes. She puts on a pair of slippers and sets her handbag on a corridor table. She strokes Leila and scratches her ears. Satisfied with the attention, Leila disappears into the guestroom.

In the kitchen, Galina finds a handwritten note beside a box of Hershey chocolate bars.

Galya –
    I brought you these chocolates. They are made in my hometown in Pennsylvania!!
    Sorry about the mess. I had some friends over to celebrate my return.

There is lots of leftover food in the fridge. Eat anything you want.

– Melissa

PS There is a plastic bag of clothes by the door. I don't want them. Maybe you know someone who does?

Melissa's notes are always written in Russian, with excellent grammar but she writes in block letters, never script. Russians never write this way. She often puts a smile beneath a double exclamation point, which must be something Americans do.

The sink is piled with dishes, and pizza boxes are stacked beside the tall refrigerator. Galina fills the kettle and clicks it on. As she waits for it to boil, she removes several plates and glasses from the sink and sets them on the counter. She clears soggy pizza crusts, a couple of cigarette butts, and other debris from the drain and fills the sink with hot water, adding an ample squirt of washing-up liquid. She opens the cabinet and sifts through the baffling array of tea: green, fruit, decaffeinated and herbal, searching for the Lipton Red Label. She always uses the mug with a maroon 'H' on it. The 'H' stands for Harvard, where Melissa went to law school. The ceramic is thick and heavy and the inside is faintly stained. She drops the teabag into the mug and pours in the steaming water.

Dipping her hands in the warm suds, she glances out of the window behind the sink. A pair of lovers are walking hand-in-hand along the embankment and a riverboat passes with a handful of tourists snapping photos on the deck. Every room in Melissa's flat has a view of the Fontanka River.

Galina squeezes the teabag with a spoon and places it on a small plate, saving it for another cup. She pulls the refrigerator door open and stands before the glowing light bulb. She had never seen such a large refrigerator before she started working for Melissa. She peels open an aluminium foil parcel, revealing a pile of pizza slices. She places one on a plate and takes it, along with her mug, to the living room.

The glass coffee table is smeared with dry drips of red wine, pizza grease, cigarette ash and potato chip crumbs. Several glasses, some stained with lipstick, are scattered on the table. An L-shaped sofa occupies a corner of the room. Above it hangs a portrait of Leila, which Galina painted last year. It covers most of the wall above the sofa. The cat sits, proud and upright, on a Turkish rug. She has her typical look of superiority and her sleek fur is shaded with blue and grey tones.

On the opposite wall hang two more paintings which Melissa bought in St Petersburg. One is a poorly painted study of sunflowers, imitating Van Gogh, which Galina loathes. The other is a cityscape of Nevsky Prospeckt, to which she is indifferent. She pushes some of the glasses aside, sets the mug on the table and takes a seat on the sofa. Sinking into the deep cushions, she balances the plate on her lap. Leila curls up beside her, rubbing her head on Galina's leg. Watching light ripple on the river below, she eats the pizza. Fat has congealed on the salami and the crust is rubbery. She finishes the tea, gives Leila's ears another scratch and gathers up all the glasses and plates from the table.

The flat has three bedrooms and a living room. One of the bedrooms, the 'storage room', is piled with Pickford moving boxes, which have not been unpacked since Melissa arrived five years ago, and two clotheshorses, laden with dry laundry. Galina must iron these clothes. Melissa has a tumble dryer in the kitchen but never uses it because it is not like an American dryer and she hates it.

The guestroom is mostly used by Leila. There is a permanent indentation on the king-size duvet where she likes to sleep. A couple of times a year, Melissa's parents or other overseas visitors will use this room. The closet is filled with coats and shoes. Once, Galina counted all the coats in the flat and discovered Melissa has thirty-two coats, including two furs, a full-length nutria and a short mink.

She always cleans the two bathrooms first. The larger is cluttered with bottles, sprays, powders and gels, which she tidies away in a narrow cabinet. The second, smaller bathroom seems to be rarely used by humans. Leila's cat litter tray is there and she must remove cat turds using a special spoon to shift out the grains of gravel.

Melissa's bedroom has a massive bed, which is never made. Every week, Galina strips the sheets, packs them into the washer and replaces them with a new set from the linen closet. In the corner, beside the bed, a chair is piled with discarded clothing. Once, she sorted through the clothes and put them away or into the laundry. The following week Melissa left a note, telling her not to mess with the items on the chair. She has not touched them since and the pile ebbs and grows from week to week.

Today she finds a used condom on the wood floor beside the bed, which repulses her. But as she strides into the kitchen and snaps a couple of thick paper towels from a roll and returns to the bedroom, she calms. Maybe Melissa has met a nice man. It always strikes Galina how strange it is for a pretty, well-educated woman to be thirty years old and single. It is a shame she is too old for Igor, they would make a very nice couple. She gathers the condom in the paper towel, delivers it to the trash in the kitchen. She asks Leila if this new man is a foreigner or a Russian. Leila sits tall, swishing her tail. Melissa's secrets are safe with her.

After cleaning the flat, Galina often stops by to visit Vera, who lives nearby. She opens the entrance door on Chekhov Street and steps into the dark corridor. The light fitting, without a bulb, hangs precariously from the wall. Skirting around a strange black patch on the dirty cement floor, she heads towards the stairs. The banister is bent, a couple of balustrades are missing. Even in the chaotic aftermath of the war, this entrance did not look this neglected and deteriorating.

She climbs the stairs to the fourth floor and knocks. She waits. Vera's slippers shuffle towards the door.

'Who's there?'

'Vera, it's me, Galya.'

The lock turns and the door opens.

'Galochka, come in,' Vera says, bending to grab a ginger cat.

She steps into the stench of cat pee, thick and strong.

Holding the scrawny feline, Vera kisses Galina on either cheek. 'Come in. It's been a hundred years.'

Knowing it is three weeks since her last visit, Galina sighs. It is precisely this sort of self-pity that keeps her from visiting more often.

'Melissa's been away for a few weeks, so I haven't come to town. Remember? I told you that on my last visit.' Galina forces a smile.

Another cat, this one is black, rubs his head and mangy body against Galina's ankle.

Stacks of newspapers, bundles of plastic bags, and empty bottles clutter the gloomy hallway. The door to Boris's room is open and several cats are curled together, sleeping on his bare mattress. The television blares from the other room. Vera leads her to the kitchen and puts on the kettle. Galina sits on a stool and a brown cat jumps on her lap, scratching its head on the edge of the table. A white cat springs onto the table, paces and finally settles, laying sprawled across the surface. The watercolour, which her father had given to Vera's mother just prior to her disappearance, hangs on the wall above the table. The garden scene, bursting with ripe vegetables, hung in the Hermitage cellar beside their mattress. Although faded, its colours are bright in the drab kitchen.

'Vera, how many cats do you have?'

A flea jumps from the fur to Galina's hand and she slaps it, leaving a bloody smear. She pushes the animal off her lap and it lands with a thud on the parquet floor.

Vera counts on her fingers, 'Sasha, Pasha, Koshka, Loshka, Kisa and Bob. Six, I guess. Claude died.' She pours the tea. 'I don't have anything to go with it.'

'I have something.' Galina takes a clear plastic bag from her purse. A cat bats her hand as she unties it.

'You always remember our favourite,' Vera says, taking a Mishka Na Severe chocolate from the bag. She unwraps it, breaks it in half and pops it into her mouth.

'You don't need so many cats, Vera.' She bites into a piece of chocolate and sips her tea.

'They find me, what can I do? Besides, they're good company.' She scratches the white cat's ears and he stands on the table, arching his back, tail aloft. 'They love me.'

Vera's skin, deeply wrinkled and leathery, sags below her jawbone. Her hair is jagged and unkempt as if she had cut it herself with a kitchen knife. Stretched and stained, her baggy mohair sweater hangs over her hunched shoulders. Several of her teeth have fallen out, leaving gaps.

'I lost another tooth, just here.' She pulls back her lip, exposing her chocolatey, purple gums. 'It was so sore, Galya, a nightmare.'

'You should've gone to the dentist.'

Vera grimaces as if Galya had just proposed a trip to outer space.

'We would help you, Vera. If you need money…'

'Who needs a dentist? It came out on its own. Everything is fine now.'

An advertisement for laundry detergent blares from the television in Vera's bedroom. The ginger cat jumps on Galina's lap and she quickly pushes it away. It hisses, landing hard.

'Valentina Grigorievna on the third floor died a couple of weeks ago,' Vera says.

'That's terrible.'

'And now her niece is living in the flat. She's all right, I guess, but she has people coming and going all hours. Nobody understands exactly what is going on in there. It isn't normal. Can you believe it? And Valentina was such a cultured woman. She wouldn't have allowed it.' She shrugs, shaking her head. 'And the worst thing, some gangster was murdered downstairs by the entrance. As I understand, he lived in the building next door. Who knows what he was doing in ours? Anyway, he was shot, right by our mailboxes. Took forever for the corpse to be taken away.'

'Did you call the morgue?'

'Of course, we called. And the police, but nobody came. The corpse just lay there. I mean, how can that be? It's impossible. Never thought I would see such a thing.'

'How long was he there?'

'Hours. It all happened in the middle of the night. I heard the shots in the stairway, so I knew something had happened but I didn't dare go out. What for? I couldn't have helped the situation. It was crazy. Nobody is in charge any more, nobody is responsible.'

'That dark patch by the door?'

'Blood. We can't get it clean. We've tried everything: bleach, vodka, floor cleaner. He was there so long that the blood went into the cement. What can you do?' She shrugs. 'It's terrible. Children live in this building! The parents couldn't even take them to school because they didn't want them stepping over the bloody corpse.'

The theme song for a television news programme interrupts their silence.

Stories of shootings and attacks no longer surprise Galina. Crime is an integral part of the new Russia.

'Vera, I'm headed out to the *dacha*. Why don't you come with me? You could get some fresh air. Maybe forage for mushrooms? Soon, it will be winter and we won't be able to go out. You haven't come to the *dacha* all year.'

Vera shifts on her stool and groans. 'Oh, Galya, you know I want to, but physically, I just can't do it. It's impossible.' She rubs her lower back and her left shoulder. 'Everything hurts.'

During the past five years, Vera has become a hermit, hiding in her flat. She only goes out to buy food from the corner shop. No matter how many invitations Galina extends, she always refuses.

Prior to the collapse of the USSR, Vera knew her place among the orderly shelves and the bookish academics at the National Library. She was a librarian, part of a system of strict order which kept the oldest library in Russia going.

When the economy collapsed, the librarians' dwindling salaries suddenly stopped being paid regularly. Many of the staff carried on maintaining the collection while some left, starting new careers in pharmaceutical companies and think tanks. Duty-bound, Vera stayed on, certain that order would be restored. But over time, chaos grew. Colleagues were stealing valuable books. The shelves became disorderly. The building suffered a leaking roof and neglect while the library's director drove a new Mercedes Benz. This slow and steady deterioration took its toll on Vera and she finally gave up. Preferring the company of cats, she stayed at home.

'Please, Vera, come with me.'

'Honestly, my dear, it is better for me to stay here. I don't have the strength and patience for the train. I'd never make it from the station to the *dacha*.'

'Boris was going out there in his eighties.'

'Well, I'm no Boris. And if Boris had lived to see our new Russian crazy streets, he would have dropped dead on the spot. *Bozhe moy*.' She slams her fist on the table, muttering something about their drunkard president.

Vera's outburst catches Galina off-guard but she is right, Boris would be horrified with all the changes. Still, there is no point complaining or dwelling on it. She bites her nail, searching for a change of subject.

'Masha turned up, completely out of the blue.' She talks about Masha's new and improved breasts, Mary Kay, and her tight dress.

'Masha is always unexpected. And let's face it, she was never your favourite.' Vera pauses, staring into space. 'It's so strange isn't it, how life is? Who would have guessed that you would've ended up living with her for all those years after Yuri was killed?'

Hearing his name spoken out loud makes Galina's throat tighten. The unnatural loss of her son is still raw, even though nearly two decades have passed. It is not the way it is supposed to be. There is a tiny part of her that, to this day, does not believe he is dead. Impossibly and irrationally, she hopes he will walk through the door. But when his name is spoken, reality is exposed. He is dead. Yuri was in that zinc coffin which was welded shut and covered with Afghan dust.

From the television, the jolly tune of a children's programme reaches the kitchen.

'Oh, I nearly forgot, Melissa gave me some clothes.' Galina opens an overstuffed plastic bag. 'Would you like this sweater?' She hands it to Vera.

Vera unfurls it and holds it up. The weave is chunky and the sleeves are slightly stretched at the elbows. She nods, folding it up and placing it on her lap.

'How is it there, at Melissa's?'

The image of the condom on the wood floor springs to mind. 'Fine,' Galina replies with a shrug. 'Oh, she brought chocolate from America.' Galina removes the Hershey bars from her handbag, opens the cellophane and hands one to Vera.

Vera studies the smooth brown label. A tear slides down her droopy cheek and she quickly wipes it away.

Galina was not expecting such a reaction. 'What's wrong?'

'Hershey bars. Don't you remember?'

She shakes her head.

'Sergei Borisovich told us that the Americans gave them Hershey chocolate bars when they left to search for the Soviets. Remember? When we met him in Gatchina.'

Galina clearly remembers meeting him. 'How can you recall such a detail?'

'I remember every word of his story.' She shrugs. 'It's all I have of my father.'

Vera strokes a brown tabby which has curled up on her lap on top of the sweater. She stares at the Hershey bar as if in a trance, perhaps pining for the father she never really knew.

Unable to think of anything more to say, Galina stands and takes the teacups to the sink. There is no washing-up liquid. She rinses them, shaking off the excess water and returns them to the cupboard above the sink.

'That's it, I guess,' says Galina. 'I'd better be off to the train.'

Vera stands, leading her into the corridor.

Galina quickly finds the money, which she had tucked away in her handbag, and places it on the table beside the chocolates before joining Vera by the door.

'Travel safely, Galya.' Vera pulls her close and kisses her cheeks.

The door clicks shut and Galina descends the stairs. The image of Vera remains in her mind. As her self-appointed older sister, she has always been Vera's protector. Even when Vera's parents were still alive and they were living in the *kommunalka* on Mokhovaya Street, Galina always looked after her. Seeing her live in such a dirty home, surrounded by flea-infested cats, she feels a failure.

Something must be done about Vera. She simply cannot go on this way.

Twenty minutes after Galina's arrival at the *dacha*, there is a knock at the front door. She glances out of the window and her neighbour, Frolov, raises his hand, giving a small wave. The man, who was once the captain of a submarine, stands soldier-straight, head high.

'Could I have a moment?' he says through the paper-thin door.

She opens it and a cold draft swirls around the room.

'Come in,' she says, closing the door behind him. 'Would you like tea?'

'No, thank you. I won't be long.' His eye glasses steam up in the warmth. He takes them off and rubs the lenses with a handkerchief. The frames are old, one side is held together with a crinkled piece of tape.

He sighs. 'Right, I guess I should just come to the point.' He rubs his tanned, leathery cheek. 'Peskin dropped by, not long ago. Are you considering his offer?'

'No, I'm not. I don't want to sell.'

His shoulders slouch forward, as if they are too heavy to support. 'Our situation is desperate, we have been trying to sell for more than a year. He is the first person to put in a decent offer. I don't want to pressure you, but Peskin will only buy if we all agree to sell.'

'I understand. But I don't want to sell.'

'Zhenya has cancer, Galina. The treatment is very expensive. I don't know how we will manage. If we sold the *dacha*, we would have $20,000 and would have more than enough to sort everything out.'

Galina had heard that his wife was unwell, but did not realise she was fighting cancer.

'Is that what he is offering, $20,000?'

He nods.

The sum is too big to contemplate, more money than she has ever seen or held, an extravagant sum.

'This *dacha* has been in my family for decades. I understand your situation but I don't want to sell. It would break my heart.'

'Just promise me you will consider it.' His voice is harder and persistent. 'Think of Zhenya. Please. After all the years of our neighbourly friendship, we'd be very grateful.'

Galina nods, knowing she will not change her mind.

As the dull morning sun filters through the autumn leaves, Galina carries her easel and paints into the back garden. Moving around the plot, she studies the *dacha* from several angles and drags her equipment towards the compost heap. Here, among the earthy smell of decaying vegetation, she has a view of the back of the *dacha*, flanked by the hammock to the right and the flowerbed on the left which wraps into the foreground. Returning to the *dacha*, she finds a medium-sized canvas and glances at her brushes standing ready in jars and tins along her workbench. The palette knife catches her eye. She has not painted with the knife in ages. The cool stainless steel is weighty in her hand. She grabs her palette and returns to the garden.

Balancing the canvas on the wooden easel, she settles on a stool. Dull grey clouds push across the sky, covering the sun. Rich gold and auburn leaves and the dark red *dacha* complement the muddy clouds. Resting the palette on her knees, she prepares the familiar arc of colours along the edge. In the centre of the surface, she mixes a light grey. The supple knife moves smoothly across the viscous oil paint as the colours combine. Her wrist moves easily, gently adding a hint of black. Using the wide edge of the knife, she applies a thin base layer across the canvas. She lightens it with a whisper of white, working it into the paint. Her fingers rounded around the knife, it dances. Wrist loose and relaxed, she applies the grey, creating a soft, textured background. It feels good in her hand as she coaxes the paint. Why has she neglected the knife for so many months?

She mixes a pale beige, adding a dash of yellow and a bit

more white. She slides paint on the edge of the knife, and forms lean birch trunks in the background on the right-hand side. The thin edge cuts into the paint, creating slender branches, just a loose outline, a skeleton of a tree. Adding more colour, she strengthens the tones in the foreground.

In the brambles behind her, leaves rustle and her knife stops, hovering over the canvas. Certain that she heard footsteps, she waits, expecting someone to appear from the forest path. Branches stir in the woods behind her. Again, her knife stops, lingering over the painting. Her hand quivers as she strains to listen. She waits but hears nothing more. Turning, she stares into the brambly thicket but does not see any movement, no explanation for the sounds. It must have been a squirrel or a mouse. She returns her focus to the palette, her knife combines cadmium red and burnt sienna.

A rough push and pull of her shoulder forces her to the ground. The palette falls. Black balaclava. Pigment smeared. Slap. Cheeks sting. Ears ring. Sharp pain jabs her ribs. Black.

Sun pierces through a break in the thick clouds. Galina squints and a stabbing pain burns her eye. Crisp fallen leaves pillow her head. Clutching the palette knife, dark red at the tip, she forces herself to sit. Her shoulder aches. Golden birch leaves flutter in a gentle breeze. Beside her, the upended stool and overturned palette. The easel remains upright and in position. The canvas is missing.

She stands. Blood drips from her chin onto her painting smock, mixing with years of paint splatters and wiped hands. Her ears ring and neck aches as she bends and picks up the palette. Gold and orange leaves cling to the paint. She collapses under the weight of heavy limbs and her head returns to the leaves. She drops the knife.

3

WARM PRESSURE ON HER HAND turns to a gentle pat, then a rub. Squeeze. A connection, touch, so humane. Galina tastes blood on her lips. Unable to open her left eye, but through the haze of the right eye, she sees wiry blond hair.

'Galina, do you hear me?'

Firm pressure, urgent patting on her hand.

'You were attacked. Frolov found you and called me.'

She forces her eyelid to open. Blinking back a cloudy film she catches a glimpse of unnaturally blond hair. Galina pulls away her hand.

'You're going to be OK,' says Elena Borisovna.

Rain pelting the roof wakes Galina. Again, a warm embrace wraps around her fingers.

'Galina, wake up. You should drink something.'

Her leathery tongue sticks to the roof of her dry mouth.

'It's me, Elena Borisovna, you're going to be OK.' Elena smiles and squeezes her hand. 'Try to sit up and have something to drink.'

She pushes herself up. The bedsheets slide beneath her but a sharp pain in her ribs forces her to stop. Elena adjusts the pillows and holds a cup to her mouth. The syrupy fruit compote mixes with the dried blood on her lips. She swallows and eases herself back.

'Galina, I don't want to upset you.' Her voice is velvety warm.

'Thank you,' she whispers.

A blue curtain gently blows, breeze ripples through an open window. Elena enters, carrying a steaming bowl on a tray. She sets it on the dresser beside the bed, the smell of chicken infuses the room. Galina stirs, hunger prods her stomach.

'I'm glad you're awake,' says Elena, holding a spoon. 'You should eat.'

Gathering her strength, Galina forces herself up, propping her back against the pillows behind her.

Elena stirs the soup with a spoon, chattering. She dips it in the broth and carefully lifts it. The hot metal rests on Galina's lips. Tasting the salty broth, she swallows.

'What day is it?' Galina asks.

'Thursday.'

Galina hesitates. 'I must go to Melissa's today.'

'*Nelzya*! You must stay in bed. Masha's going. It's all agreed.'

Masha? Why is she still here in St Petersburg? The thought of Masha, clad in her tight Lycra dress, pawing through Melissa's enormous refrigerator, drinking from the 'H' mug and stroking Leila makes Galina's head ache. Elena pats her hand. Galina resists the urge to pull it away.

Ever since the day she discovered Elena and Dima in bed together, the two women have avoided each other. The neighbours knew what had happened and participated in this separation, never mentioning the one woman to the other.

Elena lifts another spoonful of soup. Galina leans forward, gratefully accepting it.

A gentle knock on the front door is followed by quick steps and the familiar squeak of Boris's hinges. Elena's whisper and Frolov's voice, calm and measured, filters down the hallway.

'Frolov is at the door. Are you up for a visitor?' Elena asks.

Galina remembers their last conversation, peppered with his desperate pleas to sell the *dacha*. She shakes her head, declining.

Elena briskly returns to him and words are exchanged. The door opens and he leaves. Elena returns to her side, sitting on the edge of the bed.

'He's worried about you. He found you after the attack.' She gently rubs a bit of ointment on Galina's eye.

Galina winces from the pain of her touch. 'He wants me to sell the *dacha*.'

'His wife is very ill, Galya. He's in a terrible situation.'

She recoils, pulling away.

Elena's expression sours. 'You don't think *he* did this to you?'

'He wants me to sell. He could have organised it.'

Elena stands, replacing the cap on the tube of ointment. 'You have known him for thirty years, Galya. He's always been a kind, decent neighbour. How can you even consider such a thing?'

Galina hesitates, considering the question. Salty tears

sting.

'I have never been attacked. Ever. And now I have all this time to contemplate every possibility of what could have happened. Who did this to me?'

'I don't know. But I do know, for certain, it wasn't Frolov.'

Galina stirs and begins to wake. Igor sits beside the bed, holding her hand in his. His eyes are red and glassy.

'Oh Babushka, I'm so sorry this happened.'

She pats his hand.

Elena places a cup of tea beside the bed. 'Today, I'm going to reduce your pain medication. And I think you should try to walk. You need to get up and use your muscles but it may be painful, especially your fractured rib.'

'Elena Borisovna, are you sure she shouldn't go to the hospital? She looks so…terrible.'

'Bruising gets worse before it gets better. It's just going to take time to heal.'

His gaze locks on Galina and his chin quivers.

'Igor, hand me the mirror on the dresser.'

He shakes his head.

'I want to see,' Galina insists. 'I have a right to know what I look like.'

Elena hands her the mirror.

Grotesque. Her eye, which is swollen shut, is a surreal muddy yellow, blue and purple. The angry colours flow from one to the other like an ugly watercolour painting, a web of bruises on her wrinkled face. A crusty scab splits her lip. Galina does not recognise herself. Cut, rearranged and discoloured, her face is strangely Picassoesque, manipulated and unfamiliar.

Elena takes the mirror and lays it on the dresser, with a

knowing, sympathetic nod. It is enough, for now.

Galina looks at Igor directly. 'I don't want Masha at Melissa's.'

'Babushka, don't worry. Mama met with her and agreed everything. It's fine. Melissa understands. She sends her love and wishes you a speedy recovery.'

'Why didn't you ask Vera to clean?'

'Vera? You can't be serious.'

Galina sighs and her ribs ache. 'You must tell her how important this money is for us. Masha can't mess this up.'

Igor straightens. 'Babushka, Masha won't do anything to jeopardise your job. We're lucky she has offered to help.'

'Why hasn't she gone back to Moscow?'

'She's been helping me with my website idea. She knows a lot about business and has some very good contacts.'

She looks at him directly. 'I lived with Masha for thirteen years. I know her well. Be careful.'

Elena stands beside the bed, extending her coaxing hand. Galina grasps her palm, pushes herself up and takes an inventory of her pains. Her back, which has ached for years, still feels the same, her ribs are not as painful as she expected, but her shoulder hurts. Her legs are weak, but with each slow, thoughtful step, her confidence grows. She shuffles along, Elena at her side, giving support. Stepping outside, a crisp northern breeze brushes her cheeks, reminding of the impending winter.

A woman walking down the dirt road stares at her, mouth agape.

Galina hesitates, ashamed.

'Let's just go into the back garden,' says Elena, guiding her.

They walk slowly, thick grass carpet underfoot, along the *dacha* path, past the hammock. Autumn leaves swirl and rustle. Beside the compost, the stool is overturned. Elena helps her ease onto a chair.

'We brought your easel and paints in,' she says, picking up the stool and placing it by beside Galina. 'The canvas was cut. It's in your room with the painting things.'

Galina nods but she is not really listening to Elena.

Her beloved garden was always an album of memories: baby steps, family gatherings, arguments, laughter, the haze of her childhood. But now, this tranquil place, covered in a mosaic of autumn leaves, is the scene of a crime. It is no longer her peaceful sanctuary.

'I shouldn't have brought you back here,' Elena mutters.

Elena enters the bedroom carrying a wide-brimmed straw hat.

'Let's go to my *dacha*,' she says.

It is a statement, not a question, but Galina shakes her head.

'You can hide under this lovely hat, a disguise. A change of scene will be good for you.'

Elena delivers this definite plan with confidence. Negotiation is impossible.

'Doctor's orders,' she insists, helping Galina to sit up. Elena rests the hat on her head, pushing the brim down low.

'Practically the Queen of England. Nobody will even know it is you.' She extends her hand. 'Your Majesty?'

Leaning on Elena's arm for support, Galina slowly makes her way down the road. Elena reassures, patting her hand. Although her body aches, with each step Galina's muscles strengthen and her determination grows. The cool autumn air penetrates deep in her lungs, reinvigorating her spirit. Reaching Elena's *dacha*, Galina stands a bit taller.

She settles on the divan. Elena tucks a knitted blanket over Galina's legs and heads back to the kitchen. This is the first time she has been in Elena's *dacha* in decades. The kettle boils and dishes rattle in the kitchen as Galina waits for her to return.

Framed photos of Sveta, all grown-up, sit on a side table. She is smiling, cheeks like apples, posing in front of a tall clock-tower. Her hair is blonder, but Galina still sees the girl she once painted all those years ago. In a close-up, she embraces a green-eyed man. In another, wearing a full-length wedding gown, Sveta holds a bouquet of roses, kissing the same man.

Elena returns and places the tray on the table.

'Sveta looks very happy in these photos.'

'She lives in London now. Married to an Englishman,' she says, pouring the tea. 'Who would've ever guessed that my Soviet girl would get married to a foreigner and live abroad?'

'You must be lonely without her.'

Galina cannot imagine Igor moving abroad. It would be unbearable, like a piece of her own body missing.

'I visit of course. But it is a world away, so different from Russia.' Elena hands her a cup of tea and takes a seat beside her.

'Galina, I never apologised.'

'It was so long ago.'

'It was a very difficult time for me. When you found Dima and me...'

But Galina brushes her words away. 'Please, it's in the past.'

'I always knew he would choose you. He loved you very

201

much.'

'With twenty years of hindsight, it all looks different.' Galina takes a sip of tea. 'At the time, I was busy with work and worried about Yuri starting military service. I didn't give much thought or attention to Dima.'

'That spring, I had been a widow for five years. I was so lonely. Dima understood me.' She hesitates for a moment. 'I felt like a woman again. Not a doctor or a mother – a woman.'

Galina does not respond. There is nothing to say. What's done is done.

'I was surprised when he passed so suddenly,' Elena says.

Dima's death had not surprised Galina. New Russia took its toll on him. In Soviet times, he was not interested in politics. He was never a flag-waving citizen or a dissident but he understood the rules of the Soviet game. He established a place for himself in society as a respected academic and had a satisfactory apartment in the centre of town. He spent his summers at the *dacha* and took a yearly holiday by the Black Sea. He was successful. Dima and his colleagues discussed ideas and books and could spend hours in his nicotine-stained office in deep debate. But in 1991, their discussion changed. His colleagues in the philosophy department no longer discussed Mandelstam and Bunin; instead they hatched plans of buying saucepans and t-shirts in Turkey and selling them on street corners in St Petersburg. They debated where to get the best dollar-to-rouble exchange rate and considered the wisdom of Yegor Gaidar's economic plan of 'shock therapy'. Students also shifted focus to business and the numbers in the philosophy department dwindled.

Dima, who was approaching sixty, could not find a passion for such topics. He did not have the drive to learn the new rules of the game and to recreate himself in the changing Russian economy. After a lifetime of dismissing American capitalist greed and worker exploitation, he could not make the shift. He was looking forward to retirement, not starting over. When prices were liberalised in 1992 and inflation soared, the purchasing power of his pension shrank. His monthly pension would not even buy him a brightly coloured packet of imported chewing gum.

Some of his colleagues left, starting new lives in Israel, America and Germany. Dima took each departure personally, as if it was a slap in the face and against everything the Soviet Union had stood for. Others, keen to get into the market early, set up businesses. Dima turned inward and reached for the vodka bottle. He drank to escape, not celebrate, and his health suffered.

When he finally had a heart attack and collapsed, Galina called the ambulance and waited, wringing her hands and hoping they would come. After twenty minutes, Igor persuaded her that the ambulance service was no longer reliable. It would be best to carry him downstairs and hail a car. She reluctantly agreed and they rallied a handful of neighbours to help them take Dima to the lift and out to the street.

He died shortly after they arrived at the hospital. At first, Galina was angry that the broken system could not help Dima. Her tears mixed with rage. But as the new reality in Russia took hold, seeping into every aspect of everyday life, her rage turned to relief. Dima would not witness the garish advertisements which soon plastered their beautiful jewel of a city. He would not enter a shop filled with more varieties of salami and cheese than he would ever think possible, but be too poor to purchase any of it. He would not see the *babushki*, leathery and hunched, sprout like mushrooms outside the metro, hoping to sell the last of their meagre possessions. He would not see a theatre turn into a nightclub where Russian girls stripped off their clothes. He would not have to swallow his pride when Galina became a cleaner for a thirty-year old American woman.

'When Dima passed, I wanted to attend the funeral. Sveta persuaded me to stay away.' Elena wipes a tear from the corner of her eye with a handkerchief.

Galina nods, thankful she did not attend.

'I've always regretted the affair. It was selfish.'

'None of us are saints.' Galina reaches out and pats Elena's hand.

The women finish their tea, each quiet in their own thoughts.

'Elena, thank you for helping me recover.' She hesitates. 'Let's put the past behind.'

Elena raises her teacup. 'To our new friendship.'

Alone in her *dacha*, Galina slides into bed and lays her head on the pillow. A dog barks in the distance and leaves rustle outside the window. An unsettling tingle at the base of her neck makes her toss and turn. She gets up and heads to the kitchen, each step sending a stinging pain to her ribs. She switches on the kettle. Staring through the thick darkness into the back garden, her gaze rests on the compost heap in the far corner. Wind blows, the trees sway, leaves scatter, crackling as they tumble. The electric kettle flicks off and she jumps. Startled by the noise, her heart beats rapidly.

Silly old fool.

Trembling, she pours the water over a fresh mint sprig in

the cup.

She checks the front door is locked and reclines on the divan with a romance novel. She feels watched and uncomfortable. Her eyes wander from the page as she listens carefully, certain she heard something in the back bedroom. On edge, she sets the book aside.

Her thoughts soon turn to Igor. He has been noticeably absent, only visiting once. Perhaps her disgusting face is too much for him, or maybe he is busy at work. Galina is not sure but he is usually more attentive and concerned for her. A melancholy blue gives way to lonely sadness.

Silly old fool.

Finishing her tea, she returns to her bed. She turns out the lamp and darkness envelopes the room. The wind gusts hard against the *dacha* and it sways. Galina pulls her quilt close to her chin. Will she ever again feel comfortable and safe in her beloved *dacha*?

Igor arrives with a bouquet of long-stemmed roses wrapped in shiny cellophane. He is wearing a new black leather jacket. Masha, in a white rabbit-fur coat, stands at his side holding a plastic grocery bag. She kisses Galina's cheeks, lightly brushing them.

'Igor, Galina Mikhailovna looks good. You made it sound so bad,' Masha says dismissively, as if the attack was an exaggerated hoax.

Galina smells the perfectly shaped flowers but they have no aroma.

'Igor, you have a new jacket,' says Galina, caressing the supple leather.

'Of course he has,' says Masha, taking a seat on the armchair. 'He needs a new look, like a successful business man, not some sort of Soviet student.' She taps her long manicured nails on the fraying upholstery. 'He has some very good business ideas.'

Igor studies the floor, sheepishly.

'By the way, all is fine at Melissa's big, beautiful flat. Sometimes, when I'm done cleaning, I just sit on the sofa and watch TV for a while. It is so nice and comfortable there. I like it very much.'

'You must clean and leave promptly,' Galina instructs.

'And such a nice cat and beautiful fur coats. Igor, have you seen her coats? It's important for women to have nice things. You know, Galina Mikhailovna, I think she has a new boyfriend. There was some very nice lacy lingerie on her chair.'

Igor rubs his head.

'High-quality, expensive. I could tell. Natural silk.'

'Mama, please…'

'What?' Masha asks, stunned.

'We don't need to know every detail,' Igor says.

Masha shrugs and the three sit in silence for a moment.

'Galina Mikhailovna, I never would have guessed that *you* would take a cleaning job. Who would've thought you would end up painting a portrait of a *cat*?'

Galina leans back on the sofa and closes her eyes. Her head throbs.

'I want to go back to Peter,' she says. 'Once I look better.'

'I have some very good Mary Kay concealer which you can use to even out your eye. Not now, of course, but when you want to return to Petersburg.'

Galina does not want make-up and she does not want Masha here. She sits silently, not responding to her offer.

Igor clears his throat. 'So, what have you been doing?'

'Sometimes I go down to Elena's. She's been an angel. Otherwise, I just sit and wait to heal.'

'Elena?' Masha says. 'The one who you found in bed with…'

'We've put it behind us,' Galina says. 'It was a long time ago.'

Masha raises her pencilled eyebrows. 'Hmm,' she mutters.

Silence lingers.

'Well, you look much better,' Igor says.

'Honestly, I don't know if I will ever heal in here.' Galina pats her heart.

'You just need time, Galina Mikhailovna.'

She shrugs. 'I don't know. I still can't go into the garden, even looking out of the window brings back the horrible memories. Who would do this to an old *babushka* in the woods?'

Igor shifts and shrugs.

'Do you think it was Peskin trying to make me sell?'

'No,' says Igor. 'He's a very busy man with much more important things on his mind.'

'It was probably some hooligan just out for a lark. Focus on the future. It's the best way to heal,' Masha suggests, nodding her head.

Of course it is easy for Masha to say this. She is not the one who was attacked, but she speaks with authority and confidence, through pursed lips.

'I don't feel comfortable here, any more,' Galina says.

Igor waits for her to continue.

'It doesn't feel like the same *dacha*. I'll always look at the garden and think of that horrific day.'

'What are you saying?' Igor asks.

'Maybe I should sell.'

Igor shifts his gaze to Masha.

'Galina Mikhailovna, you don't even know how much he is offering. It's important to talk to the other neighbours, understand the market, and consider his offer. It should be handled very carefully.'

Galina hesitates and turns to Igor. 'He's offering $20,000.'

'I didn't expect such a large sum,' says Igor.

'I don't know what to do,' says Galina, feeling the sting of tears return to her eyes.

'Shall I speak to the neighbours and Peskin? I can find out all the details, Babuskha.'

Galina reluctantly nods.

'You shouldn't worry. Concentrate on getting well, that is the most important thing.'

Masha stands in the kitchen, triumphantly beckoning them to the table. Igor and Galina each take a seat and she places a bowl of soup in front of them. On the table, there is a box of German chocolates and a plastic container of strawberries. The perfectly shaped fruit do not resemble the strawberries Galina grows in the garden. Where in the world would these berries come from at this time of year? She has seen expensive berries like these in the shops but would never buy them herself. She would wait and get them for free from the garden. She has often wondered who would make such an extravagant purchase.

Galina glances at the chicken soup tins beside the stove. She dips her spoon into the steaming broth. Diced carrots, cubes of greyish meat, and doughy noodles swirl as she gently stirs. Galina never buys tinned soup. She takes a bite. It is saltier and sweeter than she would make but tastes good, despite the faint metallic flavour. The meat is rubbery and weirdly reminds her of rat. But that is not possible. It is from a colourful tin, a stamp of foreign quality.

Masha opens a plastic bag of sliced bread and puts a few pieces on a plate. Galina never buys this type. It has a strange, spongy texture. She dips it into her soup and it absorbs the broth quickly, partially disintegrating. She quickly delivers the sopping bread to her mouth, discreetly mopping a drip from her chin.

As they eat, Igor rattles off what he has learned about the *dacha* sale. He has spoken to the neighbours, who believe that Peskin's offer is good. The payment would be made in cash – US dollars – on the day of sale.

She did not expect Igor to move this quickly. He shifts on his stool, cagey and tense, waiting for her answer. Masha takes a strawberry and she bites into it, waiting for her response.

'OK,' Galina says. 'Let's sell.' It feels right, as she speaks the words. Her heavy heart is lightened by the idea of a suitcase of dollars under her bed and no more worries about money. As she takes a deep breath, the decision is easier than she expected. She has fallen out of love with her *dacha*.

4

⤜✦⤛

GALINA SETTLES WITH HER SKETCHBOOK on the stool in the back garden by the compost. She turns and peers into the thicket of bramble, knotted vines and thorns, searching for a pair of eyes and angry fists but sees nothing. She opens the book to a clean page, curls her wrinkly hand around her pencil and studies the view of the *dacha*. The bare silver-birch branches, like slender skeletons, flank either side of the cottage. Thick grey clouds, heavy with snow, block the sun's light, a signal for some to hibernate and others to return to the city. This is a day on the cusp of the dark, sleepy winter.

As the cold wind bites her hand, the pencil dances across the page. Her lines become trees, burst seed heads, the slanted roof, shutters and wooden slats. As she sketches, she sees herself: harvesting apples with her father, dreaming of *dacha* honey during the war, returning with Boris, snuggling like lovebirds on the hammock with Dima, Yuri's last birthday party, Igor's first steps. Despite the memories, Galina feels no hesitation or regret, which surprises her. She expected the days would grow more difficult as the final date approached but today, on the day before the sale, she feels secure in her decision. Nostalgia is pushed aside as she focuses on the security which the money will bring.

She takes a deep breath. The aroma from a distant wood-burning stove tickles the back of her throat and a crow calls plaintively in the stillness. Galina signs her name in the lower right corner of the sketch. Her hand hesitates for a moment, trembling in the opposite corner. Then she writes, 'Before Demolition.'

She returns to the *dacha*, sketchbook under her arm. Igor kneels beside the stove, lighting a pile of kindling. As the fire sparks to life, he quickly closes the door. Galina unzips her suitcase, which stands ready beside the door, and slips the sketchbook between the clothes. Little remains in the room: the divan and a pile of boxes in the corner.

'Would you rather go back to Peter tonight? I can meet with Peskin in the morning. It's not very comfortable here.'

'No, I want to see Peskin tomorrow. Elena invited me to stay at hers.'

He nods.

Igor explains that his colleague, Lyosha, is coming with a Pony Express van tomorrow. They will take the divan and boxes to Galina's studio and the money to the flat. He explained this to her before, and she agreed, so she is unsure why he is telling her again. It is as if he is double-checking, replaying the plan to be sure it is right. He nervously wrings his hands and struggles to sit still.

'Babuskha, we haven't talked about the money.'

What about the money? She waits for him to continue.

'You know, what will you *do* with it after?'

'I don't want it in the bank, Igor. I don't trust them.'

'I agree. We lost everything in the crisis last year. But money will grow if you put it to work, invest it. It won't grow under your bed.'

'I don't trust these investments, Igor. They're all crooks.'

'I agree.' He shifts in his seat. 'Babushka, I have been talking to some people about starting my own business. I think the timing is good to take advantage of a whole new industry. But I need money, an investor.'

This request drops into the room unexpectedly. She feels the dream of financial security slipping away.

'I don't know, Igor.'

'My company will design websites. This is an important service, Babushka. Many businesses want one and there aren't many companies providing a quality service. I created the site at Pony Express. I can do this work. I'm good at it. As the world wide web grows, so will demand.'

The strange foreign words grate on Galina's ears: investor, website, world wide web. She pictures dark leggy spiders casting thick webs around the world.

'I'm worried about Vera. She looks terrible. I'm tired of thinking about money and not knowing what tomorrow will bring.'

'Don't worry. I will always look after both of you.'

But her dependence on him bothers her. How can he not realise this?

'If you invest in my company and it is successful, we will have more money than we will know what do with.'

She's never said no to him. He knows this.

'I don't want you cleaning some foreigner's house.'

'Igor, it's not bad, working for Melissa. What about your job at Pony Express? You've worked for them for years. Are you going to throw that away?'

'I'm hoping they will become my first client.'

He stares at her, waiting for a response.

'Igor, we need some savings. For emergencies.'

'Invest seventy-five per cent in my business and keep twenty-five per cent for yourself. You will get it back, with interest, I promise.'

She hesitates. 'And if I don't agree?'

'I've spoken to some of Masha's contacts about investing before you decided to sell the *dacha*. I can go back to them, if you prefer.'

Galina straightens, sitting taller.

'You must not get involved with Masha or anyone tangled up with her. I understand she's your mother, but don't get mixed-up commercially with her. I don't know much about webs and business and investment. But I do know Masha.'

'She's not so bad, Babushka.' He smiles.

'Igor, she is the kind of woman that left a note and abandoned you, her child.'

He grimaces and tips his head. 'Abandoned? I was with you. It's not like she left me at Finlandsky Railway Station.'

She shakes her head and folds her arms.

'People change. Look at you and Elena,' Igor says, shrugging.

'Rekindling a friendship and going into a business agreement are not the same.' She looks him directly in the eye, searching for understanding. He nods, almost imperceptibly. She hesitates a moment longer. He is hungry for something more. He wants this business to be a success. She can see this.

She cannot say no.

'I'll give you the money but Masha cannot be involved.'

'I understand. Mama will not be connected to the business.' He holds out his arms and she leans into his lanky embrace. 'Thank you, Babushka.'

She silently calculates a quarter of $20,000 and her heart sinks. $5,000. While this sum is more than she has ever had, an uneasy feeling, tinged with regret, begins to germinate. What has she done? What if Igor fails?

Elena smiles as she hands Galina a cup of tea and takes a seat across from her at the kitchen table. Galina leans forward, resting her elbow on the wood.

'How do you feel?' Elena asks.

She shrugs. 'Honestly, it's right to sell.'

Elena waits for her to continue but she hesitates.

'The money will give you security, Galya. That's the most important thing. I should probably do the same. We'll see, maybe I'll sell too, one day.'

Galina shifts in her chair and takes a sip of tea. She does not want to think about the money and revisit her worries about investing in Igor's business.

'It's going to be strange when the *dachas* are demolished and Peskin builds his palace,' Elena says.

Galina does not want to think of the demolition either.

'Elena, thank you again for all your help these past weeks. You've been my angel. I don't know what I would have done without you.'

'Although it took a terrible event for us to reconcile, I'm glad we did.'

Galina suddenly realises she came empty-handed. 'I should have brought you something, to thank you.'

'The best gift you could give me is friendship. Promise me

we will keep in touch.'

'Of course. We can meet in Peter. Perhaps we could go to the theatre or an exhibition?'

'Yes, and I hope you will come out here next summer as well. I'd love the company.'

Galina smiles even though she does not intend to return. She has no desire to witness Peskin's plans come to fruition.

Lyosha arrives early in the white van with the Pony Express logo on the side. They load the remaining boxes and the divan. Lyosha claps Igor's shoulder, leans back into his heels and folds his arms. His slightly bloodshot eyes and gold-capped teeth twinkle. Although he looks as if he rolled directly from his bed into the van, Galina knows he does not mind getting up early on the Saturday morning to come to lend a hand. The Afghan veteran has a fatherly fondness for Igor.

'And how are you, Baba Galya? It's a big step,' he says, kissing her hand in an old-fashioned, chivalrous sort of way.

His bushy moustache tickles her age-spotted skin. He always calls her Baba Galya and she does not mind. In fact, she likes it, coupled with his sly smile and mischievous eyes. His glance lingers briefly on the faint bruising around her eye but he does not mention it.

'It'll be fine,' she says, pushing her worries deeper. 'And you, Lyosha? How are the wife and kids?'

'The usual. Children grow. The wife shouts.'

Peskin's black Mercedes pulls up beside them. The door opens and he steps out, carrying an envelope. He is dressed casually in jeans and black leather jacket, but looks tense as he scans the three *dachas*. His gaze settles on them and he approaches.

He pats the envelope. 'Everything is here. We just need to

sign the documents.'

The envelope is the size of a piece of A4 paper. Could $20,000 really fit into such a small parcel? Galina expected a suitcase filled with money.

'Shall we go inside?' asks Peskin.

'There's nowhere to sit. We've removed the furniture.'

Peskin opens the door to the back seat. 'Please, we'll finish the business in my car.'

Galina slides into the back seat. The supple black leather smells new. Igor and Peskin take their seats in the front, closing the doors behind them.

'Galina Mikhailovna must sign here, and here,' says Peskin, pointing to the documents and handing her the papers and a gold pen.

The pen is heavy in her hand and the fine blue tip skates across the paper, leaving her signature behind.

'And the money, two stacks of one hundred.' He fans a bundle of crisp bills.

'I'll count it,' Igor says, removing the rubber band from the bundle. His head drops and his back rounds as his thumb dances between the one-hundred-dollar bills. The car is silent except for the sound of his thumb sliding across the stiff paper and the bills slapping into a new stack on his lap.

Clenching his jaw, Peskin's eyes are trained on Igor, waiting for him to finish the rhythmic counting.

As Igor bundles $10,000, Galina hands the papers back to Peskin. Behind the tinted windows and solid Mercedes doors she feels separate, a world away from the *dacha*. She shifts in her seat and the leather squeaks.

Igor winds a rubber band around the last bundle of money and returns them both to the envelope.

'That's everything,' Peskin says, shaking Igor's hand.

'Nice doing business with you.'

'Is that it?' Igor smiles.

'That's it,' says Peskin. He hesitates. 'If you don't mind, I've got to meet with the other neighbours and get back to Peter.'

'While you are here,' Igor's voice quivers, 'I want to speak to you about my new website business.'

Feeling trapped in the back seat, Galina opens the door. 'I'll leave you to it,' she says, stepping out of the vehicle.

Peskin laughs. 'The artist doesn't like commercial conversation; that's understandable. Thank you, Galina Mikhailovna, and be sure to let me know about your next exhibition.' He turns his head towards her and smiles but his grin lacks warmth. Despite their transaction going smoothly, she still does not trust him and has no intention of ever inviting him anywhere.

She steps out of the car onto a bed of fallen leaves. A gust of fresh air blows and she inhales deeply, thinking about the stacks of one-hundred-dollar bills.

'Lots of happy memories here,' Lyosha says, placing his arm around her shoulders. 'But don't be sad, Baba Galya. You have lots of money now.' He claps his hands together, rubbing them with glee.

Galina does not make one last pass across the worn floorboards. She does not take one last peek at the garden. She says her goodbye to the slant-roofed *dacha* silently and takes her place in the van beside Lyosha. Igor slides into the passenger seat and slams the door shut. As the engine comes to life, Vysotsky's raspy voice blares over the tinny speakers. Lyosha quickly turns it down and shifts the vehicle into gear.

'Don't turn it too low,' Galina says. 'I love Vysotsky.'

'*Pravilno*. Everyone loves Vysotsky.' Lysosha says, turning up the music again.

Galina does not listen to the Soviet music icon very often, but every once in a while she hears Vladimir Vysotsky on the radio or television. Despite all the changes, he still holds a special place in society. He remains as loved and revered as he was when he was alive. He cuts across generations, uniting many under his sorrowful, tormented banner.

As they ease down the muddy dirt track, Galina does not watch the *dacha* get smaller in the rear-view mirror. She looks forward, sandwiched between the two men. The van bumps through mud puddles, and nobody speaks. One dirt track leads to another, which takes them to a paved road, lined with conifer forest. As Lyosha accelerates, he turns up the music again. He nudges Galina with his elbow as Vysotsky's distinctive, cigarette-stained voice and acoustic guitar fill the van. The lyrics catalogue calamities: being robbed, thrown out of the house, kicked in the jaw and holding a bad poker hand. But the tempo is upbeat, as if in happy celebration. Each stanza closes with Vysotsky shrugging off hardship and declaring that still, despite everything, he is thankful to be alive.

Feeling warm and secure, Galina relaxes her shoulders as Igor and Lyosha sing along. But the music precipitates nostalgia. It is impossible to hear Vysotsky and not think of Yuri and Dima. They loved the troubled man, and his deep, poetic lyrics sparked many lengthy, late-night kitchen-table conversations. When the hard-drinking singer and Yuri died within a few months of each other, Dima stopped listening to Vysotsky.

The windows begin to steam up and Lyosha fiddles with the feeble defroster. He shoots Galina a sidelong glance as

Vysotsky delivers the final line, his niggling question: who should he thank for being alive?

Sitting at the kitchen table on Prospect Rimsky-Korsakov, Igor counts out fifty one-hundred-dollar bills and hands them to Galina. She pinches them between her index finger and thumb. The thick, crisp paper is more substantial and cleaner than Russian bills, and smells of power. Roubles smell of nothing when they are new. It's only later, when they are supple and worn, that they take on the odour of sweat, grime and vodka. Igor takes the envelope and the remaining bills into his room.

Galina climbs up on the kitchen stool and reaches her hand into the brass samovar. For a moment, she thinks it is empty but eventually her fingers find the roll of bills from her painting sale, and she pulls them out.

Taking the money to the main room, she dreams of a new coat, boots and hat. She cannot remember a time when she bought all three at once. The mere thought of replacing the threadbare, tatty articles makes her heart race. Finally, she will feel good when out among the other stylish citizens of St Petersburg, which will make the long, sunless winter more bearable. But selecting a new coat is daunting. There are many available, how will she decide? How will she be certain that it is high-quality? Maybe she will be able to persuade Vera to come to the shops and help. She chuckles at the thought of Vera, with her jagged haircut and missing teeth, coming out of the flat to go shopping. Perhaps it would be better to ask Elena – a far more sensible choice.

Galina unzips her suitcase and removes the sketchbook. Thumbing through the pages, she finds the last sketch of the *dacha* and rips it out. She pulls a box from beneath the divan and opens it. Inside, she finds Boris's last sketch, *Everything's Ahead of Her*. The paper is brittle and yellowing. She has not looked at it since he died. How is it possible that so much can change in twenty short years? Boris's passing, followed quickly by Yuri, then Dima. The collapse of the Soviet Union. One by one, she lost them. She opens a file, which is filled with Boris's clippings of Soviet achievements. The superpower that no longer exists. She lays the bundled money on top of an article celebrating Gagarin's trip to space and closes the file. Placing everything back in the box, she closes the lid and slides it under the divan. She must spend this money carefully, especially while Igor is just getting his business established. Nothing is certain.

In the evening, Galina and Igor sit at the kitchen table with bowls of *borscht* in front of them. She gently stirs a dollop of sour cream into the broth.

'Elena Borisovna has been an angel to me these last few weeks.'

Igor nods, waiting for her to continue.

'It's quite foolish that we have not been friends all these years. Actually, we have many things in common now that we have got to know each other again.'

She takes another spoonful of soup and Igor drinks his Baltika beer.

'I want to give her something special, to thank her. I'd like to give her the painting of Sveta, you know, the one in the studio – the girl with the geese.'

Igor sets down his spoon and shifts on his stool. His eyes dart towards the window.

'Sveta is her daughter and from the very beginning I had planned to give her the portrait. But then there was the scandal with Dima.' Her voice trails off as she dips her bread in the soup. The dark red broth soaks into the dry bread. 'Do you think Lyosha would help me take it to her? I could never manage it on the metro.'

Igor looks at her and then turns his head down, resting his forehead on his fingertips.

Galina did not expect this reaction. They often asked Lyosha to transport things and he was always happy to help. 'I won't ask him if you think I shouldn't.'

Igor's shoulders begin to tremble and he looks up, his eyes glassy.

'Igor? What is it?'

'I sold the painting.'

She drops her spoon, waiting for him to continue.

'I had to.' He pours the remaining beer in his glass. 'To pay the men that attacked you.'

'I don't understand,' she says, shaking her head.

'I owed them money. They said they would come back if I didn't pay up immediately. We tried to sell it to the woman who visited the studio a couple of weeks ago, but she'd changed her mind. Mama and I took it to Moscow to get the best price.'

PART 4

1

❧

November 2016

ELENA BORISOVNA, WEARING a silk scarf over her hair, steps out of the lift. She moves slowly, leaning on a cane.

'Come in,' says Galina.

'I can't believe, after all these years, I have never been to your studio.' Elena unties the scarf, revealing her perfectly coiffed, unnaturally blond hair.

'You look beautiful.'

'We octogenarians can still look good.' Elena strikes a pose, showing off her plum skirt and jacket. 'I came straight from the beauty parlour. The girls did my make-up too. Do you think it's too much?'

'Not at all. You look gorgeous.'

'Well it's not every day you sit for a portrait.'

Galina flicks on the electric kettle and shakes some tea into a teapot. While she waits for it to boil, Elena walks over to the windows, chattering about the weather and *dacha* gossip. She turns towards Galina and the sun catches the shine of her hair and sparkle in her eye. Galina relaxes. Elena is an excellent choice for her portrait series.

'I hope I can sit still for you, Galya.'

'The most important thing is to find a comfortable pose.' She hands Elena a cup of tea.

'I haven't been comfortable in years. Everything aches!' She smiles and takes a sip, obviously worried about smearing her lipstick.

Knowing the sun will move along its low arc quickly, Galina motions to a chair on a raised platform. 'Take a seat.'

She holds Elena's hand as she steps up on the platform and sits on the chair. The sun lights her eyes beautifully.

'Lift your chin ever so slightly and turn your head just a bit towards the window.'

Elena adjusts her position and Galina moves closer to the easel.

'Are you comfortable? Can you hold that pose?'

'Maybe you could include fewer wrinkles?'

'Those wrinkles show your wisdom, dear.' She picks up a long wooden stick with a piece of charcoal taped to the end. She checks the charcoal, making sure it is secure. 'My magic wand,' she says, holding it loosely between her thumb and two fingers, standing back from the canvas. She studies Elena and the charcoal lightly dances across the surface. 'It used to have a screw at the end. But it broke years ago so I just use tape. I've looked at new ones, but the weight never seems right.'

She sketches Elena's head, neck and the slope of her shoulders. The whisper of her form fills the canvas. Her back hunches slightly and her shoulders curve forward, a reminder of her age. Galina marks the position of the eyes, nose and mouth. The charcoal skims the surface, marking her hairline and shape of her blond curls.

'Can we talk, while you work?' Elena asks.

'Of course! But don't laugh and don't move.'

Elena giggles.

'What a terrible sitter, laughing already.'

'Tell me more about this project.'

'Like I said on the phone, I'm having a solo exhibition in the spring, for Women's Day. I'm painting twelve successful women of St Petersburg.' Galina sets her wand aside and hunts through the many tins of brushes. Feeling the supple, firm bristles with her fingertips, she selects a variety of flat and round brushes. 'All sorts of different women, an actress, a writer, a politician, a scientist. You, of course, a doctor. Young and old but everyone lives here in Peter.'

'How many have you completed?'

'Seven. You are the eighth.'

'Will you really get them all done by the eighth of March?'

'We'll see. I'm not going to worry about it. I'm too old to worry.'

'I can't imagine painting a portrait, Galya. You have golden hands.'

'I can't imagine being a doctor!' Galina chuckles and takes a sip of tea. 'If you looked now, you would never believe that these lines will become your image. It could be anyone. Like a skeleton, underneath we're pretty much the same.'

She squeezes paint from the metal tubes, creating an arc around the perimeter of the palette: black on the left, followed by blues, reds, yellows and white. Elena sits silently while Galina's brush moves between colours on the palette, mixing the tones. Elena is thinner than the last time they met. Her cheeks lack their usual roundness.

'So, what about you? Do you have any news?'

Elena sighs. 'Not really. Sveta wants me to come to London.'

'For a visit?'

'I think she'd prefer if I just moved there.'

Her brush stops and she looks up. 'Leave Russia?'

'Well, yes. But honestly, I don't want to. Would be nice to be with her, of course. But, I don't know...'

Galina nods.

'Her husband is a nice man but they have their life and it is very different from mine. They both work full-time. Katya is a teenager, so she has school and her activities. It's a busy house. I'm always exhausted when I come back from visiting them. I don't think I could take it day in and day out!'

'I understand completely.'

'Besides, my friends are here. My life is here.' She pauses. 'You're so lucky to have Igor in the city. It's so much easier. And you can see little Dasha anytime you want.'

'Of course, I'm glad they're here. But they are busy too. I don't see them much.' And when she does, it is a bit like going to a foreign country, so different from her own way of doing things, but she keeps that thought to herself. 'And Dasha isn't so little any more.'

As Galina replaces the caps on the paint tubes, she yawns and stretches her back from side to side. She perches on a stool, hoping to relieve her achy legs. The door buzzer zaps the silence, startling Galina. She is not expecting a visitor.

'Hello?' she says, pressing the intercom.

'Galina Mikhailovna? It's Vasily Rozov, from the St

Petersburg Gallery of Modern Art. I'm sorry I didn't call first, could I come up for just a moment?'

'Of course.' Galina buzzes and the door releases, allowing him to enter.

She waits in the corridor, certain she can already smell his distinctive musky cologne. The lift makes its way to the sixth floor and jerks open. Vasily steps out, floating down the corridor in a light, lilting movement, with his nose slightly lifted. His dark, wavy hair is tied in a low ponytail at the base of his neck and his beard is neatly trimmed. He is an overly groomed man, perpetually picking non-existent lint from his expensive clothes, and his trousers are just that bit too tight.

'I'm sorry to just drop by. I called your flat but there wasn't an answer, so I guessed you were here. I was in the area so I took a chance and popped by. Hope I'm not disturbing you.'

'I was just getting ready to go home. Come in,' she says, stepping into the studio.

'I don't have your studio telephone number,' he says, studying the screen of his telephone.

'There isn't a phone here,' Galina says.

'And you don't have a mobile?'

'No,' she says. 'I don't need one. You found me.'

'True, I guess I did.' He smiles, returning the phone to his pocket. He notices Elena's portrait on the easel. 'I've heard about your upcoming Women's Day exhibition. Brilliant idea.'

His affirmation is not required. 'There aren't any secrets in our small town of Peter. What brings you here?'

'I received a surprising phone call. On our website, I have a short bio about you and a few images of your work. One of the pictures is a study for a portrait that you did years ago. It is of a girl, sitting with many ducks.'

'Geese,' she corrects.

'Yes, you're right, geese. Anyway, out of the blue a woman from London called me because she saw this picture on our website. It turns out that she bought the portrait of the girl with the geese many years ago.'

Galina hesitates, frozen by the stinging reminder of Igor's theft.

'So, why did she call you?'

'She wants to speak to you. She asked me to pass you a letter.' He reaches into the breast pocket of his coat and pulls out an envelope. 'She emailed it to me and I said I would print it and pass it to you.'

Galina takes it. 'I can't read English.'

'Don't worry, it's in Russian,' he says, waiting for her to open it.

She lays it on the workbench. 'I'll look at it later. Thank you, for bringing it by.'

'Oh, and I wanted to give you this invitation. We're having an exhibition of new, upcoming artists next week.' His perfectly shaped eyebrows raise, his smile broadens, revealing his pearly white teeth.

She studies the paintings printed on the card. Colourful expressionism, vivid landscapes, a couple of portraits.

He points to a portrait in the upper left-hand corner. 'This artist is very promising.'

'Empty,' she says.

He takes a breath, but does not speak. He tilts his head, folds his arms and slightly juts out his hip, looking directly at Galina.

'Don't you see it? This portrait is vacant. There is nothing of the subject here, her eyes are empty. A portrait should expose the soul, the inner spirit of the sitter. Not just the image.'

'Well, maybe something was lost in the printing.'

The problem is not the printing and she shoots him a glance which tells him so.

'Is there anything else? I'd like to finish up here and get home,' she says.

'No, that is all. I have my car with me, would you like a lift home?'

The warm car is tempting, but the thought of being enclosed with his cologne nauseates her. She declines his offer.

Galina is in the kitchen when she hears a key in the lock. It can only be Igor's wife, Irina, who never calls before she comes. The lock turns, click-click-click.

'Galina Mikhailovna! It's me, Irina!'

'I'm in here!' she calls, returning to her slicing.

'The traffic is simply terrible. Took me hours to go just a couple of kilometres. What a nightmare!' Irina moans, slipping off her boots and putting on slippers. She comes into the kitchen carrying two plastic bags. 'I brought you a few things: milk, kefir, eggs, bread, some fruit.'

She sets the bags on the table and pulls Galina close, kissing her cheeks. Irina is a striking woman. She has dark, Asian eyes, dramatically shaped in eyeliner. Straight black hair frames her face. The shiny strands angle forward towards her chin in a sharp bob. Always dressed immaculately, today she wears a black, tailored trouser suit, which flatters her slender figure, and a single strand of creamy pearls.

She pushes her hair behind her ears, exposing her pearl earrings, and places some apples in the fruit bowl on the counter.

'You didn't have to bring me anything. I just went to the market today.'

'You shouldn't go to that market on your own, Galina Mikhailovna. Call me, and I will take you to the supermarket.' Her manicured hands take a plastic container of perfectly formed strawberries from the bag. What are you making?'

'*Borscht.*'

Irina picks up a peeler and starts to cut the skin away from the beetroot. Her hands redden.

'You're dressed too nicely to peel beets,' Galina says.

Irina ignores her, dragging the peeler over the dark red vegetable. 'You know, a flat in our building has come on the market. A nice, one-room flat on the third floor. Everything is new and very modern.'

She knows where Irina is headed and braces herself.

'Igor and I *both* think it is best that you move.'

'No, thanks. It's too far from the studio.'

'Galina Mikhailovna, really it would be better. I'm rarely in this area and it is not so convenient for me.'

The kitchen is crowded with her daughter-in-law standing beside her. Galina widens her stance ever so slightly, and pushes her sharp elbow towards Irina, hoping she will step further towards the sink. But she holds her ground.

'You're eighty-three, Galina Mikhailovna. You need family around you.'

As if she needs reminding of her age.

'I'm fine on my own.'

Irina carries on peeling with added vigour, perhaps taking out her frustrations on the beetroot. 'Where's the chopping board?' Her actions are laced with inconvenienced urgency, as if she has a million more important things to do and is in a race to get somewhere else.

'I only have this one. I'll cut them.' Galina places her hands on either side of the chopping board, staking her claim, feet firmly planted on the floor below it.

'Shall I peel the carrots and potatoes too?'

'If you want.'

Irina works quickly and orange strips join the purple peelings in the sink.

'Another thing, Igor mentioned your next exhibition and I thought it would be nice if you included Dasha's gymnastics coach. She was on the Russian Olympic Team in 2004. Still very fit and beautiful, of course.' She takes another carrot. 'And Dasha's violin teacher played for the Marinsky Theatre. She would also be good. Of course, she is older but very accomplished.'

'I already have a sportswoman and a musician.'

'Galina Mikhailovna,' she says more firmly. 'I think it would be very good for Dasha as well. It would put her in good standing.'

'Practice puts students in good standing with their teacher or coach, not sitting for a portrait.'

'They all practise. This would make her stand out from the rest of the girls.' Irina scoops up the peelings and drops them in the bin. 'We'll see. We can talk about it later,' she mumbles.

Galina places a pan on the stove, drizzles a bit of oil, and turns on the gas ring. She pushes the onions from the chopping board into the oil and starts to cut the beets. Irina opens the drawer in front of Galina, pushing her aside, finds a wooden spoon and plants her feet in front of the pot, stirring the onions as they start to sizzle.

'Also, I wanted to talk to you about Dasha's birthday. Her party will be at the *dacha*; there is more room there. We'll come to pick you up next Friday and return on Sunday.'

Noticing the onions are beginning to brown, Galina reaches in front of Irina and turns down the gas ring. She had not planned on a whole weekend at Igor's *dacha* but she does not protest. She dumps the cut beets into the pot. Irina stirs.

'Of course, we must leave early on Friday. Be ready for three. The traffic will be bad if we wait longer and we must come all the way over here, to get you. Can you imagine how convenient it would be if we lived in the same building?' She looks up from the pan and smiles.

'Too bad there isn't a train near your *dacha*. I could get myself there and I wouldn't have to bother you.'

'You are no bother, Galina Mikhailovna. Don't worry. We'll sort everything out.' She speaks slowly and purposely, as if she is speaking to a child. 'I must get back to the travel agency. Another one of my girls left and now I am shorthanded again. It is just impossible to find hardworking girls, especially ones with a bit of travel experience. And of course, it's very busy this time of year.'

Irina taps the spoon abruptly on the edge of the pot and it rings like a bell. She sets it on the counter and quickly washes her hands, pushing Galina as she moves around the little kitchen. She strides to the door and puts on her boots and coat. With her fashionable black leather handbag dangling from her forearm, she blows several quick kisses towards Galina.

'Think about the portraits and the flat and we'll see you next Friday,' she calls down the corridor. She closes the door behind her, leaving Galina alone.

Later in the evening, Galina sits in her kitchen with a bowl of *borscht* in front of her. Her spoon dips into the nourishing, rich broth, stirring a dollop of soured cream into the beets, carrots, cabbage and potatoes. She blows on a spoonful, waiting for it to cool, and puts the spoon to her lips. Snipped dill is fresh on her tongue. She chews, savouring the earthy flavours.

She picks up the letter which Vasily gave her. The flap is open. She slides the paper from the envelope. The typed Cyrillic letters are bold on the white page.

1 November 2016

Dear Mrs Senotrusova,

I purchased one of your paintings, 'The Bird Girl', at a gallery in Moscow in 1999. Since then, we have enjoyed having the painting hanging in our home in London. I was very surprised to see the study for this painting on the St Petersburg Gallery of Modern Art's web page. It was fascinating to read the biography about you on their website.

I have some questions about this painting and I would be very grateful if we could speak about it. Perhaps you could email me at <u>sarahsummers@yoohoo.com</u> and we could find a way to Skype?

Yours respectfully,
Sarah Summers

On the next page there is a photograph, printed from Vasily's printer. A woman with short hair sits on an oversized olive-green chair with a young blond girl on her lap. Behind them, the painting of Sveta and the geese hangs on the wall. The woman and child smile broadly, like simpletons. How strange that the painting and Sveta both ended up in London.

The portrait conjures many memories: the warm sun on her back, the cacophony of geese, Boris, Vera, Dima and Elena. But the unsettling memory that lingers, tying her stomach in a knot, is of Igor's treachery. Even after all these years, Galina struggles to call it what it really is: stealing. In the passing decades, she pushed this pain aside and created a list of explanations and justifications to cover Igor's actions. He was young and did not know what he was doing. He was in over his head. It was the crazy Nineties. It's just a painting. And look how successful he has become. Or perhaps she simply places the blame squarely at Masha's feet. After all, she was not young or stupid. Masha persuaded Igor to sell the portrait to settle his debt. She knew exactly what she was doing.

Galina sets the letter on the table and takes another spoonful of soup. She looks at the odd curve of the @. This symbol of modernity, a computer world which she knows nothing about. She folds the paper and returns it to the envelope. Replying is too much trouble, more trouble than it is worth.

2

❦

JAMMED IN TRAFFIC, Igor's Mercedes Benz is not moving. He sits with his arm resting on the car door and fingertips on the wheel. A tweed cap covers his balding head. In the passenger seat, a laptop computer casts a glow on Irina's face. She types with purposeful strokes, occasionally mumbling under her breath, dissatisfied with someone or something somewhere. For a moment, she stops and her manicured nails comb through her hair. She sighs.

In the backseat, Dasha leans towards her door, spine curved over her luminous phone. Her thumbs dart about the screen. Expressionless but completely engrossed, she wears an enormous flannel shirt, which is very similar to the old shirt that Galina uses as a painting smock, and a woolly hat which is topped with a pompom.

The engine quietly purrs and the sturdy car shields them from the hustle and bustle of the city. Only Irina's keyboard tapping and the wipers slowly pushing snowflakes from the windscreen disturb the silence.

Irina sighs again. 'It would be very handy if you lived in our building, Galina Mikahilovna. Then, we wouldn't have to go all the way into the centre to get you and retrace our route back out of the city.'

Galina offered to take the metro to theirs, to avoid this problem, but her suggestion was dismissed.

'I mean, of course we don't mind coming into the centre. Just, it would be convenient to have you nearby,' Irina says, closing her laptop.

Igor looks in the rear-view mirror to catch Galina's reaction.

Galina takes a breath, preparing to explain when the car in front moves up, leaving a gap. A dark-green Lada quickly accelerates, and cuts in front of them.

'Igor, keep your eyes on the road,' Irina says. 'We'll never get there at this rate.'

His jaw tightens. 'We'll get there,' he mutters. 'Little by little.'

'Do you think so?' She returns to her keyboard with vigour, as if her added pressure on the keys would help propel them through the traffic. 'Did you speak to Pavel today? About the documents?'

He shakes his head. 'Later.'

Irina sighs. 'It's got to get sorted. The…'

'Later,' he orders, raising his voice.

She sits back, adjusts her legs and returns to her keyboard.

Dasha untangles the wires of her headphones and presses the little white ends into her ears. Surrounded by a cloud of music, she sinks into the leather seat. Nobody speaks for the rest of the journey.

When they arrive at the *dacha*, Dasha is fast asleep. Igor puts down his window, enters a code in a keypad at the mouth of the drive and the imposing iron gates swing open. He drives forward and the gates close automatically behind them. At the push of another button attached to the visor above the windscreen, the right-hand garage door opens and Igor pulls the car into the bay. Wide enough for two cars, the garage is always immaculately tidy. Outdoor chairs and tables, stored for winter, are neatly stacked along the far wall. A garden tractor with snow plough attachment is parked beside them.

Galina nudges Dasha's shoulder. The girl grunts, then wakes, looking confused. Galina gets out of the car and stretches her back and her legs, both of which ache from standing at the easel all morning.

As the mechanism rattles the garage door shut, the boot flips open and they each take several bags. Igor opens the door which leads directly into the house and they all file in, slipping their shoes off in the corridor. Irina slides a basket of sheepskin slippers from underneath the bench and passes Galina a pair.

Galina rests her stockinged foot on the polished stone floor, which is pleasantly warm from the underfloor heating, and puts on the thick, pristine slippers. Irina places the coats on wooden hangers and puts them in a closet. Gathering up a couple of plastic grocery bags, she steps around the luggage.

'Shall I take anything else to the kitchen?' asks Galina.

'No, this is it,' says Irina.

'I was expecting lots of groceries for the party tomorrow.'

'Oh no. We have a catering company coming. They'll sort everything out.' She says these words with a smirk and a tip of her head.

Galina should have known this. Irina would not cook for

so many people. It is silly moments like this that make her feel so different, like a nearly extinct animal from a faraway time and place.

The hallway leads to the kitchen where a white stone countertop lines one side of the wall. A deep sink, set into the stone, is just below a large window which faces the back garden. Three gleaming copper light fixtures hang from the high ceiling casting beams of light on the opposite counter. Irina opens the refrigerator's wide double doors and places milk and butter on a clean, empty shelf.

'I'll take your bag up, Babushka,' says Igor.

'She's staying in the grey room,' says Irina. 'Your mother and Joe will stay in the blue room.'

Galina had not thought about Masha coming to the party. Hearing her name, she forces herself to mask her disappointment.

'Joe is her new boyfriend. He's American.'

'We met him in Moscow a few months ago,' Igor says. 'Not a bad guy, a typical American. Let me show you to your room, Babushka.'

Galina follows Igor through the main sitting room. Under the cathedral ceiling, a white leather sofa and coordinating deep armchairs dominate the vast space. Although Galina has been to the *dacha* several times before, the grandeur and opulence still surprises her. She feels insignificant and small in the towering rooms.

Igor's corduroy trousers whisper as he walks. Back straight, he wheels the bag across the stone floor towards the main vestibule where a wide, sweeping stone staircase curves up to the next floor. Igor's loping gait is a shadowy reminder of his father, who never lived long enough to start going bald. Her knees and ankles ache and she grasps the iron banister to help her up the stairs. He turns left, following the galleried walkway which overlooks the open-plan sitting room, dining room and kitchen. Below, Irina is lighting a fire in a massive conical fireplace. Igor enters the guest room and places her suitcase on a wooden rack at the foot of the double bed, which is covered with a grey-and-white striped duvet. Frameless windows, which overlook the back garden, stretch ceiling to floor along the length of the room. Igor pulls the curtains shut, covering the expanse of glass.

He puts his hands in his pockets and turns towards her. He looks tired. Dark circles puddle under his eyes. His summer tan has already faded. She reaches out and rubs his arm. His sweater is soft – cashmere, she suspects.

'You have a bathroom just here,' he says, opening a door and turning on a light. The gentle murmur of the fan comes to life, echoing off the tiled floor and walls.

He looks distant.

'Igor,' she says.

He turns off the light, waiting for her to continue.

'Are you OK?'

The muscles in his jaw tighten and he rubs his forehead.

'Just the usual,' he says brushing his hand away. 'But worse, of course, with the sanctions and the bad economy.'

'It's just that Irina seems so…unsatisfied.'

'She's always like that. You must have noticed after… what's it been?… Fifteen years!' He chuckles. 'It's called marriage. You couldn't have forgotten.'

Galina hesitates as she studies his eyes, which are so like Yuri's – the father he never knew, her son who never aged. 'Don't forget what's important.'

He pats her shoulder. 'Let's get some dinner. I'm starving,' he says, showing her to the door.

Later in the evening, Galina climbs into bed. The thick duvet, enveloped in a crisp cover, is smooth against her skin. She turns off the lamp beside the bed and slides deeper under the blanket. The room is completely silent.

Visiting Igor's *dacha* always creates a mixture of conflicting feelings. It is beautiful and very comfortable but it seems wrong to label it a *dacha*. Like calling a castle a shed, it does not fit. She cannot help but feel nostalgic for her own *dacha*. The way the wood floors groaned as she trod on them. The softness of the uneven plaster. The little give in the thin walls in a strong gust of wind. The sound of rodents and birds digging and rustling in the leaves below her window. The squeak of the springs in the tatty, old furniture. The kitchen window at which she stood for countless hours. Boris's hinges on the front door. The slope and slight sag of the roof. She even misses the walk from the station, dodging puddles along the muddy road.

Since selling her *dacha* in 1999, Galina returned only once, when Elena invited her a couple of years ago. From the station, she walked down the newly paved road, which seamlessly joined Peskin's asphalt driveway. Her *dacha*, along with the two others, had been demolished. She knew this was going to happen, but seeing it brought back a swell of sadness and disbelief, tinged with nausea. A brick wall, two and a half metres tall, encircled Peskin's property. His enormous red-brick house occupied most of the land behind the wall, looming over neighbours. Elena's *dacha* was dwarfed by the alien monstrosity. Throughout that weekend, it was as if Galina's father haunted her. Was it right to sell? Profiting from the demolition of the *dacha* seemed like a betrayal. Elena invited her again, but she always declined.

And eventually Elena stopped inviting her.

The empty silence in Igor's *dacha* is unsettling. The triple-paned windows and thick brick walls shield all outside noises. No wind, no leaves, no birds or animals. No neighbours, cars, or trains in the distance. Utter silence. Completely protected by the building. Like a tomb.

Perched on a stool, Galina dips her spoon into a bowl of buckwheat porridge. She takes a bite, savouring the nutty grains, thankful for the familiar. She had dreaded a sticky, sweet, foreign pastry or cold breakfast cereal. Traditional buckwheat is the best way to start the day. Beside her, Dasha sits, slouched over a bowl of porridge, with earphones pressed into her ears. An electric beat mumbles around her.

'She's always plugged into headphones,' Irina says.

'It seems very loud,' Galina says. 'It can't be healthy.'

Irina shrugs and opens the dishwasher on the opposite side of the bar. 'They're all like that.' She places a bowl on the top rack and closes the door. 'The caterers will be here soon. Maria Pavlovna and Joe will arrive at noon.'

For a moment, Masha's full name throws Galina. No matter how many years pass, Masha will always be Masha, the skinny girl in the silly high-heeled sandals that Yuri brought out to the *dacha* all those years ago. She tries to picture Joe, the typical American, but can only envisage Ronald Reagan.

'Does he speak Russian?'

'More or less,' Irina says. 'Dasha practised her English with him. I think she has excellent pronunciation but of course she should take every opportunity for conversation.'

Galina nods and finishes her porridge.

'The guests will arrive around two. So, we'll have to get dressed before they arrive.'

Galina hesitates, wondering if she should tell Irina that she is already dressed. Her burgundy cowl-neck sweater is all she brought, so it will have to be satisfactory. She feels the back of her hair, which is carefully pinned up in a loose bun, as usual, and checks her nails for dried oil paint. Surely, Irina realises that she is ready for the party.

'Who is coming?'

'Mostly foreign families from Dasha's school.' She takes Galina's bowl, rinses it and places it in the dishwasher. 'And Lyosha.'

Galina smiles, relieved. 'I haven't seen Lyosha in a very long time.'

'Oh, and Melissa is in town. She is coming as well.' Irina glances at her watch, again.

'Melissa?'

'Yes.' She hesitates. 'She's helping Igor with some investments in Cyprus.'

'Really?'

Galina had not realised that Igor maintained contact with Melissa. She had moved to Cyprus a few years ago, when the sanctions were implemented and foreign investment shrank. Galina had not had contact with her since she left Russia.

'Is there anything I can do to help?' she asks.

'No, just relax, everything is sorted.' Irina pulls the earphone from Dasha's ear. 'Why don't you show Babushka your iPad drawings?' This is a command, not a question. 'I'm sure she would love to see them.'

Dasha nods, replacing her earphone and sliding off the stool.

After breakfast, Dasha and Galina settle on the sofa. The soft, supple leather seems to push them together. Dasha opens the purple glittery iPad cover and the screen comes to life.

'I have a special app for drawing,' she says.

Her pen bounces around the screen. 'It is best to draw with the stylus rather than my finger.' A still life fills a page and she hands Galya the screen. 'We did this one in school.'

Daisies in a blue glass vase and a white bowl of cherries on a beige linen tablecloth. Galina had seen Dasha's pencil drawings over the years and could always sense nascent talent.

'That's beautiful,' says Galina. 'You've really captured the different textures of the glass and the tablecloth.'

'To see the next one, just swipe left.' Dasha whisks her fingers across the screen and another image appears, a portrait of a girl. 'This is my best friend, Lillia.'

Lillia's long blond hair cascades over her shoulder, her head turned slightly to the side and tipped forward. Her complexion smooth, yet incredibly life-like, the skin tones blended to show contours of her face and her healthy, rose-blushed cheeks. Her blue eyes, illuminated by the screen, look kind yet tinged with sadness.

'She's so beautiful, Dasha. She must be a very good friend, I can tell by her eyes.'

'I can show you how to draw on the iPad, if you want to try.'

Dasha clears the screen and quickly explains the functions of the tool bar along the right-hand side. The stylus taps the glass as she demonstrates. She pushes her fingers against the screen, zooming in. She draws and zooms back out. She hands the iPad to Galina.

The stylus feels heavier than a pencil. Galina sketches a few lines and the tip glides across the screen.

'I'll try to draw you,' Galina says. 'Just a black and white sketch. A special portrait for your fourteenth birthday.'

Dasha unzips a pencil case. 'There are many different styluses here. Have a look, they're all different tip sizes.' She leans over and taps a button, clearing the screen. 'How should I sit?'

'Just be comfortable and relax.'

Dasha sits back into the corner of the sofa, with her knees pulled up to her chest, hugging them with one arm. Propping her elbow on the sofa and resting her head in her hand, she smiles. Looking staged and plastic, she is part of the permanently posing generation. Galina chooses a thin-tipped stylus from the pencil case. Holding it softly, she looks up, studying her great-granddaughter. Thankfully, Dasha has relaxed and looks more natural. She marks the shape of her tilted head and adds the position of the eyes, nose and mouth. The stylus feels awkward and she tosses it back into the bag, selecting a wider tip.

'How do I start again?' Galina asks.

Dasha leans over, taps a button and the screen clears. Galina begins again.

She starts to create the shape of the eyes, almond-shaped like her mother's. Yet there is a different quality to Dasha's eyes – a softness. Her cheeks are full, her mouth has a hint of a smile. Her eyebrows are slightly raised. The right brow arcs just a bit higher. As Galina draws, the stylus becomes more comfortable and easier to control, but she misses the texture of paper, the friction between the pencil and the page. The lines grow across the screen. Slowly, Dasha's face comes to life. She adds the finishing touches to the eyes.

Galina hands her the iPad.

'That is so cool. Can you sign it, like your real artwork?'

'Of course.' Galina signs 'Senotrusova 2016' in the lower

left-hand corner.

'I'm going to use it for my profile picture on Instagram!'
Dasha enthusiastically pokes and swipes at the screen.
'Nobody has anything like this for a profile picture.' She is
thrilled. Her face aglow. 'Baba, how did you learn to draw so
well?'

'At first, my father taught me. But when he died, my
guardian, Boris, spent many hours drawing with us. It was
during the siege, so there was a lot of time to practise. Vera
never did improve. She did not have aptitude for it and gave
up. Do you remember Vera?'

Dasha shakes her head.

Vera passed away when Dasha was six years old. The
doctors said it was her heart but Galina believed she had
simply given up and lost the will to go on. She tried to
persuade Vera to move into the flat on Rimsky-Korsokov
and take a cleaning job with one of Melissa's friends. But she
refused and spent her last years in filthy isolation in her flat.
She rarely went out, so it is not surprising Dasha would not
remember her.

Galina looks again at the sketch on the iPad.

'I still prefer a pencil and paper, I think. But it didn't turn
out too bad. It is easy to draw a beautiful portrait when I am
looking at a beautiful subject.'

3

WHEN THE CATERERS ARRIVE, Irina sends Dasha and Galina to the library on the other side of the *dacha*.

Just as they make themselves comfortable on the sofa, the doorbell rings. Irina and two other voices echo around the vestibule, followed by a deep thunder of laughter.

It must be Masha and the American.

Irina, Masha and an extremely fat man enter the library.

'What a beauty she has become,' shrieks Masha, rushing to Dasha with open arms. 'Simply the most beautiful girl I have ever seen. Let me look at you.' She stands back, motioning for Dasha to twirl around.

Dasha reluctantly turns, shoulders hunched forward.

'Not a bad figure at all. Everything is in the right place. Now, all we must do is get you ready for the party. We have time, so we don't need to panic but we really should get started.' She pats her bright-pink make-up case.

'Babushka, I don't wear make-up.'

'Just a bit, Dasha. *Choot choot*. And your hair. Asian hair is lovely but maybe some curls for a special occasion. And I have a very nice sparkle spray which would look fabulous.' She strokes Dasha's long black hair, and drops it limply. 'Don't you want to be pretty for your party?'

Masha stands, hands on hips. Her hair is aubergine, but it has a stronger, deeper red tone than in previous years. Glitter hairspray sparkles when she bobbles her head, which is often. Her scoop neck, fluffy pink sweater is form-fitting and reveals her wrinkly décolletage. A glittery gold belt is cinched around her slender waist and a straight, black pencil skirt hangs just below her knee. Her slippers are also pink and fluffy; she must have brought them.

Irina steps forward, placing her hands on Dasha's shoulders, reclaiming her. 'I'll get her ready.'

'I'll come up and help,' Masha says.

'Maria Pavlovna, it isn't necessary. You rest here, with Galina Mikhailovna.'

Masha, clearly disappointed with Irina's declaration, shrugs. 'Well, if you change your mind, I'll be here.'

Irina and Dasha head towards the door.

'Maybe *choot choot* glitter spray when you are finished?'

Irina looks back over her shoulder, forces a smile and closes the door behind them.

There will not be glitter spray for Dasha.

'Oh, where are my manners?' says Masha. 'I haven't introduced the love of my life, Joe.' She puts her arm around him, resting one hand on his shoulder and the other hand around his enormous belly, clad in a checked flannel shirt.

He steps forward, extending his hand. Galina takes it awkwardly, unused to shaking hands.

'Very nice to meet you. Igor has such a beautiful *dacha*. You must be very proud of him.' He speaks Russian but it is very stilted and simple, like that of a four-year-old child.

'Yes, they have achieved a lot.'

'He's the smartest man I know,' says Masha. 'Of course, he's successful.'

Joe hesitates.

'And, you are the second smartest man I know. A very close second.' She pats his enormous belly, as if his intellect is located somewhere among the fat.

He smiles, stroking her hand and leads her to the sofa. They sit, sinking together into the soft leather, and Masha rests her head on his shoulder.

Galina takes a seat on an armchair and folds her arms in front of her.

'So, Galya. I hear you were in the war.' Joe sits back, one denim leg propped on the other. 'Well, not in the war, fighting; the siege. You were in the siege. That really must have been…something.' He smiles broadly.

Galina nods. 'Yes, it was terrible.'

'I knew nothing about the siege, before Masha told me.'

In the silence, Joe stares out of the windows. Snow has started to fall again, flakes flutter to the ground and collect on the bare tree branches.

'It looks just like Michigan, where I'm from. Trees and snow.' He puts his right hand up, palm facing out, fingers together, thumb out. He points to the knuckle on his middle finger. 'Michigan is shaped like a mitten. I'm from here.'

Galina has no idea what he is talking about. The meaning must be lost in his poor Russian.

He quickly takes out his phone and prods at the screen. He stands and shows her a map of America on the screen and zooms into Michigan, which is, in fact, a mitten-shaped peninsula.

'And these are the Great Lakes.' He points to the blue patches. 'Very big. It's fresh water, like Baikal, but bigger.' He puts the phone back in his pocket and returns to his place beside Masha.

He is at least ten years younger than Masha. His chestnut hair and thick, full beard are tinged with grey. When his hands are free, he strokes his beard slowly.

Galina looks around the room, searching for an excuse to get up. She is tempted to stand and look at the many books on the shelves. She wishes she could help in the kitchen, find comfort and purpose in slicing an onion or washing a dish.

'I've lived in Moscow for five years. But I still miss home.' He scratches his beard. 'But my life's work brought me here. A calling. I set up a church a few years back in Moscow. It's doing really good, so we're going to set up another one here.'

'Galya, when we open in Peter, you should come and visit our church. You will feel so much better. It lightens your soul.'

Galina is certain that her soul does not require lightening.

'Masha, are you working in the church as well?'

'Not formally, more of a support.' She pats Joe's stomach. 'He's very inspirational, Galya. Has helped so many people find salvation.'

Many foreigners have flooded into Russia bringing various religions since the collapse of the Soviet Union. Galina does not see the appeal or need for such teachings. 'Including you?'

'I suppose so, yes.' Masha sits up straight. 'I always try to live by the word.'

'Truth and honesty?' asks Galina.

'Of course,' says Masha. She smiles, her powdered face

wrinkles at the corner of her eyes.

Joe's attention has strayed to his phone and he is no longer listening as his thumb prods the screen.

Masha looks directly at Galina and her eyes narrow. She takes a breath, about to speak, when Igor walks into the library.

He approaches Joe, hand extended. 'Great to see you.'

Masha leaps from her seat, draping herself on Igor. 'And me? Are you happy to see your mother too?'

'Of course.' Igor kisses her cheeks and steps away, turning to Joe. 'So, how are you?'

'I'm in the mood to party.' Joe does a dance, his belly wiggling with every jerky movement.

The men shake hands and Igor smiles, the first time Galina has noticed a genuine smile in a long time.

'It's been an interesting week in America. What did you think of the election results?'

Joe whoops and raises his fist. 'Donald Trump going to the White House!'

'You think he will be better?'

'Hell, yes, it will be better! It can't get any worse.'

Galina wonders if she understood him properly. Is it really that bad in America? So bad it cannot get any worse? She has seen some reports on the news about the election but has not followed it closely. Igor and Joe slip into English, chatting easily. Igor seems so pleased to see him and comfortable speaking English. Galina did not expect them to be so well-acquainted.

'Babushka, I'm just going to give Mama and Joe a tour of the house. They haven't been here before,' Igor says. 'Will you be OK here on your own?'

'So many books here, what else do I need?'

Igor leads them out of the library and Galina relaxes, appreciating the solitude. She wonders what Masha was going to say when Igor walked in. After all these years, she still does not trust her and prefers to keep a distance between them. Her glance shifts to the windows. Snowflakes flutter to the ground and the short Petersburg day is already darkening.

'Baba Galya!' A voice breaks into her thoughts and she turns. Lyosha slides beside her, throwing his arms around her shoulders. 'My dear! It's been too long!' He kisses her cheeks. His beard scratches her face. He smiles broadly, revealing the new teeth which have replaced his gold caps, and winks.

'I'm so glad you are here,' she says. 'I was worried it would be all foreigners speaking English.'

'Don't worry, Baba Galya. I don't know any English, except 'Happy Birthday' and 'More beer please.' He links her arm through his and pats it, snuggling beside her. 'I will look after you.'

For a moment, they sit watching the snow fall. He squeezes her hand and sighs.

'Do you remember, how we sang Vysotsky all those years ago in the Pony Express van?'

She nods.

'Do you think Igor has some Vysotsky?' He looks around the room. 'They seem to have everything. There *must* be Vysotsky.'

The living room has been completely rearranged for the party. The sofas have been removed and replaced with tables set up end-to-end to form a squared off U-shape. Crisp white cloths cover the tables. At each place setting, there is a stylish matt-black, square plate with a pair of lacquer chopsticks resting diagonally on it. Silver cutlery flanks either side, topped with a parade of glasses. In the centre of the U stands an ornate golden chair, like a throne, presumably for the birthday girl.

As Dasha mingles with the guests, she is the image of her mother. Irina did not allow Masha to smear make-up on Dasha's beautiful face but there is a dusting of fine glitter on her hair. Galina never bothered with make-up, preferring to paint canvases rather than her face, and she is glad to see the young girl's natural beauty.

Melissa enters wearing a V-neck dress which flatters her figure. Her dark hair is shoulder-length, much longer than she wore it back in the Nineties. Her face is smooth. She has an elegance and glamour which she did not possess when she was thirty. Igor approaches her and leans close as they speak. He lifts his hand and rests it on her upper arm. His thumb strokes her and he smiles. Their eyes are focused on each other. There is something familiar in this interaction and it sends a chill through Galina. The memory of Dima and Elena beside the fire, flashes before her.

'I believe she has had significant, expensive work done,' Masha whispers to Galina. 'Her eyes, for sure, and maybe a whole face-lift.'

Galina scowls and groans.

'Galina Mikhailovna, you can't tell me you don't see it.'

'Maybe she just lives a very healthy lifestyle.'

'Ha! If money can't buy beauty, then what good is it?'

Galina elbows her. 'She has always been beautiful.'

Igor leaves Melissa's side to greet another arriving guest. She glances around the room and waves when she notices Galina. Melissa weaves her way through the crowd and embraces her. They kiss cheeks and Melissa gives her an American-sized hug.

'How's life in Cyprus?' asks Galina.

'Sunny.' Her cheeks crease and her perfect American teeth shine. 'But I miss Peter.'

'Melissa, you look amazing. You must tell me your secrets,' Masha says, winking.

'What secrets?'

Igor taps his glass with a fork and the room quietens.

'Friends,' he says. 'Please, find your place at the table and we will begin our meal.'

Dasha, ensconced on the throne, is flanked by her parents with Masha and Joe opposite. Galina sits beside Joe with Lyosha to her right followed by Melissa. The other guests take their places and a pair of waiters offer wine around the table.

'Melissa, have you met Lyosha?' asks Masha. 'He's recently divorced. I only mention this because I noticed you are sitting side by side and make a very sweet couple.'

Lyosha grimaces. 'Sweet. Everyone calls me sweet.'

'And this is Joe, he is also American. We're together. He's not available,' she informs Melissa.

'I'll keep that in mind.' Melissa raises her glass and takes a sip of wine.

Galina glances around at the other guests. Everyone has a glow, clean and fresh. Dressed elegantly in tasteful, muted colours, they look as if they just stepped out of a magazine advertisement. Even Lyosha, who is usually rumpled and unkempt, has put some effort into his appearance. His hair is recently cut, moustache trimmed and shirt ironed. He appears at ease. This tableau of perfection, health, and wealth is only slightly spoilt by Joe's red flannel shirt and Galina's pilled sweater. The two shades of red, side by side at the table, clash.

Lyosha nudges Galina as he motions for the waiter to fill her glass.

'We must celebrate today, Baba Galya.'

Igor taps his glass and the chatter around the table fades.

'Friends, I propose we raise our glasses and drink to the birthday girl, to my angel of sweetness and light, my daughter Dasha. Thankfully, she gets her looks from her mother and not me. We wish you all the best, health, success and love. To Dasha!'

'To Dasha!' everyone repeats and taps their glasses.

Galina catches her gaze down the table and winks at her, raising her glass. Dasha beams and takes a sip of her bubbling champagne.

A waiter sets a black, oblong plate of beautiful food garnished with a pink orchid in the centre of the table.

'What is it?' mumbles Lyosha.

'Sushi,' says Igor. 'It's Dasha's favourite. Have you ever eaten sushi, Babushka?' He picks up the chopsticks. Cradling them in his hand, he effortlessly picks up two pieces and sets them on his plate. He pours a brown liquid into a little bowl beside his plate and fills her dish as well.

Galina takes the sticks in her hand, they feel like pencils.

'I adore sushi,' Masha squeals, easily picking up the sushi with her chopsticks and placing it on her plate.

Igor mixes a dab of green paste into the brown sauce. 'This is wasabi. It's very spicy. I don't think you'd like it.' He pinches the sushi with the chopsticks, dips it in soy sauce and quickly delivers the whole piece to his mouth.

Galina cannot imagine successfully picking up the sushi and getting it to her mouth, much less eating it in one whole piece. Joe's bear-paw hand hovers over the platter. He pinches a piece with his fingers and puts it on the plate. He adds three more pieces and pours soy sauce over a large lump of wasabi in his bowl. He pokes the chopsticks in the green paste, breaking it up. The sauce sloshes out of the shallow bowl, leaving brown spots on the white tablecloth. He sets the sticks beside the dish, where another puddle of brown forms beneath the tips.

'I can't use the sticks,' he explains. 'My hands are too big.' He pops a sushi into his mouth and chews.

Lyosha looks at the chopsticks for a moment and sets them to the side. Using his fork, he places a sushi on his plate.

'Galina Mikhailova, chopsticks are easy,' Masha says, talking over Joe's already empty plate. 'Just keep the bottom still and only move the top one. See?' She demonstrates the pincer action. Her pink nail varnish is bright against the shiny black lacquer. She reaches over Joe, takes a sushi from the platter and sets it on Galina's plate.

Once Masha retracts her arm, Joe places several more on his plate.

Lyosha cuts the sushi with the side of his fork and puts it in his mouth.

'It's rice, Baba Galya, nothing so special. I couldn't even taste that tiny bit of fish.'

Taking the chopsticks in her curled hand, she picks up the sushi and it drops, partially unravelling. She sets the chopsticks to the side and collects the sushi on her fork. She dips it quickly in the sauce and takes a bite. Lyosha is right. It is just rice.

Irina stands and gently taps her glass with her chopstick and again, the table quickly quiets.

'I propose a toast to all who have gathered here today, friends whom we have known for decades, and more recent acquaintances as well. Thank you all for coming and making this day special for our Dasha. We wish you all the very best: happiness, success, and good fortune. To us!' She raises her glass.

'To us!' everyone repeats, tapping glasses.

Galina taps her glass with those around her and Masha squeals, draining the wine. She motions to the waiter, who promptly refills it.

Throughout the meal Galina keeps an eye on Igor and Melissa, watching for them to make a silent connection across the table. But she does not see any lingering glances or coy smiles. Igor is busy with his guests on his side of the table while Melissa is chatting with the other guests near her. Perhaps Galina imagined that overly close moment when she first arrived.

Igor catches Galina's gaze. 'We wondered how you would do with sushi.'

'Well,' says Masha. 'Maybe an old dog can't learn new tricks.'

Galina looks directly at Masha. 'Your young dog isn't so well-trained.' She speaks low and quickly as Joe reaches in front of her, taking the last of the sushi from the platter.

Masha cocks an eyebrow and purses her lips. She takes a sip of wine and turns away, towards the guest to her left.

Igor clenches his jaw and ignores their exchange. 'Dasha wanted Asian dishes. We have *plov* and *manti* coming as well. That will be more familiar.'

She nods. Dasha's inquisitive eyes scrutinise Masha and Galina. She senses that Dasha heard the words passed between her and Masha. Galina turns away, hiding a flicker of shame.

The waiter sets a large, shallow bowl of *plov* in the centre of the table. The brightly patterned Uzbek bowl is piled with rice, slivers of carrot and bite-sized pieces of lamb, dotted with aromatic juniper berries and whole garlic bulbs. Lyosha spoons some onto Galina's plate.

'I'll just give you a bit,' he says. 'Save room for the *manti*.'

The waiter delivers a bowl of fresh tomato salad. Galina places a couple slices of tomato on the *plov* and passes the dish to Lyosha.

Joe eagerly starts eating the *plov*. 'So, tell me about the siege,' he says between bites. A grain of rice clings to his beard.

The question falls to Galina out of the blue and she hesitates, not knowing how to answer.

'Galina Mikhailovna is a hero of the blockade,' Masha says, speaking slowly so Joe will understand. 'She is a hero to us all.'

'Well, I don't feel like much of a hero. How could I be? I was only a child.'

'So, what was it like?' Joe persists. His smile widens.

'Cold. Like you could never begin to imagine. And hunger pains so sharp it feels like a wild animal is ripping you apart from the inside.'

'Did you really eat cats?'

'They did whatever they had to do,' Lyosha says.

Joe stares at Galina, waiting for her response.

'Cat meat is sweet. I didn't mind it. Better than rat.' She shrugs.

'And...' Joe begins.

'Joe, who needs this sort of conversation now?' asks Lyosha, glaring at him. 'This is a party. It's time to celebrate.'

After the meal, Galina retreats to the library. Alone, she sits on the sofa and closes her eyes. Her stomach, unused to large portions, aches and churns. The party hums in the neighbouring room, quiet laugher, clinking of glasses, and the shuffle of the catering staff clearing away. She prefers the solitude of her flat and studio. It is exhausting to be around so many people, making conversation.

'Finally, I found you,' Melissa says, sliding on to the sofa beside her. 'It's a beautiful party.'

Galina nods. 'Are you in Peter for long?'

'Leaving tomorrow.'

'So, tell me how are you?'

'*Normalno.*' Melissa shrugs.

Remembering the lingering conversation between Igor and Melissa, Galina gathers her courage. 'And how about a boyfriend? Anyone interesting for you?'

She shakes her head. 'I've given up on men.' She brushes her hand away, as if dismissing them all.

Maybe her fears about Igor and Melissa are completely unfounded. Silly old fool.

Melissa shows Galina several pictures of her new home in Cyprus which has a beautiful view of the sea. She proudly shows off a picture of her office, where the portrait of Leila hangs behind her desk.

'I still love this painting,' Melissa says. 'She was such a great cat.'

At the time, Galina enjoyed painting the Russian Blue and appreciated the money that Melissa paid for it. But it is only now she realises how important the painting is to her. At that moment, guilt creeps into Galina's thoughts. Sarah Summers is completely unaware of the range of emotions attached to the portrait of Sveta. Perhaps Galina should reply to her letter.

'Do you have any pets now?'

Melissa sighs, and pokes the screen of her phone. 'Meet Max.'

A wrinkly pug stares at the camera.

'He's my prince.' Melissa kisses the screen and puts it away. 'You'll meet him soon enough.'

Galina tips her head.

'When you come with Igor.' Melissa's smile melts away as she realises she has said too much. She takes a deep breath and leans back.

'I don't understand.'

'I thought you knew.'

Galina, completely confused by their conversation, hesitates, trying to read Melissa's face. 'Are you having an affair with Igor?'

Melissa's mouth falls open. She pushes her fingers through her hair, laughing.

Galina does not laugh or smile, waiting for her response.

She leans forward. 'Igor is purchasing a property in Cyprus. I'm helping him with this investment,' she whispers. 'I shouldn't say anything but I don't want you to have the wrong idea.'

Galina's brow laces in disbelief.

'Please, don't mention it to Igor,' Melissa says.

Galina nods, but is uncertain why Igor is keeping his Cyprus plans secret.

After the party, the family retreats to the library. Dasha sits with a pile of beautifully wrapped presents in front of her. She has changed into a pale-pink track suit and her hair is tied in a ponytail on top of her head. She takes a package wrapped in bright, abstractly painted paper.

'This one must be from Babushka,' she says, admiring the paper and smiling at Galina.

'Yes, that is Baba Galya's taste,' says Masha, slumped in an armchair. Her mascara is smudged and lipstick worn away. She squints, steadying herself and struggling to focus on Dasha. She holds a glass of red wine. With every movement, it bobbles precariously and the red liquid licks the sides.

Irina sits beside her, ready to catch the glass. But despite each gesture it remains balanced, as if defying gravity.

'Nobody has taste quite like Baba Galya,' Masha says, bringing the wine to her lips.

Dasha opens the parcel and finds a sketchbook and a tin of pencils.

'I thought it is time for you to have a high-quality, traditional drawing set,' says Galina.

'Babushka, I love them!' She opens the tin and admires the perfect, sharp pencils lined up in the tray.

'If you'd like, maybe you can come to the studio for some drawing lessons.'

Dasha's face lights up. 'Mama, could I?'

Irina pulls her eyes from Masha's glass and looks at Dasha. 'Between gymnastics, violin and schoolwork, I don't think you can fit anything else in. Your schedule is busy.' Her focus returns to Masha's wine.

'Correct,' says Masha, slapping her free hand on her thigh and causing the Malbec to lurch.

Joe looks up from his phone as Masha continues.

'Better for her to do gymnastics than draw. It's very important to look after her body so that she grows up to be…attractive. Don't you think, Joe? Men prefer girls with gymnastic talent to girls with drawing talent.' She stares at him, slightly swaying, waiting for his response.

'It's too late for me to speak Russian. I'm lost,' he declares, returning to his phone.

Irina glares at Igor, willing him to sort out his mother.

He gets up and takes the glass from her hand and sets it on the table. 'Mama, it's late. Joe will take you upstairs.'

Masha looks at him as if he has just sent her to Siberia. But when Igor takes her hand and pulls her up from the sofa, her face shows resignation.

'My Igor,' she says, cupping his jaw. 'I'm so proud of you.' She pulls him closer. 'You've accomplished so much. *Maladyets*. Congratulations.' She releases him and points her index finger at Galina. 'You never thought he would achieve anything.'

Galina scowls.

Joe stands, placing his phone in the breast pocket of his shirt. He says something to her in English and ushers her towards the stairs.

But she pushes him away and returns to Galina.

'You didn't even want me to have him. Your own son's child. You wanted me to abort him.'

The words slap Galina. Her cheeks warm with shame.

Igor takes his mother by the arm and Joe supports the other. As they steer her towards the stairs, Masha breaks free, stumbling back to Galina.

'You pushed me out and stole him from me. My own son.'

'Enough, Mama.' Seizing her, Igor pulls her away and forces her towards the wide staircase.

Dasha sits slack-jawed, taking in Masha's outburst. Irina pats Galina's knee and with a subtle flick of her elegant hand, she waves away Masha's comments and passes Dasha another gift from the pile.

4

꒰ ❦ ꒱

EVEN THOUGH IT IS NINE THIRTY, the weak autumn sun
does not penetrate the thick curtains in the guest bedroom.
Wrapped in the duvet, surrounded in silence, Galina does not
want to rise. The idea of lifting her spine from the mattress,
swinging her feet to the warm stone floor, and pushing herself
out of the bed to face the day exhausts her. Masha's words
infiltrated Galina's dreams, buzzing annoyingly like a fly on
a window pane, leaving her bleary from this night of patchy
sleep. Her words sting: *You pushed me out and stole him from
me.* The ungrateful, foolish girl, how dare she?

At this moment, Galina's only desire is for simplicity. Like
before. When did it all get so complicated?

Before when?

There must have been a time.

It had never been easy with Masha. Thrown together in the
flat on Rimsky-Korsakov, there was never enough space for

the two women. Dima did his best to broker peace between them, but did so at arm's length. True to his philosophical nature, he questioned rather than taking sides and bided his time over the long, dark winter, waiting escape to peace at the *dacha*. Just after Igor was born, there were several months of absolute joy when the women rallied together to look after the helpless baby. They showered him with kisses and caresses. They bonded over the smell of his downy head and the thrill of his tentative first smiles. But the bliss was short-lived. The telegram changed everything.

There had been an unexpected firm knock on the door and Galina had assumed it was a neighbour. As she walked towards the door, a voice from behind it said, 'Telegram.' She froze. He must have the wrong door; the telegram could not be for her. But he insisted. Her fingers hovered over the latch, unwilling to unlock it. He had knocked again, more urgently. Galina had opened the door and the man handed her the thin, grey paper. Yuri was dead. One of the first to fall in a faraway foreign land, Afghanistan.

Masha's girlish face had contorted as she wailed, holding Igor close and rocking. She looked wounded. At first, the sorrow had brought Masha and Galina closer together but once the coffin was buried, the quarrels returned. The two of them were stuck together, caged in the flat. Masha never did edge her way to the top of the housing list and get her own flat. The Soviet Union had to collapse for the two opposing women to be pulled apart.

Galina wipes a tear from her cheek. Silly old fool, that was decades ago. But she has never got over Yuri's death. The void remains. Not even Igor can replace her Yuri. Her thoughts turn to Igor buying a house in Cyprus. It seems so strange that neither he nor Irina have talked about it. Why would they be secretive about such a thing?

There is a gentle tap on the door. Galina flinches, and her heart rate quickens.

Silly old fool.

'Who's there?' Galina's raspy voice calls.

'Dasha.'

'Well, come in.' Galina sits up and leans against the headboard.

Dasha enters carrying a tray with a teapot, cup and a plate of cookies.

'Good Morning. Mama thought you might want some tea.' She sets the tray on the bedside table and perches on the bed. 'It's already ten o'clock.'

'Is it?' Galina says, overplaying surprise in her voice. 'This bed is just so comfortable and the room is so dark, I didn't wake up!'

Dasha pours the tea. 'Mama also wanted me to tell you that Babushka Masha and Joe have left.'

Galina takes a sip of tea and returns it to the tray.

'Where did they go?'

'Back to Moscow. It's Sunday. Joe had to get back for church this morning.'

Galina sits back, relaxing into the pillows behind her.

Fidgeting with the edge of the duvet, Dasha hesitates but clearly has something she wants to say.

'Why don't you and Babushka Masha get along?'

Galina sighs, searching for a simple answer. 'When you are young, you don't carry all the complicated relationships and feelings about the past. Stay this way as long as you can.'

Dasha patiently waits, expecting more explanation.

'I'm not a saint. None of us are. What's done is done.'

Dasha pushes her hair behind her ears and pats Galina's

hand. She has a maturity well beyond her years. Galina sips her tea and passes her one of the cookies from the plate.

Galina had had to help raise Igor. Masha could not have looked after him on her own. She had had to step up, and she certainly would not apologise if she had trodden on Masha's toes along the way. She had done what was best for Igor. Masha left of her own accord; she was not pushed. Although perhaps Galina left the door open.

'Were you serious, when you invited me to your studio for drawing lessons?'

'Of course! As long as your mother agrees.'

'We must find a way to convince her.'

Galina extends her arms, pulling her great-grandchild close. Dasha relaxes into the embrace. Her silky hair smells of coconut.

Galina descends the stairs and makes her way to the kitchen. As she fills the kettle, she glances out of the window at the dreary day. A crow perches on a snowy pine bough and animal tracks scar the snow. She cuts a loaf of rye bread and places the slices in the toaster.

As she waits for the kettle to boil and the toast to pop up, Igor enters the kitchen. His urgent steps tap on the stone floor.

'Good morning,' he says without looking at her, opening the double doors of the refrigerator. He searches the shelves and takes out a bowl which is sealed with a plastic lid.

'Good morning,' Galina says, retrieving her toast from the toaster.

Igor spoons leftover *plov* onto a plate and places it in the microwave.

'You're already having lunch and I am on breakfast,' she

says, giggling.

'I woke early and went for a run. That always makes me hungry.'

Galina settles on the stool at the marble counter as he makes them both a cup of tea. His movements are quick as if he is in a hurry, anxious to be somewhere else. And he seems distracted. He pushes the tea in front of her and the microwave dings. She assumes he will take the stool beside her, but instead he stands on the opposite side of the cold slab of stone. Holding his plate in front of him, he eats the *plov* with a spoon.

'I need to work for a couple of hours and then we will head back to Peter,' he says between bites.

Galina nods. 'Igor, about last night.'

'She was drunk,' he says. 'You know how she is.'

But there is more that Galina wishes to say. Searching for the words, she takes a breath.

'They were very young, when you were conceived.'

'Babushka, leave it in the past.'

The spoon moves sharply between the plate and his mouth.

Galina hesitates, wanting to say that she was wrong all those years ago. That she is so glad Masha and Yuri ignored her and Igor was born. But she cannot find the words and the moment slides away. Igor finishes the *plov* and places his bowl in the sink.

'So, your birthday is in a couple of weeks. Do you want to do something special? We could go out to dinner somewhere to celebrate,' Igor says.

'I'd like something more traditional. Maybe you, Irina and Dasha will come to me? I'll cook a carp. Like old times.'

'Are you sure? It's not too much work for you? I want you to rest on your birthday, not do all that cooking.'

'I can do it. I'm not dead yet! I can cook a meal, a traditional Russian meal.'

'I understand.'

He nods, taps the counter with his fingertips and steps away from her.

'Igor, I wanted to talk to you about Dasha and the drawing lessons.'

'I think she's just too busy, Babushka.'

'Yes, but it seems like something she would really like to do, Igor. I've looked at some of her iPad drawings and she has a good eye. But she needs to learn proper technique.'

'Honestly, Irina sorts these things out.'

'But maybe you could talk to her, and persuade her.

He raises his eyebrows. 'I'll try.'

'That would be the best birthday gift you could give me.'

'I understand.' He kisses Galina's cheek. 'I better get back to work.'

He forces a smile. For a moment Galina catches a glimpse of the boy she raised but he seems distant. There is much she does not know or understand. Why would he not tell her about buying the property in Cyprus? A new holiday home should be exciting news.

5

꒰꒦꒷꒷꒦꒱

IN THE MAIN ROOM OF HER FLAT on Prospect Rimsky-Korsakov, Galina lifts the table extension and slides the support beam into place beneath it. As she pulls it away from the wall, the wooden legs whimper against the parquet floor. She spreads a linen tablecloth across the surface, smoothing the handmade lace square at the centre, and straightening it. She places plates, each rimmed with a chain of violets, on each side of the table. Shining the cutlery on her apron, she lays them at each setting.

The painting that her father gave to Vera's mother, Anna, on that cold New Year's Eve in the Hermitage hangs on the wall beside the table. This garden scene hung above their mattresses in the dark cellar and then was in the flat on Chekhov Street. When Vera died, Galina brought it to her flat.

She hears the key in the lock and her heart flutters. She

glances at the table. Has she forgotten anything? The first course, *borscht*, is on the stove. The carp is in the oven. Her hand grasps her apron and she suddenly realises that she has forgotten to change into smarter clothes.

The lock clicks and the door opens.

'Babushka?' Igor calls.

He is alone at the door.

'Where's Irina and Dasha?'

'They'll be here soon.' He strips off his coat and hat. He ushers her to the divan and they sit down. 'We need to talk, about Cyprus.' His voice is low and hushed. 'Dasha doesn't know. Nobody can know.' He takes her hand and she nods, waiting for him to continue. 'There may be some problems with the company. We need a backup plan, so Melissa has helped me buy a house in Cyprus, which will lead to Cypriot citizenship.'

'You're leaving Russia?'

'It depends.' His face is stern, jawline tense.

'What do you mean?'

'I can't go into details. But you will have to come too. It won't be safe to stay here.'

Galina shakes her head. 'I'm not leaving Russia.'

Igor exhales heavily and rubs his head. His phone pings and he glances at the screen. 'Irina and Dasha are on their way up. I've only just told Irina yesterday. Please, not a word to Dasha.'

Irina and Dasha arrive carrying a wrapped birthday gift and greet Galina with a flurry of kisses. Galina passes a pair of old corduroy slippers to each of them.

'I was so busy getting everything ready, I forgot to get changed,' she says, tidying her long plait.

Irina, stylish as usual, is wearing jeans and a black, cashmere V-neck sweater. 'You look lovely.' She pats Galina's arm reassuringly, holding her glance. She knows that Igor came early to tell her about Cyprus. There is something about the way her features soften as if to say, 'Don't worry, Igor will sort out everything.'

'Please, take a seat,' Galina says.

Irina sits beside Igor on the divan, which sags under their weight, and Dasha takes a chair at the table.

'You must be hungry; shall we eat right away?' she asks.

'Open your gift first,' says Igor. He motions to the parcel. His face has relaxed as if he has not a care in world.

Galina sits beside him and he hands her the gift, which is topped with a bright pink bow. Taking it, she immediately knows by the shape and weight that it is a framed canvas.

'Yes, Papa really did buy an artist a painting!'

'Shh!' says Irina, shooting her a stern glance. 'She hasn't opened it yet.'

'She's not a fool,' mumbles Dasha.

Galina slides her finger between the gold paper and the tape, opening the package without tearing the paper, revealing a strangely familiar black shoe on a red carpet. This is a painting which she has seen before. She peels back the paper and finds two round-faced pioneers staring back at her from the canvas. One sits on a chair, the other stands beside him. Her father's signature is in the lower corner. The portrait trembles in her hand as her father's ghost slides into the room, taking a seat beside her. A chilly tingle creeps up her spine.

'It's your father's work!' says Igor, beaming.

'Where did you get this?'

'It came up in an auction and Vasily from the St Petersburg

Gallery of Modern Art contacted me.' He smiles, waiting for her response. 'Have you seen it before?'

'Of course,' Galina replies. She forces a smile but a tear rolls down her cheek, followed by another. Her hands shake and she struggles to catch her breath.

Igor takes the painting and rests his hand on her shoulder. 'I didn't mean to upset you. Are you all right?'

Her chest tightens but she forces her lungs to accept a long slow inhale of air. As she relaxes into breathing, a stream of tears flows down her cheeks. For a woman who rarely cries, the moisture is disconcerting at first as she quickly wipes them away with the back of her hand. Behind this emotional swell there is an urgency, necessity and release. It is as if the bottom of a long-forgotten box has given way and the contents plummeted to the floor.

Irina hands her a tissue and Dasha brings her a glass of water. She takes a long sip, feeling the water slide down her throat to her stomach. She takes another deep breath and begins.

'This painting saved my life. My father was ordered to paint it for a colonel while we were living in the Hermitage cellar. Before the war, he worked there as a conservationist. He wasn't really a portrait painter and he was worried that the colonel wouldn't be satisfied with his work.

'I was very weak at this time; it was just after my mother died. I could see by the way he looked at me that he was afraid I'd be the next to go. Death was everywhere. Every time he went to the colonel's, he'd bring back food. He brought *priyaniki* after his first visit and we couldn't believe our luck. I still remember the taste of the dark, spiced dough, and to this day, whenever I even smell *priyaniki* I remember the

273

cellar of the Hermitage. And then he brought chicken and potatoes and we ate it with our hands.

'Most of the time while he was working on the portrait, he was cross. I was only eight at the time, so I just assumed he was angry with me and stayed away from him. I was getting stronger with the better food so Vera and I would explore the endless corridors and empty halls with the other children, embarking on our own adventure in the enormous palace. It was much better than being in the flat, where we just sat, worried and waited for the war to end. In the Hermitage, the children played, like we did before the war. But it was strange in a way. Every time we laughed and had fun I felt guilty, as if it was wrong when so many were suffering.

'He finally finished the portrait and I just wanted him to get back to normal and stop being so mad all the time. He delivered the painting to the colonel and brought back vodka and dried fish, which I used to love. I've never eaten them again since that terrible night. I can't stand the smell of the ugly, shrivelled fish.

'Vera and I ate while my father and Boris drank. None of you knew Boris; he also worked at the Hermitage. My father's face glowed, his smile broad, full of joy as the pair of them danced around the studio, linking arms and laughing. I remember he was so thin. He had pierced extra holes in his leather belt and cinched it around his baggy trousers. The leather was so long, it flapped as he danced. I think he was just relieved to have finished the painting that he just lost himself in the vodka. But then, the mood changed, as if their limbs grew too heavy to dance, and the men settled on their stools and drank.

'Anyway, the drinking carried on and he fell off the stool. Boris fell asleep in the corner. I don't know how we did it but

274

Vera and I took my father by either arm and helped him back to our mattress in the cellar. We were so weak and small, I have no idea how we managed. He staggered down the long flight of stairs into the cellar and we dropped him on the mattress. But he didn't wake up, he died in the night.'

She brings the story to a close quickly, leaving out the ugly details of his death. The complete truth is unnecessary.

Galina, Igor, Irina and Dasha stare at the painting in silence. Galina studies the boys and remembers how jealous she had been of the chubby one. It seemed impossible that this boy could be so round when so many were starving.

Galina stands and her legs feel lighter, easier to move, but her torso is heavy, exhausted from crying, drained. The ghost of her father shadows her as she pulls the curtains across the windows, covering the inky St Petersburg night. She makes her way to the kitchen and removes the carp from the oven. Distracted by her story, she has left it longer than planned and the fins are slightly burnt around the edges. She ladles the *borscht* into the bowls and takes two to the table, placing them in front of Igor and Irina. With the siege memories fresh in her mind, this simple food seems decadent.

Irina nudges Dasha, who gets up and retrieves the other bowls from the kitchen. Galina settles on her chair and they begin to eat. Nobody speaks. Their spoons tap the edge of the bowls and occasionally someone slurps their soup. Each spoonful of nourishing *borscht* heals.

When they have finished, Dasha clears the dishes, making room for the second course, and Igor carries the carp from the kitchen. Galina cuts the fish and places a serving on each plate.

Dasha stares at the fish head on the platter. 'How can

something so delicious be that ugly?'

The three adults laugh, full-bellied and long. Too long. As laughter fills the room, the ghost seems to disappear, returning to a dark corner or cupboard where he belongs.

They enjoy their second course, savouring every bite, and conversation slowly turns to Dasha's upcoming exams and violin recital. Igor speaks of a pending business trip to Almaty and Irina enquires about the progress of Galina's exhibition portraits. They focus on the future, and the past returns to its place.

'You know, Galina Mikhailovna, there is one more birthday gift for us to give,' Irina says, finishing her last bite of fish. 'Something special for you.'

Igor and Dasha glance at her, waiting for her to continue, clearly unaware of this additional gift.

'I think Fridays would be best,' Irina continues. 'As a special treat. Would that work for you, Galina Mikhailovna? Could Dasha come to you for drawing lessons on Fridays?'

Dasha jumps off her chair and embraces her mother. 'Thank you, Mama. Thank you!'

'Fridays would be absolutely ideal,' says Galina.

At the end of the evening, hovering near the door in his boots and coat, Igor looks at the portrait pensively. 'I didn't mean to upset you with the painting.' He wrings his hands together and shifts his weight between his feet. 'I don't mind if you would prefer me to take it. Just for a while.'

She pulls him close and kisses either cheek. 'Not necessary. Thank you, Igor. When will you know about Cyprus?'

'Soon.' He inhales, as if to explain further.

'The lift is here,' Irina calls from the corridor.

But he swallows the explanation. '*Poka*,' he says instead.

He steps away, giving a little wave over his shoulder.

The lift rattles shut as Galina locks the door. She returns to the main room and takes the portrait in her hand, studying the faces of the boys she never met. She cannot even remember their names. She wraps the gold paper around the painting, reaffixing the tape. Carrying it to the corner of the flat, she places it in the narrow gap between the wall and a wardrobe, filing it away.

She takes several glasses from the table to the kitchen and submerges them into sudsy warm water. As she washes, Igor's words, '*it won't be safe to stay*', linger in her mind. She looks over her shoulder and hesitates, certain she heard something in the corridor. Fear tingles. She has not felt this prickly feeling in a long time, not since the lonely nights at the *dacha*, broken and battered.

6

⚜

DASHA BALANCES A SKETCH BOARD on her lap in Galina's studio, enjoying her first drawing lesson. She studies the basket of fruit which Galina has placed on a table. She returns her attention to the drawing in front of her.

This moment is perfect but Galina cannot help but worry that it is all temporary. Igor might take his family to Cyprus at any time. She has thought of little else and has decided she will refuse to go with them. Her home is in Russia.

Standing at the easel, she steps away from the nearly completed portrait of Elena. Mixing a touch of white to the yellowy paint on her palette, she uses a fine brush to gently highlight Elena's hair, giving it a slight reflection of light. The cool, grey background is softly textured and brings out the blue of her eyes. Galina is particularly pleased with the eyes. They reflect Elena's caring and kind qualities but also there is a strength, confidence and intelligence.

'Babushka, do you miss the Soviet Union?' Dasha asks, looking up from her sketch.

This question is unexpected.

'Why do you ask?'

'My teacher was talking about it. Soon it will be the twenty-fifth anniversary since the end of the Soviet Union.'

Twenty-five years. Surely, that cannot be possible. 'I've never been interested in politics, Dasha. Leaders come and go. Some things get better, some get worse.' Galina puts down her brush and perches on a stool, relieving her back and legs from the burden of standing. 'I'm a Soviet woman. The first fifty-eight years of my life were during Soviet times. Changing the name of the country and the leadership won't change that.'

'Do you miss it?'

'I miss being young, moving without aches and pains, having a decent figure. And yes, I suppose there are some things that I miss from Soviet times.'

'Like what?'

'Now, everything is about money. I find it...' Galina pauses, searching for the right word. 'I don't know – shallow? Before, we didn't have much but we were working for something bigger than ourselves.'

Dasha patiently waits for her to continue.

'But then again, some people didn't work very hard or do much to contribute. Some of us did. But others did the bare minimum.'

'What about Stalin?'

'You're full of questions today, Dasha.'

Dasha's cheeks redden. 'I don't know what to believe. Different people say different things.'

'I lived in Stalin's times for the first twenty years of my life.

We won the war, thanks to Stalin. I was educated and found a profession, thanks to Stalin. I didn't know any different. It's just the way it was. I was a girl, completely uninterested in government, growing up with dreams, just like you. All the secrets came out later.'

'Secrets?'

'The purges. Many people went to jail, Dasha. You must know about this. It was ugly. Even people from our family.'

'Who?'

'My father's brother was sent to the Gulag. I never met him and my parents never spoke about him. I only found out about it in the late Seventies. I still don't know much about him, even now. Many people went missing. They simply disappeared.'

Dasha sets her drawing aside and Galina senses that she is waiting for her to continue.

'But you know, no matter what, through it all I have always loved my country, regardless. It's the motherland. I suppose it is like a family. No matter what arguments and problems we encounter, we still love each other. Even though, at times, we do and say terrible, hurtful things.'

The door buzzer cuts into their conversation.

Galina crosses the studio and presses the intercom.

'Good afternoon, Galina Mikhailovna. It's Vasily Rosov from the gallery. Can I come up?'

'Of course.' Galina presses a button releasing the lock. She opens the door and waits for the lift to arrive on the sixth floor, wondering what brings him by.

'Hope I'm not disturbing. I was in the area so I thought I'd take my chances and drop in.'

'Not at all. In fact, you are saving me from answering some difficult questions.'

'Oh? What kind of questions?'

'Questions about our great Soviet Union, posed by my great-granddaughter, Dasha.'

'Ah, our former times, the times before fluffy toilet paper,' Vasily says.

Dasha giggles.

'How did we manage to beat the fascists and put the first man in space without fluffy toilet paper?' Galina quips.

'Who needs a man in space when you can't get decent hair gel?' Vasily shrugs. 'Any products that make life just a bit more convenient or nice, forget it.' He draws his index finger across his throat.

'It's true. There weren't even women's sanitary products.' Galina says.

Dasha blushes.

Galina shrugs. 'We didn't smell of pomegranate and lemons. There were fewer products, but there was community, a collective spirit that we don't have today. Everyone is out for themselves. We are even at war with the Ukrainians – our brothers, for goodness sake.'

'Inconvenient. It's all you need to know about the former times,' says Vasily. 'Personally, I prefer questions more philosophical or artistic rather than political.' He glances at Dasha's sketch. 'I see the artistic dynasty continues.'

Galina steps in closer to look at the drawing. Dasha's fine lines form the apple, orange and banana in a shallow basket. The proportions are good but the subtle shading and composition needs to be improved.

'How nice to see the talent being passed down,' Vasily says.

'What brings you by?' asks Galina.

'I got another call from Sarah Summers.'

'Who?'

'Sarah Summers. The woman in London that wrote you the letter. I gave it to you a few weeks ago.'

'Ah yes, I read it.'

'Anyway, she hasn't heard from you.'

It seems absurd, this idea of communicating with this foreign stranger, some unknown woman with whom she has nothing in common.

'She just wants to ask you a few questions,' Vasily adds. 'It is very important to engage with your patrons, Galina Mikhailovna. You would benefit from a social media presence as well.'

She brushes this comment aside, raising her brow.

'Who's Sarah Summers?' asks Dasha.

'She bought one of Galina Mikhailovna's portraits back in the Nineties, a spectacular portrait of a girl surrounded by ducks. She sent me a letter, which included her email address.'

'What's the problem?' asks Dasha, pulling her iPad from her backpack. 'It's interesting. Maybe we can go to London to meet her. I've always wanted to go to London.'

Vasily takes his phone from his coat pocket, prods at the screen and passes it to Dasha. 'Here's her email address. Her Russian isn't too bad.'

'*Klassno* but I want to practise my English,' says Dasha, her fingers dancing across the iPad's screen.

'Artistic talent, and you speak English. I should take you on my upcoming trip to New York,' he says.

'Sent!' Dasha sets the iPad aside and resumes drawing.

'Also, I want to talk to you, Galina Mikhailovna, about the exhibition in New York. Socialist Realism sells well in the States. I'd like to take some of your paintings. Maybe some of your older pieces?'

Galina leads Vasily to the rack in the corner of the studio.

'Have a look. There might be something interesting for you.'

PING!

'Oh!' Dasha gasps from the other side of the studio. 'She's already answered! It's Sarah Summers! She wants to know about your life and the painting.'

Galina finds Dasha's growing excitement bewildering. What is the point of this sort of communication?

'What should I say, Babushka?'

'Honestly, Dasha, I don't understand what she wants. I don't have anything extraordinary to tell her.'

Vasily pulls several landscapes and portraits from the rack, leans them against the wall and resumes flipping through the canvases.

'Well, you are certainly not ordinary, Babushka.'

'She's right,' Vasily says, looking at a portrait of Igor when he was four.

'How should I answer her?' Dasha asks.

Galina sighs and turns away from the rack, returning to her great-granddaughter.

'Babushka, you are something special. You survived the siege of Leningrad, taught at the best art school in the Soviet Union, lost your son in Afghanistan, and endured goodness knows what else.'

Galina shrugs off this sparse timeline of her life.

'You should listen to this wise girl, Galina Mikhailovna.'

'I want to know more, too. Even the secrets,' Dasha says, typing. She does not bother to tell her what she is writing.

PING, chimes the iPad.

As Dasha types, her face glows, alive and confident.

'She's answered again. She says she wants to know the

story behind the painting. She wants to know about the girl and why she is sitting with ducks.'

Galina thinks about the portrait. Would Dasha really want to know the truth? Would she really want to know about her great-grandfather's infidelity? Would she want to know that her father stole the painting from her great-grandmother and sold it?

'They're geese. And it's a long story.'

Dasha taps away at the screen as Galina gathers the sketch pencils into a tin.

Dasha chuckles. 'Apparently, Sarah Summers is a novelist. She likes a long story.'

AFTERWORD

❧

The Girl from the Hermitage is a work of fiction, inspired by a painting which my husband and I purchased while we were living in Moscow in 1999. It has hung in our home for twenty years but I never knew anything about the artist, Ludmila Mikhailovna Sgibneva. One night, I found a short biography of her on the internet. I learned that she had survived the siege of Leningrad and that she is still painting. Intrigued by a woman who had lived through such historic times, my imagination took over and I began to write this novel. The painting can be seen on my website: www.mollygartland. com.

ACKNOWLEDGEMENTS

The journey from idea to published book has been a long one. There are many people who have helped along the way.

The inspiration for this book found me while I was taking a beginner's creative writing course at Richmond Adult Community College (now RHACC). My teacher, Donald Smith, hated all the paperwork associated with teaching but on one of my evaluations he wrote, 'You could be a novelist.' He probably does not even remember filling in this form but at the time it put wind in my sails. I truly believe this book would not be in your hands if he had not given me that feedback. Donald, I thank you and owe you a pint.

Thank you to St Mary's University, Twickenham, with a special note of appreciation to my tutors David Savill and Jonathan Gibbs for all their careful attention, encouragement and honesty. Much gratitude goes to my fellow Creative Writing MA students who offered feedback and support, followed by a much-needed trip to the pub.

Thank you to Penny, Pirkko, Alexis, Mary, Carol, Philippa and Carina (AKA Chrysalis Writing Group) who have always offered inspiration, clever thoughts, valuable feedback and a good giggle. I thank all of the readers of earlier drafts, with special gratitude to Elizabeth Petter-Thompson who advised on the process of oil painting and all matters artistic, Anastasia Chernyakova for being my first Russian reader, and Natalia Yakimenko for giving a bit more Russian polish to the manuscript. Thank you to my eagle-eyed proofreaders, Margot, Christine and Sonya. Thank you to Dan Hiscocks at Lightning Books for taking a chance on me. To my editor, Simon Edge, and copyeditor, Clio Mitchell, thank you for working your magic. I have much respect and admiration for what you do.

And finally a big thank you to Glady, Henry and my extremely understanding husband, Steve, for giving me the time and space to chase a dream.

Originally from Michigan, **Molly Gartland** worked in Moscow from 1994 to 2000 and has been interested in Russian culture ever since.

She has an MA in Creative Writing from St Mary's University, Twickenham, and lives in London.

The manuscript for her debut novel, *The Girl from the Hermitage*, was shortlisted for the Impress Prize and longlisted for the Mslexia Novel Competition, the Bath Novel Award and Grindstone Novel Award.

GLOSSARY

Babushka (babushki): grandmother
Banya: public bathhouse
Borscht: traditional Russian soup usually made with beetroot
'Bozhe moy': 'my God'
Buterbrod: open sandwich
Choot choot: little bit
Dacha: summer cottage
Doska: wooden plank
Klassno: cool (slang)
Kommunalka: communal apartment
Kozyol: goat (slang/swear word, similar to ass)
Maladyets: congratulations
Manti: meat-stuffed dumpling
Mishka Na Severe: polar bear (literally, bear of the north)
Nelzya: forbidden
Normalno: fine
Obyazatelno: mandatory
Otlichno: splendid
Papirosa: filterless cigarette
Perestroika: Gorbachev's policy of economic reform (literally, rebuild)
Pelmen (pelmeni): ravioli-like preparation
Pirozhki: bread roll filled with meat, cabbage or potato
Plov: traditional Uzbek pilaf
Poka: bye
Pravilno: correct
Priyanik (priyaniki): traditional spiced cookie/cake, made since at least the 17th century
Samovar: a large metal container used to heat water for tea
Shashlik: shish kebab
Spasibo: thank you
'Zhizhn prekrasna': 'life is wonderful'